D0975745

# TEXAS
# FREE

Don't miss any of Janet Dailey's bestsellers

# JANET DAILEY

# TEXAS FREE

**KENSINGTON BOOKS**
http://www.kensingtonbooks.com

KENSINGTON BOOKS are published by

Kensington Publishing Corp.
119 West 40th Street
New York, NY 10018

All Kensington titles, imprints, and distributed lines are available at special quantity discounts for bulk purchases for sales promotion, premiums, fund-raising, educational, or institutional use.

Special book excerpts or customized printings can also be created to fit specific needs. For details, write or phone the office of the Kensington Special Sales Manager: Attn. Special Sales Department. Kensington Publishing Corp, 119 West 40th Street, New York, NY 10018. Phone: 1-800-221-2647.

Kensington and the K logo Reg. U.S. Pat. & TM Off.

Library of Congress Card Catalogue Number: 2018932850

ISBN-13: 978-1-4967-0958-5
ISBN-10: 1-4967-0958-6
First Kensington Hardcover Edition: September 2018

eISBN-13: 978-1-4967-0961-5
eISBN-10: 1-4967-0961-6
First Kensington Electronic Edition: September 2018

10 9 8 7 6 5 4 3 2 1

Printed in the United States of America

*As always, with deepest thanks to Elizabeth Lane for her insight, courage, and perseverance.*

# TEXAS
# FREE

# CHAPTER ONE

*Río Seco, Mexico*
*April 1985*

THE MEXICAN VILLAGE SLUMBERED UNDER THE LIGHT OF A WANING crescent moon. In the empty plaza, windblown shadows flickered over the cobblestones. The cantina was closed for the night, its outdoor tables and chairs locked away behind corrugated metal doors. A bat fluttered from the tower of the old adobe church and melted into darkness. A skinny dog foraged for leavings in the deserted marketplace.

The night was almost peaceful. But the stillness was heavy with tension—especially in one small adobe house on a dusty side street. Nothing in Río Seco was the way it had been before the Cabrera cartel took over the town. And for Rose Landro, after tonight, nothing would be the same again.

The click of a boot heel on the tiled patio startled Rose to full alertness. Lying fully dressed in the dark, she checked the impulse to sit up, fling aside the covers, and bolt out of bed. She was a small woman. Face-to-face, she'd be no match for the burly intruder who was stalking her. Her only chance of survival lay in surprise.

The loaded Smith and Wesson .44 was a cold lump under her

pillow. As footsteps clicked across the patio, she closed her hand around the grip, cocked the hammer, and slid to the floor. Her free hand bunched the pillows into a semblance of her sleeping body and covered them with the blanket.

She knew who was coming for her. Lucho Cabrera, younger brother of the local cartel boss, was built like a short pile of bricks. He wore high-heeled cowboy boots to make him appear taller. The sound of those boots, clicking across the kitchen, chilled Rose's blood.

Gripping the heavy pistol, she crawled across the floor and pressed upward to stand against the wall, in the shadows behind the door. Her breath came in shallow gasps. Her pulse hammered in her ears.

The cartel would kill anyone who stood against them. They had already murdered Ramón and María Ortega, who'd taken Rose into their home twelve years ago. Rose would have fled for her life before now, but she could not leave without avenging the couple who'd cared for her like their own daughter.

*Honor.* The Ortegas had lived by that code. Now it was Rose's turn to carry on the tradition.

The footsteps were coming closer. Would Lucho stand in the doorway and fire at the lump in her bed, or did the sadistic pig plan on raping her first, as he'd done two months earlier when he'd caught her walking home alone after dark?

At the memory of his filthy, sweating body, her finger tightened on the trigger. If ever a man deserved killing, it was Lucho Cabrera. Only his older brother, Refugio, was worse.

The bedroom door creaked open. Rose held her breath as Lucho stepped into the room, his pistol drawn. The faint moonlight, falling through the high, barred window, cast black shadows across his fleshy face. As he neared the bed, he holstered the gun. One hand fumbled with his belt buckle. *Good.* This was almost too easy. She could shoot him now, in the back. But something in her wanted more. She wanted him to see her. When the bullet tore into his body, she wanted him to know who had fired it.

She forgot to breathe. Every muscle was a coiled spring as she waited for the right moment.

"*Brujita fea . . .*" he muttered. The name, given to Rose because of the birthmark on her face, meant "ugly little witch." Over the years she'd learned to bear it with a measure of pride. Superstitious people tended to fear her, especially some of the men. But that wouldn't stop Lucho. He might even be planning to take a trophy back to his brother—an ear, a hand, or even her head—as proof of his bravery.

Still muttering, he loosened his trousers and jerked back the blanket. That was when he realized he'd been tricked. He spun around, cursing as Rose stepped out of the shadows, the .44 gripped between her hands.

"*Muera, pendejo.* Die, you bastard," she said, aiming the heavy revolver at his chest.

Lucho had no time to draw his weapon, but in the instant her finger tightened on the trigger, he lunged for her. The pistol roared, but Lucho's move had thrown off her aim. The bullet struck his right shoulder, barely slowing the brute's charge.

Slammed by the recoil, Rose staggered backward. Her feet tangled in the loose rug on the floor. Losing her balance, she went down hard, landing on one arm.

She managed to keep a one-handed grip on the gun, but now he was standing over her, blood streaming down his sleeve. She could hear the hiss of his breath between his teeth as he reached for his holster, then paused, cursing. That was when Rose realized her shot had disabled his shooting arm. The flicker of distraction as he switched to draw with his left hand gave her the only chance she had left.

She cocked the .44 and pulled the trigger.

This time she didn't miss.

Steeling her shattered nerves, she scrambled to her feet. Her knees quivered as she stepped over Lucho's supine body. He was dead, all right, his trousers gapping open to tell the story. Rose fought back a wave of nausea. This was no time to fall apart. The sound of gunfire was bound to alert the cartel. If she wanted to live, she had to collect her wits and get out of there.

Her duffel was already packed with the few clothes and necessities she owned. What she needed most was hidden outside.

The patio was eerily silent. Knowing she'd have to run, Rose

had already given her beloved goats and chickens to the neighbors. All that remained was to move aside a potted palm, lift up
the tile underneath, and scrape away the earth that covered a
small, rusting metal box.

The box contained her U.S. birth certificate and the American
dollars that her self-appointed guardian Bull Tyler had given
Ramón toward her keep. Ramón, kindly man that he was, had refused to spend a cent of it, instead putting the cash aside for the
day when Rose would need it. Now, after twelve years, that day
had come.

Rose opened the box and checked to make sure nothing was
missing. Then she snapped it shut and shoved it into the hip
pocket of her jeans. Back in the house, she glanced around for
anything else she might need. The .44 lay on the kitchen table
where she'd left it. She thrust it into her belt and flung Ramón's old
woolen serape over her shoulders to hide what she was carrying.

From the next street over, she could hear dogs barking. Someone could be here any minute. After snatching a set of keys from
a nail inside the cupboard, she grabbed her duffel and raced
across the patio, out the back door.

One key opened the padlock on the shed behind the house.
Inside, covered by a canvas tarp, was the 1947 Buick that had
been Ramón's pride and joy. The cartel knew about it, but none
of the swaggering thugs who trailed after *Don* Refugio wanted an
old car. They wanted new cars, sleek and fast and showy. None of
them had tried to claim it.

There were tools in the shed, as well—hammers, saws, picks,
shovels, a coil of rope, and more—tools she would need where
she was going. With the car uncovered, Rose flung them all, along
with her duffel, into the Buick's cavernous trunk. Last of all, she
took her grandfather's double-barreled 12-gauge shotgun from
its hiding place under Ramón's workbench, wrapped it in a blanket, and laid it at the back of the trunk along with a box of shells.
After closing and locking the trunk, she opened the shed door
wide, climbed into the car, and turned the key in the ignition.
The powerful V8 engine purred to life. Ramón had taught her

how to maintain his treasure, and Rose had learned her lessons well. The tank was full of gas, the oil changed, and the battery charged. With luck, she could make it across the border without needing to stop at a station, where the distinctive car and the port-wine blaze down the left border of her face would make her all too easy to remember.

The cartel would be after her—that much she knew. *Don* Refugio would not rest until he'd hunted down his brother's killer and made her pay.

With the shed door locked behind her and her headlights turned off, she drove through an alley and took a back lane out of town. Where the lane met paved road, she swung onto the narrow highway, switched the lights on high beam, and punched the gas pedal to the floor.

By now someone would have heard the shots, found Lucho's body, and most likely broken into the locked shed to discover that the old Buick was gone. It could be a matter of minutes before Refugio's goons were on her tail. While she could, she needed to gain as much time and distance as possible.

Her plan was to stay on the highway until first light. After that she would cut off into the maze of rough back roads that connected the scattered villages between here and the border at Piedras Negras. Her birth certificate was proof of citizenship and should be enough to get her into the United States. The car was another matter. Ramón had never licensed it in Mexico. But its Texas plates were eleven years old. The registration in the glove box bore the name of Carlos Ortega, Ramón's late brother who'd worked for Bull Tyler's father on the Rimrock Ranch. And Rose was driving it without a license.

Getting the Buick through customs could be trouble. Should she concoct a believable story and hope for the best? Or should she turn aside and look for a spot where smugglers and *coyotes* crossed the river? Never mind, she had time to make a plan. Right now all that mattered was staying ahead of the cartel.

Once she crossed the border, her final destination would be the Rimrock Ranch and the thirty-acre parcel of land she'd inherited from her grandfather—the land she'd left in Bull Tyler's care. But there'd be no safe refuge for her anywhere, not even on the Rimrock.

She'd been just fourteen when Ham Prescott, Bull's powerful neighbor, had shot and killed her grandfather before her eyes. When Ham came to silence her, Rose had blasted the old man to death with her grandfather's shotgun.

The incident was seared into her memory—the gleam of moonlight on Ham Prescott's pistol, the weight of the heavy shotgun in her shaking hands, and the blast that had nearly knocked her over backward. Afterward there'd been the sight of the old man's body sprawled on the ground and Bull running toward her across the yard.

To save her from arrest and vengeance, Bull had spirited her to Mexico and left her with his friends, the Ortegas. For twelve years she'd been safe. Now she'd be returning to face the consequences of what she'd done. Would she be jailed and hauled into court to stand trial? Would Ham's son, Ferg Prescott, be waiting to avenge his father's death?

She was taking a dangerous risk returning to the Rimrock. But she had no other place to go—and no other spot on earth that was hers by right of inheritance.

Bull had promised her that, when it was safe to return, the land would be waiting for her. But over the years he had never come back for her or contacted her in any way.

Could something have happened to him? That was possible, she reasoned. But it made more sense that Bull had simply taken the land for himself and left her stranded in Mexico.

Rose's hands tightened on the steering wheel. She owed Bull Tyler her freedom, and maybe even her life. But the one thing she did not owe him was her grandfather's land.

He might have taken advantage of a powerless girl, but she wasn't fourteen anymore. She was twenty-six years old and strong enough to fight for what was hers.

Bull closed the gate on the sad little graveyard and moved down the hill. By now, Bernice would have fed the boys their supper and sent them off to do their homework. Bull's own supper would be warming in the oven. He would eat it alone, or maybe with Jasper if they needed to talk. He didn't see much of his sons; but then, he'd never had much use for children. When they were older, he would teach them to be men and to run the ranch. Right now the most vital thing he could do for them was to build and preserve their legacy.

Family and land. In the end, nothing else counted.

Jasper was waiting at the bottom of the hill, a lanky, scarecrow figure against the fading sky. Knowing that Bull liked to be alone here, he wouldn't ordinarily have come this far. Not unless there was trouble.

"What is it?" Bull sensed that the news wouldn't be good.

Jasper scuffed out the cigarette he'd been smoking. "Just got word from the boys coming in off the range. We're short six head since last month. No sign of carcasses anywhere, not even bones."

Bull mouthed a curse. "Rustlers. Got to be."

"Rustlers—or maybe the Prescotts." Jasper hated their powerful neighbors as much as Bull did.

"It doesn't make sense for the Prescotts to be stealing our cattle when they've got so damned many of their own," Bull said.

"That doesn't mean Ferg wouldn't do it just to rile you," Jasper said. "He's hated your guts ever since you stole his girl and married her."

"I'm aware of that. But rustling's a serious crime. I can't imagine Ferg would risk going to jail for a few cows." Bull began walking back toward the house. "First thing in the morning, I'll call the Special Rangers and have them get somebody out here pronto."

In his younger days, Bull might have enjoyed tracking down the rustlers himself. But the Special Rangers who worked for the Texas and Southwestern Cattle Raisers Association were hired to combat rustling and related crimes. They were sharp, tough professionals who knew how to handle dangerous thieves and deadly situations. This was their job, not his.

Jasper nodded. "Good idea. I'll go on ahead tomorrow and get the boys started on the branding and marking." Jasper seemed about to say more, but he broke off suddenly, staring toward the headlights that were coming up the long, gravel drive from the main road. "Now who the devil could that be? You weren't ex-pectin' a visit, were you?"

"Not tonight." Bull lengthened his stride, ignoring the twinge in his hip. Unexpected company tended to mean problems, un-less maybe some lost traveler had taken a wrong turn.

They reached the house as the vehicle was pulling into the yard. At the sight of it, Bull's gut clenched. He knew that old Buick. He knew its history, and he knew who must be driving it. He swore under his breath. As if he didn't have enough trouble on his hands.

Lord help him.

Rose was back.

# CHAPTER TWO

*B*ULL GLANCED AT JASPER AS THE OLD BUICK PULLED INTO THE
yard. Jasper was grinning, making no effort to hide his pleasure.
"I'll be damned!" he muttered. "Never thought I'd see the day!"
He started forward, then checked himself, as if waiting to see
what Bull would do.

Bull wasn't surprised that his foreman was happy. When Rose
was here as a girl, Jasper had taken her under his wing. The two of
them had been as thick as thieves. Jasper had even argued for her
rights when Bull had altered the deed to her grandfather's property and registered the thirty-acre parcel as Rimrock land.

Rose would be wanting that land back—otherwise she wouldn't
have come here. And she'd be madder than a wet wildcat when she
discovered what he'd done.

The driver's door opened on the far side of the car. Catching
the remembered scent, the two dogs bounded toward her. Rose
paused long enough to scratch their shaggy ears and send them
off. Then she walked around the car, into full sight.

In his thoughts, Bull had always pictured her as the scrappy
runt of a girl he'd driven to Mexico twelve years ago.

*The girl who'd been tough enough to blast the life out of Hamilton
Prescott with a double-barreled twelve-gauge shotgun.*

She turned to face him from a distance—about the same distance as she'd been from Ham when she shot him. The toughness
was still there. But this Rose wasn't a girl anymore. She was a woman
in her midtwenties.

Even grown to womanhood, she couldn't have stood much over five-foot two. Dressed in ragged jeans, a Mexican serape, and cowboy boots that had long since molded to her feet, she had the look of someone from another time and place—or maybe a character from an old Sergio Leone western.

A mane of sun-streaked, tawny brown hair framed chiseled features etched with shadows of grief and hardship. The port-wine birthmark Bull remembered blazed like a banner of defiance down the left border of her face. A more typical woman might have arranged her hair to cover such a blemish. But Rose wore hers like war paint.

She was formidable.

"Rose." Jasper spoke her name. She turned and saw him. He opened his arms. "Damn it, girl, come here."

She hesitated, but only for an instant, before she ran to him. He hugged her close. "Welcome home, darlin'," he said.

Bull caught the glint of a tear on Jasper's cheek. Rose had been like a daughter to him—or maybe a kid sister, given their age difference. In the conflict over the land that was bound to come, Bull knew he could expect no help from his oldest friend.

After a moment, Rose broke away from Jasper and turned toward Bull. In the security light that flooded the yard, the striking eyes she fixed on him were the color of strong, dark coffee, framed by indecently long lashes and crowned by thick, dark brows. "Hello, Bull," she said.

"Hello, Rose." There were no embraces. He wasn't glad to see her, and she couldn't help but know it. After all this time, he'd hoped that maybe she'd found a man and settled down somewhere. But he should've known better.

"You must be hungry and tired," he said. "Come on in. I'll have Bernice rustle you up some supper."

"Bernice?" She looked crestfallen. "I was hoping you'd married Susan. I was looking forward to seeing her again."

Bull's throat tightened. He glanced at Jasper for help.

"Susan passed away six years ago, Rose," Jasper said. "Bernice is my sister. She came to take care of their two boys."

"Oh—oh no, I'm so sorry." Caught off guard, Rose showed a flash of vulnerability. She'd known Susan for only a short time, but Bull recalled that there'd been an instant connection between them.

"Those two boys would make any man proud," Jasper put in, breaking the awkward silence. "Are your bags in the trunk, Rose? I'll carry them inside for you."

"The key's still in the car," Rose said. "Just bring the duffel, thanks. Everything else can stay."

"Take her bag to the duplex. That'll give her some peace and quiet," Bull said, thinking it would also give *him* some peace and quiet. He needed time to come up with a plan to keep that thirty-acre parcel of land with its vital access to water.

Bull saw Rose hesitate, as if uncertain whether to follow Jasper or stay. He jerked his head toward the house.

"Come on in and eat before you turn in, Rose. Jasper, you come, too. We've all got some catching up to do."

Rose sat at the long table, thinking how much grander the place was than when she'd stayed here twelve years ago, cooking and helping with chores to earn her keep. There was matching china on the table and leather furniture in the parlor. A beautiful portrait of Susan in a blue dress and pearls hung on one wall.

By now, Rose had met Bernice, a chatty woman who already seemed to know a great deal about her. And Bull's sons had come out of their room long enough to say hello. The two were as different as brothers could be. Nine-year-old Will was cast in the image of his father—dark hair, a sturdy frame, and a resolute look about him. Seven-year-old Beau was his mother's child—fair and slender, a natural charmer with an easy smile.

Rose felt herself drawn to the motherless boys. But caution warned her back. A lot of things had changed in her absence, and there was no way of knowing whether the stern man who faced her across the table would turn out to be her friend or her enemy.

"How are things in Río Seco, Rose?" Bull buttered a slice of crusty sourdough bread. His tone was casual enough, but Rose could sense that she was being grilled.

"Things are bad," Rose said. "A drug cartel's taken over the town. Ramón and María are dead. Shot."

A shadow seemed to pass across Bull's rugged face. Ramón had always spoken well of him, as if they were friends. "And the boys, Raul and Joaquin?" he asked.

"No word from them in months, not since the last time they went off to work on that sheep ranch. I don't know if they're dead, too, or if they've gone over to the cartel."

"I'm sorry," Bull said. "I remember them well. They were good boys."

"Yes, they were." Ramón's two nephews had been like older brothers to Rose, laughing and teasing, teaching her to ride, throw a rope, and herd sheep. But they were no longer boys and had gone their own way. She tried not to wonder what had become of them.

"So you can understand why I had to leave," she said, knowing better than to mention what had happened last night in Río Seco.

"Sounds like you've been through a hell of a time, girl," Jasper said. "But don't worry. You've always got a home here, with us."

Dear Jasper. Kind and loyal to the bone. He never changed. But Rose didn't want to make a home on the Rimrock. She wanted to build a cabin on her own land and run some stock, or find some other way to support herself. Tonight, however, was no time to bring that up.

Instead she helped herself to another slice of pot roast, added a squirt of mustard, and folded it into a slice of bread to make a sandwich. "I can barely remember the last time I had beef," she said. "Most of the time, if we had meat in Río Seco, it was mutton, or pork when we could afford it. Compared to beans and tortillas, this is a meal fit for royalty. And this house is a palace. It appears you've done well here, Bull."

"We've managed, with a lot of work." Bull fell silent. Rose sensed that he was waiting for her to bring up the secret that hung between them—the secret that must come to light if she was to stay.

Telling herself it was time, she asked the question that had gnawed at her all the way from Río Seco. "What happened here after you took me to Mexico, Bull? Can I still be arrested for shooting Ham Prescott?"

Bull exchanged glances with Jasper. "What happened is a story for another time," he said. "But no, you're not likely to be arrested. The shooting was ruled self-defense."

"Which is exactly what it was," Jasper added.

"And Ferg Prescott? When he learns I'm back, will he come after me?"

Again, Bull glanced at Jasper, then shook his head. "You did Ferg a favor. He hated his old man and wanted him out of the way. If he was set on revenge, he'd have taken it long before now. The story's old news, Rose. As long as you keep your head down and don't make a fuss about it, you should be fine."

"I understand," Rose said. But in truth, she didn't understand at all. Large pieces were missing from the picture, and Bull didn't seem inclined to fill them in. Maybe later, when she got the chance to talk with Jasper alone, she could ask him for the full story.

For now, the evening's conversation seemed to be over. Bull rose from his place at the table and massaged the invisible kinks in his lower back. "Roundup time in the morning," he said. "Unless you're up before first light, you won't see us for breakfast, Rose. But Bernice will be here in case you need anything."

"Didn't you say you were going to call the Rangers?" Jasper reminded him.

"Oh—that's right. You'll have to get the men started without me. I'll join you as soon as I've talked to them."

"No problem," Jasper said. "Coming, Rose? I'll show you to your side of the duplex."

"Thanks," Rose said. "Just leave it open. I'll be along after I've cleaned up here."

After the men had gone, Rose put the leftover food in the fridge, rinsed the dishes, and loaded them in the dishwasher. She could hear the muffled sound of the TV from Bernice's apartment off the kitchen. She hoped Bernice would appreciate not having to clean up after the late supper. The woman had been friendly to her. Rose would do her best to keep things that way.

She left by the kitchen door, stepping out into the cool spring night. A stone's toss from the back steps was the chicken coop she and Jasper had built together, its wire mesh sides anchored securely in the ground to keep out marauding coyotes, snakes, and weasels. The chickens had gone to their nest boxes. From the deep shadows, Rose could hear their soft clucking, like the muted conversation of old women at a quilting bee. The comforting sound gave her a sense of home. Were these chickens descendants of the ones she'd rescued from her grandpa's place and left behind when Bull had rushed her off to Mexico? Maybe Jasper would know.

At the far edge of the backyard, she could see the blocky outline of the duplex. A glowing red dot and the faint aroma of burning tobacco told her Jasper was waiting for her on the porch.

She could see him now, leaning back in the old cane rocker she remembered from the past, with his boots on the porch rail and the dogs sprawled nearby. He put his feet down and gave her a grin as she mounted the steps.

"It's early yet. I know you're tuckered out from driving, but I was hoping you might want to sit and visit a spell." He nodded toward the empty chair beside him.

"Thanks. I'd like that." Rose came up onto the porch and sank onto the chair.

"Can I offer you a cold beer, now that you're legal to drink it?" He held out a bottle of Dos Equis, streaming with condensation. Rose took it from him and popped the cap. The first sip was icy on her tongue—a delicious shock.

"Thanks," she said. "Nothing ever got this cold in Río Seco."

He let her drink in silence for a few moments. Clouds drifted across the sky. An owl called in the darkness.

"Are you all right?" he asked her.

There was a world of concern in Jasper's question, but Rose wasn't ready to tell anyone about what had finally driven her out of Mexico. "I'm as well as could be expected," she said. "But the whole time I listened to Bull tonight, I was trying to fill in what he wasn't telling me."

Jasper tossed the butt of his hand-rolled cigarette over the rail into the dirt below. "I take it you're asking me for the whole story."

"Yes, if you don't mind. To start with, what happened after Bull took me away? All I remember is that Ham was lying there, bleeding on the ground. Then Ferg showed up and hauled him to his truck, and Bull was yelling at me to get my things."

Jasper took his time, as if piecing the story together. "When Bull took you away from here, he was acting in your best interest. In fact, he may have saved your life."

"I understand," Rose said. "That's what I've always believed."

"Ham was hurt beyond savin', but as you know, he didn't die right away. He was still conscious and talking when Ferg drove off with him."

"So he could've told Ferg that I shot him."

"Maybe, but only one person knows for sure what Ham said, and that's Ferg."

"So then what?"

"When Bull got back from Mexico a couple days later, Ferg was waitin' for him with the sheriff to arrest Bull for Ham's murder. Ferg claimed that Ham had named Bull as his killer."

Rose stifled a gasp. "But why would Ham lie about that, especially when he was dying?"

Jasper shrugged. "Maybe he didn't lie. Or maybe he never said a damned thing. But as long as nobody knew for sure, Ferg could pin Bull to the wall, like he's always wanted to do."

"But why wouldn't Bull just tell the truth? I was out of the country, where the law couldn't reach me."

Jasper rolled another cigarette from the makings in his shirt pocket. "This is where it gets complicated. Bull lucked onto a sharp lawyer, an old geezer named Ned Purvis. Ned advised Bull to take the blame and plead self-defense."

"But why? Bull didn't shoot Ham Prescott. I did."

"I know. But by Purvis's reckoning, no jury would've believed that a fourteen-year-old girl, who was gone without a trace, had pulled the trigger. And he was right. It took some doin' to prove that Ham had drawn his gun, but when the pistol finally turned up at the scene, Bull was acquitted. Self-defense. Pure and simple. And you're in the clear."

"So it's over."

"Dead and buried, just like old Ham."

"How many people know the truth?"

"Ned Purvis passed away five years ago. Susan would've known, but she's gone, too. That leaves just you, me, and Bull."

"What about Ferg?"

Jasper lit the cigarette and took a long drag. "Let's say, just to speculate, that Ham told him the truth. For Ferg to accuse you now would be to admit he lied eleven years ago. Besides, Ferg's hands weren't exactly clean that night. We know enough to smear his reputation, even if it's too late to send him to jail."

"But there's no statute of limitations on murder. If the truth came out, where would I stand in the eyes of the law?"

"The evidence that saved Bull—the fact that Ham had drawn a gun—would save you, too. So don't worry your pretty head about it."

Rose finished the beer, then laughed. "You're probably the first man to call me pretty, Jasper. Most of the men in Río Seco called me a witch."

"Then they were superstitious fools." Jasper stroked the dog that had nosed his hand for attention. "So what's your plan now that you're back?"

"To claim my land and live on it. Is that going to be a problem?"

"With Bull?"

"What do you think?"

"I think you're going to have a fight on your hands. Bull's a good man, but when it comes to land, it's like he's got a bit in his teeth and a burr under his saddle. If you could make some kind of deal, maybe a partnership—"

"No deal." Rose stood. "That land is mine. My grandfather left it to me. Bull may've had the use of it, but now it's time for him to give it back. I won't settle for anything less."

Jasper tossed away his cigarette and rose to go inside. "Then Lord help you, darlin'. And Lord help Bull, too. You're both going to need it."

After a beastly night of tossing and turning, Bull rolled out of bed and pulled on his clothes and boots. It was barely light, too early to call the Rangers' office about the rustlers. But maybe he could get a start on chores, freeing Jasper to leave for the roundup with the men who'd come down to the ranch.

After splashing his unshaven face and raking back his hair, which was already showing strands of gray, he strode down the hall to the kitchen, where he found Jasper at the table drinking the coffee he'd made. There was a kitchenette in the duplex, but after years of breakfast in the big house, Jasper had never broken the old habit.

"Have some coffee," he said to Bull. "There's scrambled eggs and bacon on the stove if you want something solid. From the look of you, you could use it."

"Didn't sleep," Bull grumbled, pouring himself a cup. "So, did you talk to Rose last night?"

"We visited some." Jasper forked up the last of the scrambled eggs on his plate. "She mostly wanted to know what happened after she shot Ham."

"Did she mention that parcel of land?" Bull took a seat at the kitchen table.

"She did. She wants it back. For whatever my advice is worth, I think you should give it to her."

"I figured that's what you'd say. But that land is our only access to the creek and the cattle tank we built to hold the water. We can't afford to lose it." Bull got up, heaped a plate with bacon and eggs, and sat down again. "The best I could do is offer her a different piece of land in exchange. Do you think she'd go for that?"

"I wouldn't bet on it. That thirty-acre parcel was her grandpa's. He's buried on it. And I don't think she'd take kindly to your digging the old man up and moving him."

"Well then, I'll just have to tell her no."

"Good luck with that." Jasper rose from the table and carried his plate and cup to the sink. "I'll be off with the boys as soon as the chores are done."

"Go on ahead and get an early start on the roundup. I've got some time to kill. I'll take care of the chores myself."

"Fine. Let me know when we can expect a ranger out here." Jasper left by the back door. Moments later Bull heard the sound of his truck starting up.

He made easy work of the chores, checking the pastures and adding water to the troughs and feed to the empty stalls in the horse barn. Rose's old Buick was pulled up outside the duplex, but he saw no sign of life there. After driving straight through from Río Seco, she was probably worn out. Fine, let her sleep. He was in no hurry for the confrontation that was sure to come.

By the time he finished, it was nearly seven o'clock. Lights were on in the house. By now Bernice would be feeding his sons and readying them to catch the school bus at the end of the lane. Bull went into his den, sat down at his desk, and made a call to the regional office of the TSCRA Special Rangers. Clive Barlow, the man who answered the phone, was a longtime acquaintance.

"Howdy, Bull," Barlow drawled. "What can I do for you?"

Bull had never been a man to waste words. "Yesterday we came up six cows short."

"That's a lot of cows—and a lot of cash to lose," Barlow said. "Since you're calling us, I'm guessin' you think it's rustlers."

"What the hell else could it be? Cows don't just sprout wings and fly away."

"Simmer down, Bull. We've already got a man on it. Ferg Prescott called us last week. Seems he's missin' cows, too. We sent one of our rangers undercover to look into it, a new guy named Tanner Mc-

Cade. When he checks in, I'll let him know you're havin' troubles as well."

"Blast it, Clive, don't just pass the word. Send him over so I can set him straight on what's happening."

"Can't do that, Bull. He's undercover, workin' as a hand for Prescott. It wouldn't do for him to be seen talkin' to you."

Bull mouthed a curse. "So, does Ferg know who he is?"

"Ferg had to know to hire him on. But nobody else is supposed to know, not even you. Don't worry, I'll tell him about your trouble when he checks in."

"Do that." Bull slammed down the phone. Damned waste of time. Meanwhile, he was losing cows—and money. Hell, he'd be better off strapping on a gun and taking matters into his own hands. It wouldn't be the first time he'd sent a rustler to the promised land. In the old days . . .

But the old days were gone, and these new times were different. Too many rules and regulations, with the law and the government looking over your shoulder. For now, all he could do was tell his men to keep a sharp eye out.

Still seething, he strode out to his pickup, swung into the driver's seat, and roared out of the yard.

Standing in the shadow of the porch, Rose watched him go. She'd been awake since early dawn, but she'd stayed out of sight, not wanting to confront Bull until she knew more about what he'd done with her land.

She could see lights and movement through the window of the kitchen, where Bernice was probably making breakfast for the boys. Rose knew she'd be welcomed at the table. But she wasn't ready to mingle, let alone get into a conversation about her own plans. She'd found a jar of instant coffee in the kitchenette of the duplex and made do with that for breakfast. Now that Bull had left, she was ready to visit the place where she'd taken refuge with her grandfather after fleeing the foster system, and where she'd stayed until he was murdered by Ham Prescott.

The sunrise faded to a blue morning as she drove the Buick behind the outbuildings and onto a deeply rutted dirt road that led north along the east boundary of the ranch. Her grandfather's land wasn't far—a couple of miles at most—but the going was slow. Rose had to balance the wheels between the high center and the outside edge of the road to keep from scraping the Buick's undercarriage.

Maybe the next time she came here, she could ask Jasper to lend her a horse. The old car would have to be sold or traded for a pickup that could handle the road and haul supplies for building her cabin. With luck, she might even find a collector and get a good price for the restored vehicle. But she was getting ahead of herself. First she needed to secure and hold the parcel that was her inheritance.

When familiar landmarks told her she was getting close, she parked the car next to a clump of mesquite and slid the .44 out from under the seat. Rose had long since learned not to take her safety for granted. The cartel was like a giant spider, the strands of its web reaching far beyond the Mexican border. Their agents could be anywhere, and look like anyone. If they'd traced her car, they could already be closing in.

And Ferg Prescott, whose ranch bordered her land on the far side of the creek, could have his eyes on the place his father had killed for. Alone out here, she couldn't be too careful.

As she climbed out of the car, the splash and gurgle of the creek reached her ears. Memories swept over her, the old log cabin on its banks, the vegetables and chickens she'd raised, and the nighttime treks to the outhouse in the trees. Most poignant of all was the memory of her grandfather—his deep, gravelly voice, his kindness, and his defiant courage at the end of his life. She would never stop missing him.

The cabin would be gone. Bull Tyler had torched it, with her grandfather's body inside, to hold off Prescott's men while they made their escape. Only her chickens, which Jasper had caught and taken to the Rimrock, had been saved.

Rose had braced herself for whatever she was about to see. But even so, the sight of the trampled bank, the head gate, and the ugly pipe leading from the water to the cattle tank, with only a few tilted posts remaining where a fence had once marked the boundary, almost crushed her heart. This had been a beautiful place once, a place she had loved. But all that had changed.

Near the edge of the clearing, a massive cottonwood trunk lay where the tree had fallen, its limbs cut away. Here, in a space dug out underneath, was where Bull had buried her grandfather's charred remains. No casket. No service—perhaps not even a prayer. And only a temporary marker, long since gone.

Kneeling beside the spot, Rose laid a hand on the makeshift grave. "I'm back, Grandpa," she whispered. "And now that I'm here, I'm going to make a home in this place—a home you'd be proud of."

She was about to rise and go when a familiar prickling of her senses warned her of danger. She'd seen nothing, heard nothing. But all her instincts told her that she wasn't alone.

Someone was watching her.

She froze, one hand thumbing back the hammer to cock the .44. She had learned to depend on her danger instincts. If she sensed that someone was watching her, she was probably right.

She'd seen no one on this side of the creek. But the other side was Prescott land—hostile territory ever since the old days, when she'd lived here with her grandfather and Ham Prescott's hired thugs had harassed them with guns and torches in an attempt to force them off the property.

In the end, when he wouldn't sell, Ham Prescott himself had shown up on the far side of the creek and shot her grandfather with a rifle. Her grandfather had made it back into the cabin but died a short time later. That was when Bull and Jasper had shown up, rescued her and her chickens, and set the cabin ablaze to cover their escape.

And that was when Bull had found the hidden deed to the property and kept it for himself.

Rose could still feel a hidden presence on the far side of the creek. Ham Prescott might be long gone, but his son Ferg was in charge now, and Ferg was no different from his father. He could easily have his men watching her.

She kept the pistol cocked, her grip steady and sure. If she had to, she would shoot first and ask questions later.

# CHAPTER THREE

SCREENED BY WILLOWS, TANNER MCCADE WATCHED THE WOMAN ON the far side of the creek. Who was she? And what the hell was she doing out here?

On the pretext of riding fence, he'd been checking the boundaries of the Prescott Ranch, looking for places where rustlers might have parked a truck and crossed over with stolen Prescott cattle, when he heard the approaching motor. Leaving his horse in the trees and moving into the willows, he'd watched the vintage Buick pull up and park next to a clump of mesquite.

Ferg Prescott had warned him that, when it came to cattle rustling, the neighboring rancher, Bull Tyler, was the prime suspect. True or not, there was clearly no love lost between the two men. Some asking on Tanner's part confirmed that the Tyler–Prescott feud dated back to the previous generation. And one of the biggest bones of contention had been this nameless creek and the land on the far side of it.

Tanner had seen an aerial photo, showing the creek and the place where a length of PVC pipe led to a circular cattle tank on the Tyler property. Both the Prescott Ranch and Bull Tyler's Rimrock got most of their water from wells. But the creek, which gushed year-round from its source in the escarpment, was an important water source for range cattle. Control of the land along the banks meant control of the water. That control was split between two powerful men who appeared to hate each other's guts.

Now Tanner was seeing the disputed spot for the first time. Everything was pretty much as he'd expected.

Except for the woman.

She was kneeling beside the old fallen tree on the far side of the creek, so close that he could have tossed a stone and hit her. Her back was toward him now, but he'd seen her walking toward the water with a heavy pistol in her hand. Small as she was, her powerful, confident stride seemed to say, *Don't mess with me!*

He had to admit she was pretty—not like most women, but more the way a wild hawk was pretty, fierce and alert, her sun-streaked hair tied back with a length of black ribbon, her denim shirt and faded jeans skimming the curves of her sinewy little body. She wasn't young, but young enough . . .

For what? Tanner gave himself a mental slap. He was looking for rustlers, not a bed partner. And her actions in this place were enough to put her under suspicion.

Now she was bending lower, reaching under the tree trunk as if feeling for something, maybe a message. He could step into sight, aim his pistol, and order her to drop that big .44 she was packing. But he'd never shot a woman, and he didn't want to chance doing that now. Besides, if he spooked her, he would never learn what she was up to or whether she had any unsavory friends lurking around.

Her body stiffened abruptly, as if she'd heard something. Tanner hadn't moved or made a sound, but she seemed to sense his presence. From her kneeling position by the fallen tree, she rose to a crouch. One hand cocked the pistol as she glanced around. Satisfied, but still alert, she stood, giving him his first head-on look at her striking face.

Her skin was sun-bronzed to a golden hue. Her features were sharp and proud, her eyes as dark as the heart of a sunflower. When she glanced to one side, he saw the wine-colored streak that spilled down the left side of her face. Rather than mar her features, it lent her a wildness that was almost erotic.

But he wasn't here to ogle her, Tanner reminded himself. If this woman was in league with the rustlers—perhaps as a lookout—it would be his job to round her up and bring her in with the rest.

Still gripping the pistol, she backed away from the creek, toward the mesquite clump where she'd left her car. Tanner began to breathe again as she lowered the gun, climbed into the Buick, turned the car around, and headed back toward the Rimrock Ranch. At least the woman and the car would be easy to recognize if he saw them again—and something told Tanner he would.

But right now he wanted a closer look at whatever was under that fallen tree trunk.

Tanner straightened to his lean, six-foot height. Holstering the gun, he crossed the creek at a shallow spot and moved up the bank to the clearing where he'd seen the woman. It was his first time on Tyler property. The sense of being in a forbidden place triggered a prickle that raised the hair on the back of his neck. For all he knew, he could be shot just for being here.

He knew the lay of the land from the maps he'd studied. This narrow parcel ran like a finger, north along the creek from the main border of the Rimrock. Beyond its boundaries, the land was federal, open range all the way into the Escarpment, where the creek, fed by artesian water under the caprock, flowed in a steady stream. According to Texas law, nobody owned the water. It was the *access* to the water that made the difference in this dry country.

The cattle tank had been filled recently. Tanner could see horse tracks along the bank and boot tracks by the head gate, which could be opened to let water flow into the pipe. There were cattle tracks, too, and here and there the small, pointed prints of Mexican cowboy boots where the mysterious woman had walked. Her prints were most numerous next to the fallen tree, which must have been a giant when it was growing.

The trunk lay a few inches off the ground, its girth supported at either end by its roots and the broken stubs of its branches. Crouching, Tanner peered underneath. He could see no sign that the ground had been dug up or disturbed in any way except for a single small, fresh handprint pressed into the earth.

What was he seeing here?

Was it some kind of message?

Backing off, Tanner studied the ground beneath the tree trunk. A narrow section of earth, about six feet long, had settled over time, as if the dirt had once been dug up, replaced, and left.

It looked a grave, he realized, more than likely an old one. He couldn't be sure without digging it up. But he had too much respect for the dead to disturb the place without a good reason.

Instead he focused on the mysterious woman. Was she a messenger, a spy, or a mourner? Was she part of the Tyler crew, or was she, like him, a trespasser on the land?

Nothing else Tanner saw here gave him any answers. But if there was any chance the woman was linked to the rustlers, he'd be smart to keep an eye on her.

The Buick had vanished around a bend in the road, probably going back to the Rimrock. For now, there was nothing left to do here. Still pondering, Tanner crossed the creek to his horse, mounted up, and set off to find Ferg Prescott and report what he'd seen.

After visiting her land, Rose drove the twenty-mile road into the town of Blanco Springs. She hadn't seen much of the place when she'd last stayed at the Rimrock. Most of the time, Bull had insisted on keeping her out of sight. He'd even made up a story about her being Jasper's visiting niece. Only later had she learned that this wasn't just for her safety. Bull, she'd long since learned, rarely did anything unless it served his own purpose.

After eleven years, the town was much as she remembered— the working-class homes, the grocery and dry goods stores along Main Street, the ramshackle Blue Coyote Bar, and the Burger Shack, which sold sandwiches, pizza, shakes, and sodas. The thought of a real hamburger and an ice-cold Coke made her mouth water, but she didn't want to attract the kind of attention she'd get at a place like that. Not today, at least.

At the end of Main Street she found the city and county building where, she assumed, the property records would be kept. The

County Recorder's office was in the basement. When she asked to see a map of the Rimrock Ranch, the clerk, a bespectacled young man who made an effort not to look at her birthmark, gave her a plat—a hefty book of surveyors' maps with legal descriptions that meant nothing to her. Sitting down with it at a long table, Rose leafed through the pages until what she was seeing began to make sense. After forty minutes of searching, she opened a map and recognized the creek and the strip of land her grandfather had left her.

Marking the page with a scrap of paper, she carried the plat to the counter, pointed out her land, and asked the clerk who owned it.

"Have a seat and I'll look it up," he said. "Forgive me if it takes a few minutes. I'm new at this job."

"Is there anybody around who was here twelve years ago, when the deed was recorded?" Rose asked.

"Sorry. Beth Hazelton, who ran this place for decades, passed away last month. I was part-time help. Now I'm running it myself, at least until the next election for County Recorder."

When Rose failed to make chatty conversation, he rummaged in the files and books for a few more minutes. Rose's gut told her what he would find. But she had to hear the news for herself before she could confront Bull.

"Found it!" the clerk said. "The deed to that parcel of land was recorded in 1974."

"And the owner?" Rose's pulse quickened.

"Mr. Virgil Tyler of the Rimrock Ranch."

Rose had known what she would hear. Still, she couldn't help clasping at a last thin thread of hope. "Is anyone else's name on the deed?" she asked.

"No name's recorded except Mr. Tyler's. These days we make photocopies of deeds, but from back then, we'd have only the record. Mr. Tyler would have kept the deed himself."

"I see. Thank you." Rose strode out of the basement room, a bitter taste welling in her throat. She'd hoped against hope that her suspicions weren't true. But it was time to face reality. Bull

Tyler, the man who'd sheltered her under his roof, saved her life more than once, and stood trial for the act she'd committed, had stolen her land and was very likely plotting to keep it.

"You say you saw a woman by the creek?" Ferg Prescott's beetling brows met above a nose reddened by too much Kentucky bourbon. In middle age, he was putting on weight, developing jowls and a paunch that overhung his belt. Now, seated behind his massive desk, he looked like what he was—the absolute ruler of the biggest ranch in Blanco County, a powerful presence whose word was law.

Tanner had met him less than a week ago. But he already knew enough to watch his step with the man. Ferg Prescott was sharp, volatile, and ruthless. His ranch hands were well paid, well housed, and well fed, but fear of their boss took a toll on them all.

"Far as I know, the only woman on the Rimrock these days is the housekeeper," Ferg said. "Could that be who you saw?"

"This was no housekeeper. She was wearing jeans and boots and driving an old green Buick that looked like something from the forties."

"Doesn't ring a bell." Ferg stubbed out the butt of his illegal Havana cigar in an ashtray made of polished Mexican onyx. Lifting a fresh cigar out of a box, he said, "Tell me more."

"She was small, midtwenties, tawny brown hair, not bad looking," Tanner said, understating his description. "The one thing you'd notice about her was a dark red birthmark down the left side of her face."

Ferg's expression didn't change at first. But his fingers clamped so tightly around the cigar that they crushed the fine, brown leaves, releasing their leathery aroma into the air.

"Do you know her?" Tanner asked.

Ferg nodded.

"Do you think she could be connected to the cattle rustling?"

Ferg's eyes narrowed to slits of anger—or maybe it was something deeper and darker. Almost like fear.

Taking his time to answer, he laid the crushed cigar aside, lit a fresh one, and took a slow puff, drawing it out as if weighing what he was about to say. "I don't know about the cattle rustling," he said. "But yes, I do know her. I can't prove it, mind you, and it would never hold up in court, but I have every reason to believe the little she-devil murdered my father."

Tanner crossed the ranch yard to the two-story frame bunkhouse, the one place on the ranch where he had access to a phone. Most of the hands would be out on the roundup. Tomorrow he'd be joining them. But right now he had the time and privacy for a couple of calls.

The pay phone was mounted on a wall outside the first-floor dormitory-style bedrooms. It made sense that Ferg wouldn't want homesick cowboys running up the ranch phone bill. Still, it struck Tanner as petty that the hired hands couldn't even order a pizza from town without paying for the call.

After checking to make sure no one was nearby, he placed a collect call to Clive Barlow at the regional office.

"Anything new?" Clive asked.

"Still chasing leads. If any of the Prescott men are rustling their boss's cattle, they're doing a good job of covering their tracks. Ferg's still claiming that Bull Tyler is the rustler. In the absence of anyone else, I'm inclined to believe him."

"Well, this might change your mind," Clive said. "I got a call from Bull this mornin'. Seems he's missin' cows, too."

"That doesn't mean he's telling the truth, or that somebody else on his ranch isn't stealing them." Tanner told Clive about the strange woman he'd seen that morning. "When I told Ferg about her, he almost crushed his cigar. He told me he suspected her of killing his father."

"Now that's middlin' strange," Clive said. "I remember that case, ten . . . no, twelve years ago. Ham Prescott was an old bastard. Came onto the Tyler property with a pistol and got himself blasted to smithereens with a shotgun for his trouble. But it was Bull Tyler who admitted to the deed. Bull pleaded self-defense and the grand jury let him off. Now Ferg is sayin' the woman done it? That doesn't make sense."

"Ferg did say there wasn't any proof."

"Well, whatever he says, you'd best keep an eye on the lady. Her showin' up about the same time as cattle disappearin' is a bit too much of a coincidence to suit me."

"Agreed. I'll keep my ears open. Maybe I can pick up something on the roundup tomorrow." Tanner hung up the phone, wishing he'd had better news to report. True, there were gangs of rustlers who swooped in and drove off cattle to load into trucks for out-of-state markets where they wouldn't likely be traced. But nine times out of ten, the thieves would turn out to be local, often working on the very ranch where the stock went missing. Tanner had done his best to fit in with Prescott's men. But he was new on the job, and if there was any business going on behind the boss's back, they wouldn't trust him enough to let him know. Most of them, in fact, seemed terrified of crossing Ferg Prescott in any way.

That was why he'd turned his attention to the neighbors. But now Bull Tyler had reported cattle missing, too. Tanner's gut instinct told him something wasn't what it appeared to be. But what was it? What was he missing?

For now, all he could do was trust his eyes and ears and get back to work. But there was one more call he needed to make. This call was personal.

After fishing in his pocket for a handful of change, he made a long-distance call to a small ranch at the foot of Wyoming's Wind River Mountains.

A woman's voice answered. She sounded anxious, or maybe just tired. Tanner knew his sister-in-law didn't have it easy. Life on a struggling ranch with a husband and four active kids could take a lot out of any woman.

"Is everything all right, Ruth?" he asked. "How's Clint?"

Ruth sighed. "He could be better. His back went out just in time for calving season, and now that I'm pregnant again, I can't be much help. Your brother needs you, Tanner. You need to come home."

"I'll try to send more money. Maybe Clint can hire some high school kids for the heavy lifting."

"Maybe." She sounded weary and frustrated. Tanner couldn't blame her.

Guilt bored deeper, like a sharp-bitted auger, as he ended the call. Five months ago, he'd seen the ad for this job in a newsletter for ranchers. The requirements—knowledge of the cattle business and law enforcement experience—had been a perfect fit for him. Taking the position as a special ranger for the TSCRA had meant leaving Wyoming and moving to Texas. Clint and Ruth had tried to talk him out of it. But he'd argued that the extra money would contribute more to the ranch than his presence and his meager salary as a deputy sheriff.

He'd made good on that promise, at least. Most of his salary went back to the ranch for new stock and equipment, supplies, and repairs and to help his brother's family through the lean winter months.

But Tanner had kept his real reason for leaving to himself. Desperate to escape his memories, his nightmares, and his gut-wrenching guilt, he'd jumped at the chance to get away and start over. Maybe in a new place, with new people and new responsibilities, he could begin to heal.

So far, that wasn't working so well.

Ferg Prescott poured himself a second shot of bourbon and tossed it down in a single gulp.

*Why now?* He punctuated the thought with a string of the vilest curses in the English vocabulary. Why, now that the plan was in place to destroy Bull Tyler and get his hands on the creek property, did that ugly little bitch of a girl have to show up?

He knew who she was, of course. After his dying father had named her as his killer and the girl had disappeared, Ferg had hired a top-notch investigator to track down her background information. It had taken months of work, cost a pile of money, and taken some conjecture on Ferg's part, but he'd finally gotten some answers.

Rose Landro, child of a single mother and an untraceable father, both presumed dead, had run away from foster care to stay with her maternal grandfather, an old hermit who'd bought the creek parcel years earlier and lived on the land in a tumbledown shack. As his only known relative, Rose would have been heir to the land.

But that was where things got interesting.

When Ham Prescott had shot the old man for refusing to sell, and Rose, hiding in the shack, had witnessed the crime, Bull had taken her in and used her to blackmail Ham. That had led to Ham's going to the Rimrock to silence her and running smack into her shotgun blast.

Restless, Ferg stood up and walked to the window, gazing out at his kingdom. Beyond a stand of budding cottonwoods lay the back road from the Rimrock, where he'd stopped the truck that night, delaying long enough to make sure his father died before reaching home. That was when Ham had told him it was the girl who'd fired the fatal shot.

Ferg had kept his dying father's confession secret and blamed the shooting on Bull. With Bull in prison it would have been easy to get the land and control the water from both sides of the creek. But Bull had not only gone free, he'd gotten rid of the girl and taken the land for himself.

And now, the rightful owner of the contested property had shown up.

Ferg sat down again, lit a fresh Havana, and blew a smoke ring into the air. On second thought, Rose's return might not be so bad. His present scheme was risky. If it failed, he could use her as a backup, maybe become her ally against Bull to help her get the land back . . .

A tentative knock at the door broke into his thoughts. That would be Garn, his son and heir. But Garn could damn well come back later. Ferg knew what the young fool wanted, and he wasn't in the mood to talk about it now.

His twenty-one-year-old son had been conceived by accident when he and Edith were little more than hormone-crazed kids, not even married yet. Spineless and bookish, with no interest in ranching, Garn had none of the drive and fire that had made the Prescotts the most powerful family in the county.

Even more disappointing than Garn was the fact that Edith hadn't given him the strapping, manly sons he'd wanted. After four miscarriages, she'd had her tubes tied for the sake of her health. Not that it had done much good. She'd died a few years later from ovarian cancer.

Her photo hung on the side wall of his office, in a spot where he rarely looked. Now he gave it a passing glance. She looked the way she had in life, her colorless blond hair drawn back in a bun, her face bare of makeup. In younger days, she'd been pretty in a buxom sort of way, and always up for a romp in the backseat of his car. But the miscarriages had convinced her that she was paying for her sins. A preacher's daughter, she'd turned back to her religious roots, taken a separate bedroom, and spent her nights reading the Bible. Not that Ferg had minded. He'd never been faithful to his marriage vows and had no trouble finding comfort elsewhere.

Still, life wasn't fair, he groused. Susan Rutledge Tyler, the woman he'd once hoped to marry, had given Bull two strong sons before the crash that took her life. Unless he wanted to marry again and start over, he was stuck with Garn.

But back to the girl. He needed a way to break the ice with her. Blowing another smoke ring, he pondered what the ranger had told him. He'd mentioned a Buick, an old one. And Ferg had discovered an interest in collecting vintage cars. Maybe . . .

The rap on the door had become more insistent. Garn wasn't going away. Ferg sighed. "Come on in."

His son stood in the open doorway of his office. Pale like his mother, with a long face and gangly body like his preacher grandfather's, he was wearing a yellow polo shirt.

*A goddamned yellow polo shirt with some kind of animal on the pocket! He couldn't even look like a rancher!*

Bull sucked on his cigar and blew out the smoke in a cloud. "If you're here to talk to me about that fool Washington internship, you can forget it. I told you it was a waste of time, sending in that application."

"But it wasn't," Garn said. "I've been accepted. I won't be starting until fall, but I need to respond in the next few days." He took a breath, as if gathering courage. "This is my dream, Dad. I've wanted to go into politics ever since President Reagan came to the ranch on that bird-hunting trip."

"I don't give a damn what your dream is," Ferg said. "You're not going to Washington. You're going to stay here and learn to run the ranch."

"I knew you'd say that," Garn said. "That's why I mailed my letter of acceptance this morning. It's a done deal. I'm going."

"Over my dead body!" Ferg thundered. "I let you go to college when you begged me. But now that's done. You're staying right here!"

Garn shook his head. "Let's not fight about this, Dad. I'm twenty-one years old. I can do what I want. Meanwhile, I'll be here through the end of summer. That's almost five months. If we can make peace, I'll knuckle under for that time and focus on the ranch."

*Spoken like a budding damned politician,* Ferg thought. He'd always equated political types with rats and maggots. But at least the young fool had the *cojones* to stand up for what he wanted. Maybe that was better than nothing.

"We'll talk later," he said, as a new idea sprang up in his mind. "Meanwhile, I've got an errand for you to run."

He scrawled a note on ranch stationery, folded it into an envelope, and wrote a name on the outside. "Take this to the Rimrock Ranch," he said. "Deliver it personally to Miss Rose Landro."

Garn didn't mind being asked to deliver the note. He'd been dying of boredom, and any excuse to get away from the ranch and his father's bombastic presence was welcome.

He drove slowly on the dirt road that connected the two ranches. Much as he loved flying along in his sleek Porsche, he didn't want to raise dust that would settle on the car's shiny black finish that had just been waxed the day before.

With one hand on the wheel, he glanced at the note his father had given him. *Miss Rose Landro*. The name was intriguing. He pictured some exotic movie star type, but Miss Landro could just as easily be eighty years old.

Since the envelope was unsealed, he took the liberty of unfolding the note and reading it. Interesting, he thought. Whomever this Miss Landro was, it seemed he was about to get to know her, perhaps know her well.

# CHAPTER FOUR

*I*T WAS ONE-THIRTY WHEN ROSE ARRIVED BACK AT THE RIMROCK. BER-nice was standing on the front porch, a gingham apron over her slacks. Her apple-cheeked face broke into a smile as Rose climbed out of her car. "So there you are, honey. I knew you might be too tired for breakfast. But when you didn't show up for lunch, and I saw that your car was gone, I started to worry. Come on in the kitchen. I'll make you a sandwich."

Rose would have answered that she could make her own sand-wich, but she knew Bernice meant well and was trying to be friendly. With a murmur of thanks, she followed the woman into the kitchen and sat down at the kitchen table she remembered from the old days.

"Where are the boys?" she asked, making conversation. "Are they in school?"

"Yes, they take the bus into Blanco Springs. They'll be home around four. They're good boys. You'll enjoy getting to know them." Bernice busied herself at the kitchen counter, slicing cold roast beef and homemade bread. "Jasper's told me a lot about you," she said.

"A lot?" Rose's pulse skipped. "How much?"

"I'd say just about everything, including some secrets I'd never tell a soul. My brother thinks the world of you. He's always hoped you'd come back."

"Jasper was my best friend when I was here before," Rose said.

*you're interested, please follow my son home in your car. If your vehicle*
*turns out to be what I'm looking for, I can offer you cash on the spot.*
    *Sincerely,*
    *Ferguson Prescott*

Garn Prescott appeared to have read the message before giving
it to Rose. "My father collects old cars," he said. "He's building a
special barn for them." He glanced at the Buick, which was parked
next to his shiny Porsche. "I can promise you he'll be interested in
this one."

Was it a trap? Rose hesitated, weighing the offer. It seemed almost too good to be true. But she did need to trade the Buick for
something more serviceable, like a pickup with a camper on it.
The trouble was, without a title or registration, she had no idea
how to get rid of the old Buick, especially for a decent price. Ferg
Prescott's offer, if legitimate, could be a lifesaver. But she knew
enough about Ferg to be cautious.

"The car is a dirty mess," she hedged. "Besides, there's no paperwork. I took the car after the owner died."

"My father can handle the paperwork, and he'll have one of
the boys wash your car before he gives it his final okay." Garn unfolded his lanky frame from the chair. "Come on. What've you got
to lose?"

*Plenty*, Rose thought. But if she meant to settle on her land,
sooner or later she would have to deal with Ferg. So why not now,
especially if his offer to buy her car was genuine?

"Fine," Rose said, rising. "Lead the way. I'll be right behind you."

For an instant, she weighed the idea of telling Bernice where
she was going, then decided against it. The good woman would
only worry, or worse send someone to rescue her if she was late
getting back. It was an easy decision. But as she climbed into the
car and fished the key out of her pocket, she remembered her
tools in the trunk and the pistol she'd left under the front seat.

Garn was pulling away, but he stopped when she jumped out of
the car and waved him down. "Stay here," she told him. "I need to
unload the car before we go."

Without waiting for his response, she drove around behind the duplex, hauled the tools out of her trunk, and piled them against the back wall. The question of the gun gave her some pause. She would feel more secure going to the Prescott ranch with a weapon. But there was no way to hide the heavy pistol on her body, and she'd never get away with wearing it openly. The .44 would have to stay here.

After wrapping the gun in her serape, she carried it into her side of the duplex and stuffed it under the bed. Feeling vulnerable and more than a little nervous, she went back to her car and followed the Porsche along the back road to the Prescott Ranch.

She'd seen the two-story frame house before, from a distance. It looked the same as she remembered, impressive with its white exterior and gingerbread trim above the broad, shaded porch. As Garn escorted her up the front steps, she noticed that the paint around the door was peeling.

"Step into my parlor," Garn joked, recalling the old poem about the spider and the fly. It expressed Rose's feelings exactly, but she wasn't about to say so. How much did this unsettling young man know about her past? What had she been thinking, letting herself be lured here with no way to protect herself?

The living room, with its heavy walnut cabinets, massive leather furniture, and mounted trophy heads—bison, cougars, coyotes, javelinas, bobcats, and a hideous black bear with its mouth open in a snarl—was overpowering in its masculinity. It wasn't hard to imagine her own head, stuffed and mounted on the wall.

"This way." Garn's hand, settling on the small of her back, sent a jolt of alarm through her body. His touch lingered as he guided her down the hall toward an open doorway and nudged her through ahead of him. Only then did he drop his hand and take a step back.

Ferg Prescott rose from behind the desk, his features arranged in a smiling mask. He had aged in the past twelve years, his presence taking on a weight that was more than physical. *Ponderous* . . . That was the word that sprang into her mind. He was far from old. But it was as if the flesh of his face and body had been sucked downward by some invisible force. The pricey-looking wool shirt and leather vest he wore were as spotless as his hands, as if they'd never been exposed to a lick of outdoor work.

How much did he know about her part in his father's death? How did he plan to use it?

"Thank you for coming, Miss Landro," he said. "Let's have a look at your car."

Nerves quivering, she let him escort her back outside. Garn walked behind her, so close that she imagined she could hear him breathing.

When they stepped out onto the porch, Rose saw that one of the ranch hands, who must have been given the order ahead of time, was already hosing down her car. She stood next to Ferg, watching the dirty water flow off the chassis of the old Buick.

"Not bad," Ferg said. "Looks to me like a forty-seven Buick Super. Is that right?"

"I don't know," Rose said. "I was never told. But it's been well maintained. It runs fine. The key's in the ignition, if you want to try it out."

"Since I wouldn't be driving it much, that's not an issue," Ferg said. "The body looks to be in decent condition. Has it been restored?"

"I don't know for sure, but I think so."

"And the interior?"

"The same."

"If it was all original, the car would be a treasure," Ferg said. "Restored, I can offer you eight thousand cash."

Eight thousand. Not as much she'd hoped for but enough for what she needed. "I got the car in Mexico," she said. "There's no title."

"I can take care of that," he said. "I took the liberty of drawing up a bill of sale. When we've filled in the blanks and you've signed it, the money's yours. Do we have a deal?" He held out his hand.

Rose returned the handshake. His palm was smooth and cool, his clasp businesslike. She didn't trust the man or his son, but she needed the money to carry out her plan. She had little choice except to gamble that Ferg was playing straight with her.

Back in his office, they signed duplicate copies of the bill of sale. Ferg counted out hundred-dollar bills from a strongbox in his desk, slipped them into a manila envelope, and handed them to Rose. The leaden eyes that met hers were flat and unreadable.

"You can count it again if you want," he said.

"I watched you count it. That's good enough." Rose jammed the envelope into the hip pocket of her jeans. All she wanted to do was get out of there. But first she needed another favor.

"If you'd like to drink to our bargain, I've got some excellent Kentucky bourbon in my liquor cabinet," Ferg said as they walked back into the living room.

"Thanks, but I've done what I came for. Now I need to get going."

His smile was razor thin. "Another time, then. I can have somebody drive you back to the Rimrock."

"I'll do it." Garn had joined them again. His father ignored him.

"Thanks," Rose said, "but what I need now is to buy another vehicle. Is there anything like a used car lot in town?"

"The man who runs the garage usually has a few out back for sale, or he can tell you who else is selling one," Ferg said. "I can't vouch for his honesty. If you find one you like, you'll want to have a man check it out for you."

"I know enough about cars," Rose said. "All I need is a ride to town."

"I can drive her," Garn said.

Again, Ferg ignored his son's offer. "McCade's around," he said. "Go find him, Garn. Tell him he can take the new truck. The keys are on the hook by the door."

Garn's expression soured, but he did as he was told, hooking the key ring with a finger as he strode out the front door, leaving Rose alone with Ferg.

She stirred uncomfortably. "You must have things to do," she said. "I can wait for my ride on the porch."

Ferg gave her a smile. "That's fine. But know that you can call on me anytime, for anything you need. Consider me your friend, Miss Landro. And trust me when I say that I can do more for you than Bull Tyler can."

"Thanks, I'll keep that in mind." Rose started for the door, then paused. "How did you know me and know about my car?"

He smiled again. "No mystery. One of my hands saw you this morning. When he described you, I knew who he was talking about. And when he mentioned the car, I knew that I wanted to see it for myself. Does that answer your question?"

"I suppose so." Rose remembered the feeling she'd had that someone was watching her. She'd learned to trust her instincts. This time they must've been spot-on. "I'll let you get back to work," she said, moving toward the door.

"Good luck finding your vehicle. If you need anything else, let me know." With that, he vanished into the shadowed hallway.

Rose walked onto the porch, closing the door behind her. Leaning on the rail, she gazed across the distance at the russet cliffs of the escarpment that jutted skyward along the west boundary of the Rimrock. Two vultures circled above the foothills, riding on the warm spring updrafts.

The old Buick was gone from where she'd left it, taken to someplace where it would be cleaned or stored. And the envelope of money—more cash than she had ever seen in her life—was straining the rivets on the hip pocket of her jeans.

In the past hour, her life had taken on a surreal quality—money in her pocket and Ferg Prescott offering to be her new best friend. She'd have to be crazy to trust the man. Bull and Jasper didn't hate him for nothing. But he'd just given her what she needed and hinted at more to come. Maybe he'd even be willing to help her get her land back.

But what would he demand in return?

Had she just sold her soul to the devil?

A shiny, dark blue pickup had come around the barn and was headed for the house. That would be her ride to town. Rose came down the steps as the truck pulled up to the foot of the porch. She was about to open the passenger door and climb in when the driver swung to the ground, strode around the truck, and opened the door for her.

Without a word he reached out to help her into the high seat. Glancing up, Rose glimpsed a craggy face, dark hair lightly silvered at the temples, and steel gray eyes. He was no movie star, but the skip of her pulse told her that his sheer masculinity had touched off a response.

She lowered her gaze. Hard experience had taught her to be wary of attractive men. They tended to think they could take whatever they wanted from a woman—especially a marked girl who would probably be grateful for the attention. Rose would never have called herself shy. But her self-protective instincts were razor sharp.

Avoiding eye contact, she clasped his forearm to lever herself upward. Through the worn flannel sleeve, his muscles were like ropes, taut and hard. His faded shirt and worn leather vest smelled of clean, fresh hay, as if he might have been working in the barn when he was called to drive her.

As she groped for the seat belt, he closed the door, went back around the truck, and climbed into the driver's seat. "Tanner Mc-Cade's the name, Miss. You want to go to town, right?" The sharp inflection of his words told her he wasn't from Texas.

"That's right," she said. "I need to go someplace where I can buy a used truck. Mr. Prescott told me about a garage."

"I know the place. I'll wait while you look, in case you don't see what you want." He paused as if waiting for her reply, which didn't come. "Believe me, you don't want to be stranded in Blanco Springs," he said.

She shrugged. "I don't want to be a bother."

"A bother? When it's this or muck out the stable, it's an easy choice."

"Thanks." He had made her smile, a rare accomplishment. But that didn't mean she trusted him any more. Something told her that with this man, she would have to watch her every move and her every word.

*Tanner McCade.* The name sounded as if it belonged to a movie cowboy. For all she knew, he could've made it up. Was he what he appeared to be, a simple cowhand working for Ferg Prescott, or did he have his own agenda? Whoever he was, or however he might try to charm her, one thing was certain. She couldn't afford to trust him.

Tanner turned the truck onto the main highway. The woman sat in silence beside him. *Rose.* Garn Prescott had mentioned her name. It didn't suit her, Tanner thought. Or maybe it did. She was a prickly little thing, more like a wild rose than one of the hothouse beauties Ferg Prescott's late wife had planted below the porch.

He knew, of course, why Prescott had asked him to drive her to town. Prescott wanted him to get her talking and report back on anything she told him. So far, the lady wasn't cooperating.

Was she in league with the cattle rustlers? That was what he was really supposed to find out. But Prescott seemed to want something else. Was it because he suspected Rose of murdering his father, or were his reasons even deeper and darker?

Never mind. He was here to investigate the rustling, not serve as Prescott's private spy. Unless she mentioned cattle, he was under no obligation to pass on anything he heard.

"I have a question," she said. "Mr. Prescott told me that one of his hands saw me this morning, and that the man told him about my car. Was that you?"

"It was. I was riding fence and saw you drive up." *A necessary half lie.*

"Why didn't you show yourself or say something?"

"I didn't want to startle you. And I figured that whatever you were doing, as long as it wasn't on Prescott property, it was none of my business." *Another necessary lie.*

"But you told your boss. And you weren't riding fence when you saw me. There isn't a fence on that part of the boundary, just the creek."

The woman was damned sharp.

"I mentioned you in passing. And no, I wasn't riding fence. The boss wanted me to look into some missing cattle. I was checking for tracks."

"And what did you find?"

"Nothing worth mentioning." *Except you.*

He was tempted to ask her what she'd been doing on the Rim-rock side of the creek, but he had a feeling she would either lie or shut down and refuse to talk to him at all. As for asking her whether she'd really murdered Ferg Prescott's father, that would open a whole different can of worms.

He glanced at her firm yet delicate profile and small, work-worn hands. Not that it was his business, but so far he could hardly believe Rose was capable of killing anybody, especially the large man that Ferg's father must've been. She was like a feisty, little brown-eyed cat, so vulnerable that he felt an awakening urge to protect her.

Not that he was capable of protecting anybody. He'd already proven that to himself, his family, and the town he only wanted to forget. That was one reason he'd chosen to be here in Texas, rounding up cattle thieves instead of putting away wanted criminals in Wyoming.

They were coming into Blanco Springs now, passing the Blue Coyote, the movie theater, the dry goods store, and the Burger Shack. Rose could see the gas station and garage on the corner, partway up the street.

"You don't have to wait for me," she said as Tanner pulled into a parking space at the side of the building. "I can handle this."

"I get it that you want to," he said. "But I'll hang around all the same. You might need a ride home, and for me, it beats going back to work."

When she shot him a glare, he added, "Don't worry, I'll keep my distance. You won't even know I'm here."

"Fine." Clearly, he didn't think she was capable of buying her own vehicle. She was aware that car dealers viewed women as suckers and tended to take advantage of them. But Ramón had taught her about cars, how to maintain and repair them, and how to tell a sound vehicle from a *limón*. And eleven years in Mexico had taught her how to haggle and bargain like a pro. She could do this.

She was tugging at the stubborn seat belt buckle when he came around to her side of the truck and opened the door.

"Here, I've got it." He leaned in and reached across her lap. His head brushed her breast as he found the release button and clicked the buckle open. The contact sent a jolt through her body. She didn't like being touched in an intimate spot—not even accidentally. It stirred too many bad memories—the man who'd moved in with her mother when she was ten, the foster home she'd run away from, and more recently the swaggering goons who'd taken over Río Seco and abused every female they could get their hands on.

She climbed out of the truck, ignoring the arm he offered. "Stay here," she said, and strode around the corner of the building to the front.

A big-bellied man in greasy coveralls was working on a Jeep in the open garage. He straightened, his stubbled face breaking into a grin as he saw her.

"Well now." His eyes looked her up and down, making her cringe inside. "What can I do for you, little lady?"

Rose squared her shoulders and drew herself up to her full height. "I was told you might have some used vehicles for sale," she said in a chilly voice. "I'm looking for a pickup truck. One with a camper would be best, but I'll look at whatever you've got."

His gap-toothed grin broadened. "I'd be happy to show you what I've got." The bastard actually winked. "But I reckon you'll want to see the trucks first. Come on, they're out back."

Reminding herself how much she needed something to drive, Rose followed the man out the back door of the garage. Half a dozen vehicles stood in a weedy yard cluttered with old tires and parts, surrounded by a sagging chain-link fence.

"I take 'em on commission," the man said. "Since it's the only car lot in town, I do a pretty good business here. Take a look."

He stepped aside to let her walk forward. Two of the vehicles had been wrecked and were probably being sold for parts. There was a flatbed farm truck, a work van, and a truck with a tow rig attached. None of those would do her. But her heart skipped when she saw the last truck. An older red Ford pickup, showing some dings and wear, with a small camper on the back.

Rose could sense the man watching her as she looked it over. She willed herself to ignore him. This truck would be perfect if it ran decently and if she could get it for a good price. "Can I start it up?" she asked.

"I can do it for you. Is this a present for your boyfriend?"

Why did he have to make this so difficult? "Just get the key," Rose said. "I'm buying it for myself—*if* I buy it."

"Sure, sweetheart." He stepped into his office and came back with a set of keys on a worn leather fob. "The brass one's for the camper," he said.

"I figured as much." Rose took the keys and climbed into the cab. The truck started on the first try, the engine running smooth and true. Rose revved the gas pedal and felt the quick response. Against her better judgment, she was falling in love.

After popping the hood lever, she climbed out of the running truck and felt beneath the hood for the release.

"I can do that," the man said.

"I'll do it." She propped the hood open while she looked underneath. So far, so good.

"How much?" she asked, still peering under the hood.

"Ten thousand."

Her heart sank. "For cash, on the spot? How much?"

"The same," he said. "But if your offer includes being nice to me, I just might lower the price for you."

Rose swore under her breath. She had no intention of being "nice" to this foul man; but if she wanted the truck, getting it might take some tough negotiating.

She was bending in for a closer look at the engine when she heard the rasp of deep breathing behind her. A hard ridge pressed against the seat of her jeans, butting and rubbing. At the same time, a clumsy hand tugged at the envelope of bills she'd stuffed into her hip pocket.

A murderous, fear-driven rage exploded inside her. With a

grunt of fury, she twisted out from under the hood, and flung her strength into one desperate, upward-swinging blow.

She was less than half the man's size, and her fist might have glanced off, but she managed to hit him in the eye, hard enough to hurt. As he staggered back, bellowing in surprise and pain, she charged in and landed a kick to his groin.

He doubled over, cursing, but didn't go down. Rose stumbled back, falling against the truck as he lumbered toward her. "You little bitch!" he snarled. "I'll show you!"

Rose glanced around for any kind of weapon she could use. A length of rusty pipe lay nearby, half buried in the greasy dirt. Snatching it up, she braced herself to fight for her life.

# CHAPTER FIVE

"*H*OLD IT RIGHT THERE, MISTER. BACK OFF, NICE AND SLOW."

Tanner stood framed in the open doorway of the garage, an icy scowl on his face and a revolver in his hand. Startled, Rose stared at him. In her panic, she'd forgotten he was outside.

"Are you all right?" he asked Rose.

Rose gripped the pipe she'd found. Her pulse was still racing, pumping adrenaline through her body. Somehow she managed to nod.

"You." Tanner's eyes were riveted on the man. "Zip your damned fly and get down on your knees."

The man did as he was told. "Don't hurt me," he blubbered. "I was only havin' a little fun with the lady."

"Shut up!" Tanner snapped. "Rose, do you want me to beat the shit out of this bastard before we go?"

"I was about to do that myself, but he's not worth the effort." Still breathing hard, Rose tossed the pipe to the ground. "Actually, I had my eye on that truck. But I can't make an offer until I've driven it on the road."

"No problem." Tanner kept the gun level. "I'll keep an eye on our friend here while you take it for a test run."

"Thanks. While you're at it, maybe you can talk him down on the price. Ten thousand's a little too steep for me."

"I'll see what I can do."

Rose climbed into the driver's seat again. The truck had stopped running. She started it again, backed up, and drove out through the opening in the far side of the fence.

Only after she'd turned the corner, out of sight, did she begin to shake. With the engine still running, she pulled off the road, shifted into neutral, and laid her forehead on the steering wheel.

*Breathe . . . just breathe . . . It's all right. You're safe,* she told herself.

After a few minutes, she felt calm enough to drive. She put the truck in gear, pulled back onto the road, and took a shortcut to the highway. The truck handled fine. But as she turned around and drove back toward the gate, she felt the anger returning—anger not only at the man who'd assaulted her but at herself.

Why had she assumed she could handle the garage owner when one look should have alerted her to what he was? Why hadn't she asked Tanner to come inside with her, or gone back to the Rimrock and waited for Jasper to drive her to town?

But she knew the answer to that question. Life had taught her some bitter lessons. But one stood out. In the end, she could count on no one but herself. People lied to her, brutalized her, or simply went away. Even the best of them, like her grandfather and Ramón and María, had died and left her devastated and alone. As for Jasper, she knew he cared for her; but his first loyalty was to Bull. And Bull was as unpredictable as lightning.

Tanner had saved her today. But his actions had shown her that he wasn't the simple cowboy he pretended to be. Ham Prescott had kept a few hired guns around his ranch—she remembered that because they'd threatened her grandfather. It came as no surprise that Ham's son would do the same.

The knot in the pit of her stomach tightened as she drove back through the gate. Tanner and the garage owner were waiting where she'd left them, Tanner still holding his pistol on the big man.

"So how do you like the truck?" Tanner asked her as she climbed out of the cab.

Rose tightened her jaw and narrowed her gaze, assuming the mask she wore when she was nervous. "Not bad. But can I afford it?"

"We did some negotiating," Tanner said. "Our friend here is

willing to give up his commission on the truck and sell it for the owner's price of seven thousand. Does that suit you?"

Rose could only imagine what Tanner had threatened the man with to get the price down, but this was no time to ask questions. All she wanted was to get the truck and leave. "It suits me fine," she said. "Let's do some business."

In the garage's grimy office, it took only a few minutes to sign the paperwork and hand over the money. The garage owner was sullen and silent but made no move to challenge them. They were just finishing when a beat-up black Camaro with squealing brakes pulled up to the front of the garage. The man glanced at Tanner, as if asking permission to go. When Tanner nodded, the man left them and hurried forward to deal with his customer.

Tanner slid the pistol into the holster under his vest and handed her the signed title. "I'll walk you to your new truck," he said, holding the office door and closing it behind them as they walked outside. "After that, you're on your own."

"I guess I should thank you," Rose said as they paused outside the truck. "I might've had a rough time of it if you hadn't been there."

"Then I'm glad I was." He opened the door of the truck. "Be safe, Rose."

As Rose turned to climb into the cab, he laid a brief hand on her shoulder. It was an innocent gesture, but the contact with her hypersensitive nerves triggered an alarm. She gasped and jerked around, poised to defend herself.

He stepped back. "Sorry. I didn't mean to spook you."

She remained frozen an instant longer, then exhaled and lowered her arms. "I'm just jumpy, that's all."

"I understand." He kept his distance as she climbed into the truck. "Will you be all right getting your truck licensed?" he asked her.

"Fine, assuming the folks at the motor vehicle department have better manners than our friend here. I don't suppose I'll see you again."

"You never know." He closed the door and stepped out of the

way as she backed up and headed for the gate. Glancing back, she saw him standing where she'd left him. He gave her brief wave and disappeared from sight.

Tanner drove back to the ranch, side windows rolled down to let in the fresh breeze. Traffic was light on the narrow highway. Two stray cows grazed on the grass that grew in the bar ditch along the road. He pulled left to give them a wide berth.

Ferg Prescott would be waiting to hear what he'd learned from Rose. Not that there'd be much to tell. Rose Landro wasn't much of a talker. He'd learned only that she was tough, guarded, independent to a fault, and feisty as hell.

Was she working with the cattle rustlers? If she was, she'd made a good show of hiding it. As for whether she'd really killed Prescott's father, Tanner would never have believed such a thing. But then, as she'd brandished that pipe to defend herself, he'd seen the fury in those stunning eyes. She'd reminded him of a cornered animal, terrified and enraged.

He recalled how she'd jumped away, more scared than startled, when he'd touched her shoulder. His best guess was that Rose had been hurt in the past. She'd learned to protect herself and fight back. It wasn't beyond belief that she'd even learned to kill, or maybe been forced to.

But that was none of his business. He was here to arrest cattle rustlers, and so far all Prescott had done was send him on wild-goose chases. He'd seen no solid evidence of thieves or, apart from Prescott's word, found any proof that cattle were even missing. He was beginning to feel like a prop in some larger scheme. It was almost as if he was being used, and he didn't like it.

He could confront Prescott and demand to know what was really going on. But if the powerful rancher was involved in something illegal, and masking it with the cattle rustling claim, voicing his suspicions would only get him booted off the ranch, or worse.

Whatever was happening, something didn't feel right. It was time he stopped chasing shadows and got to the truth.

Tomorrow he'd be joining the Prescott cowboys on the roundup.

After that, it might not hurt to pay to visit the Rimrock, especially if he could find an excuse that wouldn't blow his cover.

He'd pulled up by the barn of the Prescott Ranch and was climbing out of the cab when he saw something lying on the passenger seat. The sight of it triggered a fleeting smile as he picked it up and tucked it in his pocket.

It was the black silk ribbon that had slipped off Rose's hair.

It was well after dark when Bull drove his pickup into the ranch yard. He was hungry, dirty, and sore after a hellish day on the roundup. One of the hands had broken an arm wrestling a steer, and Jasper had driven him to the hospital, shorting the crew by two men. A yearling calf, fleeing the rope, had fallen into a ravine and had to be shot. Several other calves had diarrhea, a condition known as scours, which was never a good sign. He'd isolated the animals and told the cowhands to keep an eye on them, but he'd probably need to pay a vet to come out and check the herd. And vets didn't work cheap.

His arthritic hip throbbed as he eased out of the truck and felt his boots crunch gravel. He didn't want to see anybody, didn't want to talk to anybody. All he wanted tonight was something in his belly, a hot shower, and a few hours of blessed sleep before crawling out of bed at dawn to face another day.

But that was not to be.

As he walked around the truck, he noticed an older pickup with a camper parked next to the house. There was no sign of the old Buick, but Rose was waiting in the circle of the porch light, ready to pounce on him like a hungry cat.

He swore as she came partway down the front steps. "We have to talk, Bull," she said.

"Not tonight." He tried to move past her, but she blocked his way. Short of shoving her aside, there was little he could do. "I'm worn out, Rose," he said. "Anything we have to talk about can wait till morning."

She faced him, standing at his eye level on a higher step. "I've waited eleven years. That's long enough."

"Tomorrow, Rose. I've had a rotten day. I don't need this."

"All I'm asking is ten minutes," she said. "Long enough to make it clear where we both stand. You owe me that much."

"*I* owe *you*? Damn it, I saved your life.*"

"And you took my land. Come sit down. There's a cold Tecate waiting for you on the porch."

Grumbling, Bull followed her up the steps. The woman was like a pesky mosquito that wouldn't go away without a taste of his blood. Too bad he couldn't just swat her and go in the house.

The beer, as promised, was waiting on the side table next to the rocker. Bull sank into the chair, popped the cap, and downed half the bottle in one long swig. It wasn't his favorite brand, but it was cold and tasted good. Night-flying insects buzzed around the porch light. The muted sound of a radio, playing twangy country music, drifted from the bunkhouse across the yard.

"What happened to your car?" he asked as Rose took a seat opposite him.

"I sold it to buy the truck. But that's not what we're here to talk about." When Bull didn't reply, she continued. "I stopped by the courthouse earlier and checked the deed to my property. My name isn't even on it. Just yours."

Bull had anticipated that much and had his answer ready. "You'd just killed a man, Rose. The only way to protect you was to get you out of the country and wipe out any evidence that you were ever here—that included your name on the record. If I hadn't done that, there could still be a warrant out for your arrest."

Her derisive snort told him what she thought of that explanation. "Jasper told me how you were arrested and tried for the shooting, and how you were acquitted. You could've brought me back then."

Bull finished off the beer. "It still wasn't safe for you here. Ham was alive and talking when Ferg hauled him into the truck. There's no way he wouldn't have told Ferg that you shot him."

"So why did Ferg blame you?"

"Because he could. He could put me away for good and then hire somebody to take care of you—or do it himself, although that wouldn't be Ferg's style. He doesn't like getting his hands dirty. What I'm saying, Rose, is that as long as you're here, you'll be in danger."

"I can't go back to Mexico."

"I understand. But you could go somewhere else. Anywhere you want. If it's money you need—"

"No!" She was on her feet, the porch light reflecting fire in her eyes. "That parcel of land is my legacy. My grandpa meant for me to make a home there, and that's what I intend to do. Keeping it from me is nothing short of thievery, Bull Tyler!"

Tossing the empty bottle off the porch, Bull rose to his feet. His height and bulk dwarfed her petite size, but she didn't back off. "I think your ten minutes are up, Rose," he said.

Her stubborn chin jutted higher. "Fine. We can talk again later. Meanwhile, I'm expecting you to come up with a fair and honest plan to return my property."

*In your dreams, lady.* Bull kept the thought to himself as he strode to the front door. Fairness and honesty didn't enter into his decision to hold the land. That acreage on the creek, with its year-round water supply from below the caprock, was vital to the survival of his ranch. To turn it over to a defenseless woman, who couldn't hope to hold it against the Prescotts, would be like slitting his own throat.

As he opened the door, a question struck him. Even before he turned back to ask, Bull knew the answer. "You didn't waste any time selling that old Buick," he said. "Who bought it from you?"

"Ferg Prescott made me a fair offer, and I accepted it," she said. "He paid me in cash."

Bull turned away, stepped into the house, and slammed the door behind him.

Bernice had left dinner warming in the oven, on a pie plate wrapped in aluminum foil. Bull shoveled down the food, his appetite gone. Ferg and Rose—Lord, didn't the fool woman know she was dealing with the devil?

It didn't take a genius to guess what Ferg had in mind. Befriend Rose, win her trust, help her get her land back, then move in and take control, maybe even have her killed. Ferg was capable of anything.

Would Rose listen if he tried to warn her? Not likely, Bull groused to himself. And certainly not tonight. For now, all he could do was keep an eye on the situation and hope Rose would see the danger. It wouldn't hurt to put in a word to Jasper. Maybe Rose would listen to him.

Shoving his worries aside, he dragged himself down the hall to the master bedroom. The door to the boys' room stood ajar, the dim light casting a beam across the floor. Pausing, he inched it open far enough to look into the room.

His sons lay asleep in their twin beds, their eyes closed, their hair falling like rumpled silk against the pillows. Will was sprawled beneath his quilt, his arms and legs outflung as if he were flying in his dreams. Beau had drifted off reading a book, which lay open on the floor where he'd dropped it.

Tired as he was, Bull lingered a moment, his heart contracting. Now that Susan was gone, these two boys were all he lived for. The land, the cattle, the backbreaking work that kept it all going, was for them—a legacy to enrich their lives and pass on to future generations. To protect that legacy, he would fight for every inch of ground, against all comers.

Even Rose.

Closing the door, he crossed the hall to get ready for bed.

The rooster in the chicken yard woke Rose at dawn. Barefoot and dressed in her ragged flannel nightshirt, she pattered out onto the front porch of the duplex. In the east, the unrisen sun streaked the clouds with a blush of fiery pink. An early meadowlark called from the lower pasture.

The morning air was cold enough to make her shiver. She inhaled its freshness, easing herself into the day after a night of hellish dreams that had seemed all too real.

The nightmares were nothing new. Sometimes she dreamed about Mexico and Lucho's ugly face grinning down at her. Other times it was Ham Prescott and the awful impact of the blast striking his body, or her grandfather staggering into the cabin, barely alive. Last night's dreams had been a kaleidoscope of memories. She'd woken with a jerk, shaking in the darkness, grateful to be awake and happy that it was almost morning.

Jasper's truck was already gone. She knew, without looking beyond the house, that Bull's truck would be gone, too. The roundup started at first light. And after last night's clash, it wasn't surprising that Bull would want to make an early getaway.

She would give him a day or two to think about the land before she cornered him again. There was always the hope that he'd come around and do the right thing. But knowing Bull, she was going to need a backup plan.

Would Ferg Prescott be part of that plan? He had offered to help her with anything she needed. She didn't trust Ferg, but if his offer included access to legal help, she couldn't afford to walk away—not if Bull left her with no other option.

The lights were on in the kitchen. The aromas of fresh coffee and bacon drifted on the morning breeze. Rose had planned to clean her new truck today, but it wouldn't hurt to pitch in and offer Bernice some help, as well. It was time she started earning her keep.

She took time to make the bed, shower, and put on clean jeans and a long-sleeved shirt. The ribbon she'd used to tie back her hair was missing. Regret stabbed her as she remembered how María had given her the ribbon to wear on her sixteenth birthday. That aside, having her hair loose was a nuisance while she was working. She would have to make do without it today, or maybe find a rubber band or a length of twine in the house.

By the time she left the duplex the sun was coming up. Behind the house, she stopped to watch the chickens, scratching and pecking for grain in their fenced yard. There were about fifteen of them, their colors—blacks, reds, and rusty browns—reminding her of the birds she'd loved and nurtured as a girl, living on her land with her grandfather. She'd had other chickens in Mexico, and goats, too. She loved goats, with their wise faces and mischievous ways. Maybe when she got her land fenced, she could have chickens and goats again.

She entered the kitchen through the back door. Bull's two sons were sitting at the table, wolfing down bacon, eggs, and pancakes swimming in maple syrup.

"Pour yourself a cup and help yourself, honey." Bernice gave her a smile. "You're just in time."

"Thanks. I'm starved." Rose filled a mug with coffee, took an empty chair, and heaped her plate. The kitchen brought back memories of the old days, when she'd made breakfast for Jasper and Bull and any hired hands that showed up. The fixtures and appliances were new, but the cozy warmth and the smells of good food were the same.

Bull's sons studied her with curious eyes. She'd met them the night she arrived here, but only for a moment before they'd gone off to finish their homework. "Aren't you boys going to school today?" she asked, making conversation.

"It's Saturday. We don't have school on Saturday. Everybody knows that." Will's expression was so much like his father's that Rose had to smile.

"So what do you do on Saturdays?"

"Our dad has chores and stuff for us to do," Beau said. "If we get done, we can ride our horses."

"You have your own horses?"

"Uh-huh," Beau said. "They're ponies, not big horses. Mine's Brownie. Will's is Chief. We take care of them and everything."

"So where do you go riding?" Rose hadn't spent much time around children, but she found herself warming to Bull's bright, handsome sons.

"Mostly just around the ranch," Will said. "But if Jasper or one of the cowboys goes with us, we can ride into the escarpment. There are some neat canyons there. Some even have Indian drawings on the walls."

"But we can't go there today." Beau nibbled on a strip of bacon. "All the men are on the roundup, and our dad doesn't let us go without a grown-up."

"Dad says that next year, when I'm ten, I can help with the roundup," Will said. "But this year I have to stay home with the baby."

"I'm not a baby!" Beau's hand clenched his fork in an angry grip. "I can do anything you can do!"

"That's enough, boys," Bernice warned. "Unless you want to spend the day in time-out, you can learn to get along."

Rose speared a second pancake and doused it with syrup. "I want to do my share while I'm here," she said to Bernice. "How can I help you today?"

Bernice was cleaning the cast-iron pancake griddle with a paper towel. She paused. "I can handle the housework fine. But with a mountain of bread and cake to bake for the roundup celebration tonight, chasing after these boys will be more than I can do. If you could keep an eye on them and maybe help them with their chores—"

"I don't need a babysitter," Will grumbled.

"I wouldn't be babysitting, just helping out," Rose said. "You can show me what to do."

"Can you ride a horse?" Will asked.

"Sure." Rose had helped the Ortegas herd sheep on horseback, spending long days in the saddle.

"If you can ride a horse, we can go to the canyon," Beau piped up.

Rose glanced at Bernice. "Would that be all right?"

"If you don't go too far. It's easy to get lost out there."

"We won't get lost," Will said. "We'll go to the canyon with the horse pictures. I know the way."

"All right. You can go after lunch. But only if you get your chores done."

"Yay!" Beau clapped his hands.

Will gave him a stern look. "We have to get our chores done first. Jasper gave me the list last night. It's in the bedroom. I'll get it after we eat."

After breakfast, Rose waited in the great room with Beau while Will fetched the list. The portrait of Susan, in blue silk and pearls, hung behind them on the wall. Rose turned to look at it, remembering the day Susan had pitched in to help her and Bull bathe the muddy dogs, and how she'd laughed as smelly mud spattered her from head to toe. In the portrait, probably painted when she'd graduated from high school, she looked like a princess. But there'd been more to Susan Rutledge Tyler than beauty. No wonder Bull was desolate without her.

"That's my mom," Beau said. "I look at this picture every day. It helps me remember her."

"I remember her, too," Rose said. "She was beautiful."

He looked surprised. "Were you her friend?"

"Not really. I didn't know her very long. But I liked her."

"My dad met her when he went back to Georgia to buy a horse," Beau said. "He saw her and they fell in love. Her folks said she couldn't marry him because he wasn't rich, but they got married anyway."

Rose gave him a smile. That wasn't the story she remembered, but if this version had become the family legend, who was she to challenge it?

"Let's get going." Will headed for the front door with the list in his hand. The boys were expected to work hard on their day off. The list included raking the chicken yard and gathering the eggs, picking up any trash that the dogs or hired hands had left on the ground, shoveling up the dog droppings, filling the water troughs in the stalls and paddocks, and sweeping out the open space in the barn. Even with Rose pitching in, it was a lot for two boys to do. The dogs tagged after them around the yard, happy to have their young masters outside for company on a warm spring day, with the bright sky overhead and the smell of pit barbecue wafting from behind the bunkhouse. Today would be the final day of the spring roundup, and everyone on the ranch looked forward to the celebration that would follow.

"You missed that cigarette wrapper, Beau." Will pointed to a scrap of white by the bunkhouse door. "Go back and pick it up."

Beau did as he was told, but his face was a thundercloud. Young as he was, the boy had a mind of his own. Rose couldn't help wondering what would happen on that inevitable day when he finally stood up to his brother. For now, the best she could do was distract both boys.

"Hey, we're almost done!" she declared. "Come on, I'll race you to the water tap."

Spurred by her challenge, they took off running. Beau, a small streak of lightning, was all smiles when he won. "He always gets ahead of me," Will complained. "I'm the oldest. It isn't fair."

"I'm just faster than you. That's all, you old slowpoke," Beau said.

Rose, who'd finished last, made a show of being breathless. "Well, you're both faster than I am!" she said, panting. "Let's get our work done."

Tanner had been with the roundup crew on the far range most of the morning, cutting out last year's calves for vaccinations, branding, and castrating. It was hard, dirty work, though no worse than what he'd done on the family ranch in Wyoming. But the real job he'd come to do, keeping his ears open for any talk of rustling, was even more frustrating. He'd learned nothing. Meanwhile, Ferg was getting free labor courtesy of the TSCRA.

It came as a relief when the graying, sun-weathered foreman hailed him and beckoned him out of the melee of hides, horns, sweat, and dirt.

"Just got word that the boss wants you back at the house, McCade. Pronto," he said. "Leave your horse. The boy who came to fetch you will drive you back in the truck."

*What now?* Tanner dismounted, handed off his horse to another cowboy, and headed for the pickup that had just pulled in. What was going on? Was this some new, important development, or was Ferg just pulling his strings again?

Ferg was pacing the front porch as the pickup pulled up to let Tanner off. "It's about time you showed up," he grumbled.

"What's going on?" Tanner didn't figure he owed the man an apology. Ferg seemed to forget that Tanner was only pretending to work for him.

"What's going on is a chance to catch those cattle-thieving bastards red-handed. There's a dozen cows missing from the west pasture that borders on Bull Tyler's place. One of my hands reported seeing fresh tracks leading right toward the Rimrock. Follow them, and you'll likely have your rustlers. There's a horse saddled and waiting outside the stable. Get going!"

Tanner found the horse, a handsome dun, with a canteen of water and a pair of binoculars slung from the saddle horn. His pistol was already holstered at his hip. Not that he planned to use it in single-handed combat against a gang of rustlers. This wasn't Hollywood. He would try to get a look at the men if they were still there, maybe hang around, out of sight, until a truck—the only practical way for thieves to transport a dozen animals—showed up. He'd get the description and license number, call Clive, and have the truck picked up with the goods on the road. With luck, the trucker would make a deal and nail his contacts on the Rimrock—if that's where they could be found.

It sounded simple enough, but the thought of what could go wrong—from a no-show to a deadly gunfight—was always there in the back of any lawman's mind.

So who was behind the stolen cattle?

Tanner knew better than to jump to conclusions. He knew that nothing would make Ferg happier than putting Bull Tyler away for stealing his cattle. But why would Tyler risk prison for a few cows—especially when he'd reported missing cattle, too? More than likely, someone else was responsible.

As he rode west toward the Rimrock Ranch, he kept his eyes on the trail of split-hooved cattle tracks, mingled with the curved prints of shod horses. There'd been at least two riders driving the small herd, maybe more. One of the horses had a loose shoe that was missing a couple of nails and would probably soon come off. At least that one would be easy to track.

The country here was open, the flat ground rising to the foothills of the escarpment, dotted with clumps of sage, cedar, and mesquite. Spring-hatched flies swarmed on droppings that looked to be hours old. It made sense that the rustlers would have moved the cattle sometime in the night. By now the valuable animals could already be gone, loaded in a truck under cover of darkness. He'd be lucky to find anything more than tracks.

At the boundary between the two ranches, Tanner passed a posted sign, probably one of many, facing west. He shook his head as he read the stenciled lettering:

PRESCOTT RANCH. PRIVATE PROPERTY.
TRESPASSERS WILL BE SHOT ON SIGHT.

The old West was alive and well in this country, Tanner mused as his gaze swept the landscape beyond the sign. Here the scrub was thicker. Clumps of mesquite, which hadn't been chained out, grew almost as high as a man's head. At least it would give him some cover if he needed to get in close. But that wasn't likely. By now, he suspected, the thieves and the stolen stock would be long gone.

Barely had the thought crossed Tanner's mind when a faint sound, carried by the breeze, reached his ears. He swore in surprise. It was the unmistakable bawling of cattle.

More cautiously, he rode closer. He could hear the animals clearly now. They sounded distressed, as if they might be trapped or thirsty. Why would they still be here? Had the truck been delayed? Had there even been a truck?

Keeping to the heavy brush, he slowed the horse to a walk. A covey of quail burst out of the undergrowth and scattered in a flurry of sounds and feathers. Tanner paused, waiting for them to settle before he went on. Ahead, he could see the rugged red-and-white cliffs of the escarpment and the opening of a shadowed cleft that might be a narrow canyon—a handy place to hide stolen livestock.

Some instinct caused him to glance up. Still distant, he caught a movement in the rocks along the rim of the escarpment. Sunlight glinted on metal—could it be the barrel of a gun?

He shaded his eyes, trying to see more of what he'd glimpsed. It made sense that the thieves would place a guard on the stolen cattle. If he could see an actual person, for later identification it could help him break the case.

He reached for the binoculars and brought them to his eyes. But the horse, which kept shifting and dancing even after he halted the animal, made it difficult to focus the lenses. Tanner decided he might have better luck from the ground.

He had replaced the binoculars and was about to dismount when a rifle shot rang out. The roar of sound exploded in his head as he pitched into blackness, struck the ground, and lay still on dry, red earth.

# CHAPTER SIX

*B*Y THE TIME THE LAST WATERING TROUGH WAS FILLED AND THE BARN was swept, Bernice was calling Rose and the boys to wash up for lunch. They hosed off at the outside tap and sat down to tomato soup, grilled cheese sandwiches, and chocolate cake for dessert.

"Can we ride our horses now?" Beau asked.

Rose glanced at Bernice for approval. Bernice nodded. "Just make sure not to go too far. And you boys, remember that Rose is in charge. When she says it's time to go back, you don't argue. And no fighting, or the ride's over right then. Understand?"

The boys nodded, excused themselves, and dashed out the back door. Rose got up to follow them.

"Are you sure they'll be all right?" she asked Bernice.

"They'll be fine, honey. They're good boys, but they can be headstrong. Don't be afraid to let them know who's boss."

"Thanks." Rose hurried out the door. Headstrong? Of course they were. They were Bull Tyler's sons. Why should she expect anything else?

When she got to the stable, the boys were already saddling up. Even Beau, young as he was, had no trouble putting the down-sized saddle and bridle on his brown pony. Will's red-and-white pinto was bigger but still not a full-sized horse. He handled the animal with the skill of a seasoned cowboy. Somebody—probably Jasper, since she couldn't imagine Bull having the patience—had taught the boys well.

"You can ride Belle." Will pointed out a docile-looking bay mare in a nearby stall. "Can you saddle her by yourself? I can help if you don't know how."

"I can manage." Rose found the gear she needed in the tack room. She'd suspected the boys might trick her with an unruly mount, and she was ready. But Belle was a sweetheart. She stood calmly while Rose slipped on the bridle and laid the pad and saddle on her back. Only when she bent to fasten the strap and the cinch did she notice the mare's bulging belly.

"Oh, my goodness!" she exclaimed. "She's—"

"She's pregnant," Will said. "That's why she's not on the roundup. But Jasper says it's okay to ride her around the ranch."

"He says the exercise is good for her," Beau added. "'Specially since she'd not due for another six weeks or so."

"She's a great little cutting horse, but the roundup can be rough, and this is her first foal," Will said. "She was bred with a champion stud, so we don't want anything to go wrong."

Rose had to smile. These two boys, not even out of elementary school, talked like the cowboys they'd grown up with. At least she hadn't heard either of them curse.

She eased into the saddle, taking time to settle her weight. "I promise to treat her gently," she said.

With Will leading the way, they set out across the greening lower pastures and onto the open flatland. The afternoon sun was bright and warm, the landscape dotted with clumps of mesquite and ablaze with bluebonnets, Indian paintbrush, and firewheel. Humming bees pillaged the blossoms. White butterflies rose in clouds where the horses passed.

The boys had told her they were headed for a small box canyon in the escarpment. A cliff face was there with pictographs of horses on it. The canyon was on Rimrock land and not too far for an easy ride. Even for a lone woman and two young boys it sounded safe enough.

Saying little, they rode at a slow pace set by Beau's short-legged pony. Where the land rose, they picked up a faint trail that wound through the foothills. Here sagebrush and rabbit brush grew in clumps among the mesquite. A jackrabbit, bounding across their path, startled Will's pony. He calmed it with the skill of a seasoned rider.

Rose was bringing up the rear when she noticed cattle tracks in the loosened dirt along the trail—not just one or two sets of tracks, but many of them, all going the same direction. "Whoa." She stopped the boys. "Take a look. Does your dad run cattle out here?"

"Not usually. The grazing's not that good. And since Ferg Prescott dammed that little creek in the canyon, there's no water." Will slid off his pony, dropped the reins, and crouched to examine the tracks. "These haven't been here long. Less than a day, I'd say."

"I heard Dad say he was missing some cows." Beau had stayed on his pony. "Maybe this is where they went."

"He'd be happy if we found them," Will said, mounting up. "Let's follow the tracks and see where they go."

Bull's son was taking over. So far, Rose couldn't see any harm in it. But it still made sense to be careful. "All right," she said. "But if there's any sign of trouble, and I say turn back, we do it. Hear?"

Will didn't answer. He was pushing ahead, his eyes fixed on the trail the cattle had left.

They were getting closer to the escarpment now. Amid the russet stone cliffs and hoodoos that rose above the foothills, Rose could make out a shadowed cleft that she assumed to be the canyon. The tracks were leading in that direction.

Intent on trailing the cattle, Will was lengthening his lead. Soon he'd be out of sight, lost among the stands of mesquite that were higher than his head. "Slow down, Will!" Rose shouted. "Stay with us!"

Will kept on as if he hadn't heard.

Knowing she couldn't leave Beau behind, Rose did her best to hurry him. But the stubborn little pony was getting tired. Even with Beau kicking his flanks, he refused to move.

At her wits' end, Rose dismounted and strode forward. "Come on, Beau, you'll have to ride with me until we catch up with Will."

"What about Brownie?" He climbed off the pony and allowed her to drop the reins and boost him onto the mare.

"He'll be all right. We can catch him again on our way back." Which would be soon if she had her way. Will's disobedience had already crossed the line.

Rose was about to climb up behind Beau when she glanced down at the tracks and noticed something else next to the trail. Among the cattle tracks were the prints of a shod horse's hooves, too big to have been made by Will's pony and too far ahead to be the mare's.

The cattle hadn't just been wandering. Someone on horseback had been driving them.

Somebody who could still be around.

"Will! Come back here!" Rose kept her voice low. By now Will, set on finding his father's missing stock, had disappeared behind a thick stand of mesquite. Warning Beau to be still and keep his head down, she led the mare forward. There was only one reason for men to drive cattle to a place like this—to steal them.

A moment later, she came upon Will's pony, tied to a sturdy branch of mesquite. Her heart crept into her throat. Will had gone ahead on foot. He must have noticed the riders' tracks and wanted to get close to the cows without being seen. By now he could be anywhere, and she didn't dare leave Beau alone to follow him. All she could do was stay out of sight and pray for Will to come back safely.

Knowing Beau would be safer on the ground, she hoisted him out of the saddle to crouch beside her. Fear gnawed at her gut as the time crawled past and Will didn't return. Why hadn't she thought to bring her pistol? At least then, if they were caught, she would have had a way to defend the boys and herself.

Her anxiety mounted with each second. Should she go after him? Or would that only increase the likelihood of their being seen? Not that it mattered. She couldn't take Beau with her, and she couldn't leave him behind. Heart in her throat, she waited. Over the distant bawling of the cows, she could hear the hammering of her heart.

What if something had happened to the boy? It would kill Bull to lose his son, and she would be to blame for letting him go. Why hadn't she found a way to stop him?

At long last, the bushes rustled, and Will appeared, scratched and dirty but unhurt. Sick with relief, Rose fought the urge to seize the boy's shoulders and give him a good shaking. "Didn't you hear me telling you to come back? Anything could have happened . . ."

Her words trailed off as she saw his expression. Will's face was pale, his blue eyes wide with shock and fear.

"What is it? What happened?" she demanded.

"I saw a man on the ground." Will's voice was a shaky whisper. "His horse was by him. He looked like he was dead."

"You're sure?"

"I didn't get close. I've never seen a dead person before. Not even my mom. Dad wouldn't let me see her." Will's manly bravado had vanished. He looked like the scared child he was.

"Did you see anybody else?"

Will shook his head. "Just cows. They were in the canyon, with a rope strung across the rocks so they couldn't get out. But two of them came far enough for me to see their brands. Our brand is a rocking R, for Rimrock. These cows were branded with a bar-P. They were Prescott cows, not ours. We need to go find Dad and tell him."

"What about the man?" Beau asked. "What if he isn't dead? What if he's just hurt?"

"What if he's a rustler?" Will countered. "What if he stole those cows?"

Rose sighed. She couldn't leave a wounded man to suffer a lingering death in the desert. But her first concern had to be the safety of Bull's sons.

"Right now you boys have got to get out of here," she said. "Take Chief, go back to where we left Brownie, and wait while I check on the man. If I'm not back in five minutes, start down to the ranch without me. I'll catch up."

"What if something happens?" Beau asked. "What if you don't come back?"

"Then you just keep going. Get home as fast as you can and tell somebody what happened. Understand?"

The brothers nodded, both of them looking worried.

"Good. Now get going!"

The sturdy pinto had no trouble carrying two young boys. Rose watched them until they rounded the biggest mesquite clump and disappeared. *They'll be all right,* she told herself. Will knew the way home. And she didn't plan to be here long. If the man Will had found was dead, she could take his horse and have someone at the ranch call the law. But what would she do if he turned out to be wounded and dangerous?

Rose cast around for a makeshift weapon. All she could find was a solid leg bone from what appeared to be a deer or a sheep. Bleached clean and probably dragged here by a coyote, it wouldn't hold up in a serious fight. But it was all she had.

Leaving the mare, she crept forward. A thorny branch scratched a stinging trail across her cheek, drawing blood. A scorpion skittered across her boot and vanished into the underbrush. Rose ignored it and kept moving. Ahead, the bulky outline of a horse loomed through a screen of mesquite. Sensing her approach, the animal snorted. "Easy, boy," she whispered, hoping the big dun wouldn't startle and bolt. "I won't hurt you."

In a sandy clearing, she found the man. His rangy body, vaguely familiar, lay sprawled facedown on the sand, as if he'd been shot off his horse. A streak above his temple was crusted with blood that had seeped into his dark hair. Two circling dots in the sky became vultures, keeping a grim death watch.

Dropping the bone, Rose crouched over the man's body and slid a hand beneath the back of his leather vest. Through the sweat-drenched cotton shirt, she felt the subtle rise and fall of his rib cage. He was alive—and the wound, she realized, was no more than a crease where a bullet had grazed his scalp. But unless she could bring him around and get some water down him, he might not be alive for long.

A canteen hung from a strap on the horse's saddle. Rose was about to move away and get it when she noticed the butt of a holstered revolver jutting from beneath his hip. The weapon lay partway under his body, but the grip was within easy reach.

Moving with care, Rose closed her shaking fingers around the grip and gave it a tug. The gun didn't move. Either it was a tight fit in the holster or it was wedged beneath his body. She tugged harder. The man shuddered and groaned. Then, in a lighting move his hand flashed out and clamped around her wrist.

Dazed but still powerful, he twisted like a cat, yanking her arm as he righted himself and sat up. "What do you think you're . . ." His voice broke off. He stared at her, a half-muffled string of curses purpling the air. Only now, as she saw his face, did Rose recognize Ferg Prescott's man, Tanner McCade.

Releasing her hand, he shoved her backward and jerked the pistol out of its holster. "You've got about five seconds to explain what you're doing here, lady. If I don't like what I hear, I'll be taking you in and turning you over to the law."

Rose pushed herself to her knees, glaring into his bloodshot eyes. "Turning me over for what?" she demanded.

"For cattle rustling—or at least as an accessory. Hear those cows? They belong to the Prescott Ranch. And they've been herded onto Rimrock property. That's rustling in anybody's book. And here you . . . are."

He blinked and lowered the gun, his body slumping. One hand went to the wound on his head. He winced as his fingers touched the blood-encrusted crease. "My head hurts like hell. . . . Good Lord, have I been shot?"

"Shot, but just winged from the looks of it. Hold on, I'll get you some water." Rose stood, strode to the horse, and retrieved the canteen. It was heavy with the cool weight of the water inside. When she glanced up at the sky, she saw that the buzzards were gone.

"As for my being a rustler, you're out of your mind. All I'm doing here is trying to save your life." As she spoke, she twisted the lid off the canteen and thrust it toward him. "Drink up.

There's plenty, and it'll make you feel better. Then I'll sponge off that wound, just to pretty you up a little. You're lucky to be alive."

He drank long and deeply, wiping his mouth as he lowered the canteen. "So if you aren't a rustler, as you say, what the hell are you doing out here?" he asked.

"I was out riding with Bull's two sons. We came across the tracks and thought they might be some missing Rimrock cows, so we followed them. We got this far and found you."

He glanced around. "So where are the two boys?"

"I sent them back the way we came. As soon as I get you on your feet, I'll be going after them. They're just kids. They shouldn't be out here alone. Do you have a clean handkerchief?"

He fished in his shirt pocket and came up with a folded square of white cotton. She poured water on it and began dabbing at the wound, not opening the bullet crease but cleaning up around it. His hair was thick and clean, just beginning to gray at the temples, and the skin of his face had weathered to a patina like fine leather. Even under these crazy conditions, Rose was aware that she enjoyed touching him. But maybe that was because he was no longer a threat.

"I suppose I should ask what *you* were doing out here," she said.

"Prescott sent me to check out the tracks leading from one of his pastures. I followed them this far, heard the cows, and saw somebody up in the rocks. Then everything went black. Judging from where the sun is now, that would've been at least an hour ago. Did you see anybody when you came along with the boys?"

"Not a soul. If the rustlers are still with the cows, they're not showing themselves." She rinsed the bloodstained handkerchief, untied his red bandanna from around his neck, and rolled it into a makeshift bandage. "I've got to catch up with the boys," she said, tying it around his head. "Do you think you can ride?"

"I'll be fine." Grimacing with effort, Tanner pushed himself to his feet and took a few steps. He swayed as he walked, but he kept going, his teeth clenched against the pain. Rose stayed at his side to steady him as he crossed the clearing to his horse. As if to prove he didn't need her help, he clasped the saddle horn, lifted a boot to the stirrup, and swung his body into place.

"What are you going to tell your boss?" She reached up to hand him the canteen.

"The truth." His eyes were laced with pain. "He'll be grateful that you came along and helped me. Where's your horse?"

"Back there in the brush." She glanced over her shoulder, the way she'd come. "Hang on, you'll want this." She fetched his hat, which had caught on a nearby bush.

He took it and placed it on his head, working it gingerly over the top edge of the bandanna. "Almost forgot . . . I've been saving something for you." He reached under his vest, groped in his shirt pocket, and came up with a crumpled black ribbon. "I found it in the truck," he said.

"Thanks." She took it. "It might not look like much, but it holds a memory of someone I cared about. I thought it was gone for good." She tucked it into her pocket, aware of the warmth that lingered from his body.

"Maybe we'll see each other again, Rose," he said.

His words, innocent on the surface, raised her protective barriers. He was a man, after all, and she knew almost nothing about him. She forced herself to speak. "Under the circumstances, it might be better if we didn't. Right now, as long as you're all right, I've got to catch up with the boys."

"I'm fine. Go on."

To Rose, he still looked unsteady, but she'd already left Bull's sons on their own too long. Leaving Tanner, she raced back the way she'd come, found the mare, and sprang into the saddle.

A few minutes later, crossing the brushy flat, she caught up with the boys. Beau was riding Brownie again, the little pony trotting eagerly toward home.

"Was the man dead?" Beau seemed more curious than worried.

"No. He was unconscious, but I woke him up and gave him some water. He's going to be all right."

"Was he a rustler?" Will asked.

"He was just a cowboy looking for Mr. Prescott's missing cattle."

Rose knew better than to tell them more. "Right now, we need to find your father and tell him about those cows."

"I know where to find him," Will said. "I'll go with you and show you the way."

Rose gave him a stern look. "I'll find him myself, Will. You're in trouble for disobeying me. You and Beau are going home and putting away your ponies. Then, when I tell Bernice what you did, you're probably going to your room."

Rose's truck bounced over ruts and holes as she tore up the winding dirt road to the Rimrock's canyon pasture. Bernice, who'd taken charge of the boys, had told her where to find Bull. Driven by urgency, she'd broken all sensible speed limits getting to him. Any way you looked at it, finding stolen Prescott cattle on Rimrock property was serious trouble.

The pasture was in a basin ringed by the cliffs of the escarpment. It provided grass and winter shelter for most of the herd of red-and-white Hereford cattle that had made Bull Tyler a prosperous man.

As Rose parked her truck next to Bull's pickup and then cut the engine, she could see the meadow where mounted cowboys were separating the remaining cattle to be moved to spring pasture and cutting out the last of the animals to be branded, vaccinated, ear-tagged, and, if meant to be steers, castrated. The spare horses from the remuda were being loaded in trailers to be hauled back to the ranch paddock.

Climbing out of her truck, Rose spotted Bull standing with Jasper on the far side of the branding chute. As she hurried to close the distance between them, the clamor of bawling calves and the odors of wood smoke, hot iron, and seared flesh flooded her senses. She waved her arms to get Bull's attention.

He strode toward her, then, sensing her urgency, broke into a run. "What is it?" he demanded. "Are my boys all right?"

"Don't worry, the boys are fine." She told him what they'd seen and heard, leaving out the mention of Will's disobedience. That could be dealt with later.

Bull swore. "Damn it, you know Ferg's going to think it was us that stole those blasted cows." He turned to Jasper, who'd caught up with him. "Have all our men been here the past couple of days? Nights, too?"

"Far as I know, except for Lee Roy, who broke his arm. I don't do bed checks, but after a day on roundup those boys would've been too tuckered to sneak off and steal cows."

Bull swore again, then sighed. "I reckon it's time for some damage control. Jasper, you're in charge here. Rose, you follow me down to the house. I might need you to back me up on what you and the boys saw."

In the next instant, he was hauling himself into his pickup. By the time Rose got her own truck started, he was already a quarter mile down the road. Gearing down and bracing her body against the bumps, she stomped the gas pedal and roared after him.

So far, so good. Ferg poured himself a congratulatory shot of bourbon and tossed it down in a single swallow. Once those stolen cows were discovered on Rimrock property, it would be natural to assume that someone on the Rimrock was behind the theft. If the discovery wasn't enough to raise the stakes, finding the murdered body of a TSCRA ranger was sure to bring down every law agency in the state.

Deke Triplehorn, Ferg's security man, had been a sniper in Viet Nam. The man was a dead shot with a scope-equipped high-powered rifle. Today he had orders to gun down McCade from the rocks, then move out of range and circle back to the ranch, where Ferg would provide him with a solid alibi and report McCade missing. A search would lead to the discovery of the ranger's body. At that distance, there was always the chance that even Triplehorn might miss or only wound the ranger. But the plan could be shifted to cover that possibility.

Ferg's idea had been to back Bull into a tight corner, then offer his legal assistance on condition that Bull sell him the creek property. At the time, the idea had seemed like a good one. Call the TSCRA and file a complaint about stolen cattle. Ask to have a ranger assigned, then set up a fake crime and a real shooting, with evidence pointing to Bull or one of his employees.

But the plan wasn't perfect. Tanner McCade was sharp, curious, and unpredictable. It remained to be seen whether he could be counted on to be in the right place at the right time.

The request for a ranger hadn't been all pretense, Ferg reminded himself. He had definitely been losing stock—a few animals here, a few there, never enough to make a noticeable difference. But his foreman, who kept a close tally, had mentioned that the numbers were off. Maybe he should've given McCade time to catch the real rustlers before setting him up to be shot.

Ferg was pouring a second shot of bourbon to calm his nerves when his phone rang. There was no mistaking Bull Tyler's angry voice on the other end of the call. As soon as he heard it, Ferg knew his scheme had gone off the rails.

"If you're missing any cows, Ferg, you'll find them in that box canyon where you dammed the spring. Whoever stole them and left them there, it wasn't me or anybody on my ranch. You've got two hours to get them the hell off my property, or they'll be dead meat."

The slam that ended the call made Ferg's ear ring. He sighed as he replaced the receiver in its cradle. The plan, a long shot to begin with, hadn't worked. But never mind. An even better plan had rolled into sight driving a vintage 1947 Buick. This one was even legal. All he had to do was charm Rose Landro into letting him help her get her land back. The rest would be like shooting fish in a barrel.

He pushed his hefty frame up from behind his desk and walked out onto the front porch. The hands who'd driven the cows into the box canyon last night were close by and could be called to herd them home. No problem. But one question remained.

What had happened to McCade?

More than an hour had passed since Tanner had watched Rose leave and heard her ride off. Sitting on his horse and drinking from the canteen, he'd given her time to gain some distance. Then, after allowing a few minutes more for his head to clear, he'd turned the horse back toward the canyon and the lowing of the stolen cattle. He'd felt as if the devil were drilling on his skull. But he had a job to do. That job was to investigate and stop the cattle rustling.

Instead of going straight in, as he had when he'd been shot, he'd made a wide circle and approached the canyon from the side. Pistol drawn, he'd taken his time, checking the ground and the rocks before moving in close. He'd found the Prescott steers alone in the canyon, with rope strung between the rocks at the mouth to keep them from escaping. There'd been no one guarding them and no sign of vehicle tracks.

Puzzled, he'd backed off, holed up in a stand of cedars, and waited on the off-chance that the rustlers might return. When, after forty-five minutes, nobody had shown up, he'd decided to go back to his room in the Prescott bunkhouse, take something for his splitting headache, and return in time to wait for dark, when the cattle would most likely be loaded and moved.

Waiting, he'd had plenty of time to think about Rose and how she'd leaned close to sponge his wound, her breast brushing his shoulder, her breath warm against his ear. The lady had definitely stirred his blood. But he'd be a fool to buy her story about riding out here with two young Tyler boys and having to leave to catch up with them. For all he knew, she was the lookout for the rustlers and she'd hurried off to warn them away.

Now, as he rode back toward the ranch, Tanner saw three riders approaching. He recognized them as cowhands from the Prescott ranch.

"Well, look at you, McCade," one of the men hooted. "Did you get run over by a cattle stampede?"

"Long story, Lem," Tanner muttered. "What are you boys doin' out here?"

"The boss sent us out to fetch some cows that ended up on the Rimrock," the man named Lem answered. "Seems somebody found 'em and called the boss to come herd 'em back. He said we was to keep an eye out for you on the way. Sweet Jesus, you look like you got kicked by a mule, or maybe got yourself shot."

"Right the second time," Tanner said, tilting his hat to show the bandanna. "The bullet just put a crease in my scalp and gave me a hell of a headache."

"That sounds like somethin' Bull Tyler would do," one of the man said. "He's a mean son of a bitch. You're lucky you didn't get your brains blowed out."

"You think it was Tyler who shot me?"

"Who else? Unless it was his foreman, Jasper Platt. He's a mean one, too."

"You don't look so good," Lem said. "Can you make it back to the ranch by yourself?"

"I think so. Long as the horse knows the way," Tanner said.

"We'd ride back with you," Lem said, "but the boss will skin us alive if we don't get them cows back pronto."

"Don't worry. I can make it on my own."

Tanner watched the three cowhands ride off toward the escarpment. Then, turning the horse, he nudged it to an easy walk and headed back toward the heart of the ranch. At least he wouldn't have to return to the canyon tonight, as he'd planned. He could clean up in the bunkhouse, swallow a fistful of ibuprofen, report to Ferg, and then maybe get some sleep.

Only by chance did he happen to look down at the ground, where the three riders had left a fresh trail, superimposed over the tracks of the cattle and the thieves herding them.

One set of hoofprints showed signs of a loose shoe—a shoe with two nails missing.

Ignoring the ache in his head, Tanner dismounted and compared the new and older prints to be sure of the match. It was perfect. Something strange was going on here. Assuming the horse hadn't been switched between riders, the men he'd just met, the ones who were headed out to bring in the so-called stolen cattle, were the same ones who'd herded them onto Rimrock land in the first place.

Lem had mentioned that Ferg wanted the animals brought back at once. That would imply that Ferg knew exactly where they could be found. And Ferg wouldn't have known that unless he'd ordered his cattle moved there in the first place.

Tanner swore out loud. What in hell's name was going on? Was Ferg trying to frame his neighbor, Bull Tyler, for cattle rustling? If so, it was a lame-brained idea. Any of the men who'd done the herding could testify that they'd been acting under orders from Ferg.

So what had his own role been in this charade?

Ferg had sent him after the so-called stolen cattle, knowing exactly where he would find them. If things had gone as planned, he would have found the animals and assumed the thief was Bull. Tanner could only guess that somebody, most likely Bull himself, had learned of the scheme and ordered Ferg to come and get his livestock.

He'd been set up, Tanner realized. The TSCRA had been set up as well, sending him here and wasting valuable time and resources. The more Tanner thought about it, the angrier he became. Ferg Prescott was going to answer for this.

But what about the gunshot that had nearly killed him?

And what about Rose?

Overcome by a wave of pain-shot dizziness, Tanner leaned against the big dun's shoulder and pressed his face against the horse's warm coat. Nothing he'd learned so far could explain what had happened to him or who had fired the shot, let alone the reason why.

Perspiring with effort, he dragged himself back into the saddle and gave the horse its head. In an effort to focus, he thought about Rose, bending over him, giving him water and cleaning around his wound. Had she been the one who'd shot him?

In a way it seemed to fit. After winging him and knocking him off his horse, she could have ridden down to make sure he was dead. After he opened his eyes and saw her, she could easily have shot him again, at close range, to finish the job. Instead she'd decided to save him.

That didn't make sense. But who else could it have been? Someone else from the Rimrock? Maybe Bull Tyler himself?

Tanner unscrewed the lid from the canteen and gulped the

water to the last drop. If he could make it to the stable without passing out, he would put the horse away, wash up in the bunkhouse, take something for the pain, and get a few hours of rest. As soon as his head cleared, he would do whatever it took to unravel this mystery.

The first step would be to confront Ferg Prescott.

# CHAPTER SEVEN

*T*HE ROUNDUP ENDED WHEN THE LAST ANIMAL WAS BRANDED, tagged, castrated, inoculated against disease and parasites, and moved to new pasture. After that, even if the hour was late, it was time for celebration.

Ignacio, the bunkhouse cook, and his two young helpers had been busy since last night, pit barbecuing a prime beef. Bernice had helped out by providing fresh-baked rolls to go with the beef and beans and a chocolate cake for dessert. According to tradition, the cowhands would save their carousing until the family had eaten and left. After that, there would be loud country music, free-for-all gaming, and enough beer to last until the tired men staggered off to bed.

Bull, Rose, Bernice, Jasper, and the two boys had filled their plates at the head of the line and sat at the plank table near the bunkhouse to enjoy the feast. After they'd gone back to the house, the merrymaking had begun in earnest, with a boom box blaring old country music and the cowboys helping themselves around a tin washtub filled with ice and Mexican beer.

An hour later, after the boys had gone to bed and Bernice and Jasper had retired to their quarters, Bull sat alone on the unlit porch with his boots on the rail, an empty Corona bottle at his feet and a half-smoked Marlboro between his lips. The spring night was clear, the stars like a spill of gold dust across a velvet sky.

A bat swooped low over the porch, chasing clouds of newly

hatched spring insects. In the distant foothills, two coyotes sere-
naded each other with lovelorn wails.

The party outside the bunkhouse was in full swing, with a glowing bonfire, raucous music, and laughter, punctuated by an occasional curse over an unlucky throw of the dice. Some horseplay
was allowed, but brawling was forbidden, and any cowhand who
brought a gun or knife to the celebration would be fired. In the
years Bull had been giving these post-roundup parties, he'd yet to
be called upon to deal with a problem among his men.

All in all, today had been a good day, he mused. The roundup
was over with all the stock accounted for. Even the missing cows
Jasper had reported earlier had been found in a hidden gulley
where they'd wandered in search of succulent spring grass.

Best of all, perhaps, he'd foiled Ferg Prescott's latest plot to
frame him for a crime, then blackmail him into giving up that
creek property. As soon as Rose had told him about those Prescott
cattle in the box canyon, he'd known what the conniving skunk
was up to. That one phone call was all it had taken to cut the bastard's scheme off at the pass.

But one thing still troubled him. As he and Will were washing up
for the party, Will had told him about finding a man lying on the
ground—a man who'd looked as if he might be dead. Rose had
sent the boys on their way while she went back and helped him.

Why hadn't Rose mentioned the incident earlier? Was she hiding something? Had Ferg bought more from her than her old car?

"I was hoping I'd find you out here, Bull." As if his thoughts
could conjure her, Rose came striding around the house and
mounted the porch steps. "Now that the roundup's over, there
are things we need to discuss."

"All right. Sit down." Bull knew what she had in mind, but he
was set on a different conversation. Rose had a pushy way about
her, but she wasn't the one in charge here, he reminded himself.
He was the boss of the Rimrock, and within its borders his word
was law.

"Before you start on me, I want to talk to you about what happened today." He tossed his cigarette butt into the gravel below

the porch and watched the smoldering dot die into darkness. "I know what you told me about finding the cattle. But tonight Will mentioned that he'd seen a man on the ground—a man he'd thought was dead. I could tell he was pretty upset about it. Why didn't you say something to me?"

Rose settled back in the chair, her hands clasped around one knee. "I was hoping Will would tell you that he found the man because he disobeyed me and rode ahead of Beau and me. Did he?"

"He did, and he'll be punished for it. I've taught my boys to be honest, especially with their father. But tell me about the man, Rose. Was he really dead?"

"No." She gazed past him, as if studying the flow of moon shadows on the gravel. "He'd been shot, but the bullet had only grazed his head and knocked him out. I gave him water, cleaned him up some, and made sure he could ride. Then I left him and caught up with your boys. That's the last I saw of him."

"Did he say who shot him?"

"He said he'd glimpsed a movement in the rocks above the canyon. But beyond that, he didn't even remember being shot. Is there any chance you might have cattle rustlers on the Rimrock?"

"If I do, they don't work for me. All my men were busy with the roundup. And herding those cattle into the canyon was Ferg's doing. He was just up to his old tricks, wanting to get me in trouble." Bull was growing impatient. This was a puzzle, and he didn't like puzzles. He liked to know what he was dealing with so he could face it head-on.

"You didn't think to ask his name?"

She turned and looked at him then, with eyes like dark flint. "I didn't have to. He was the man who drove me to town when I bought the truck."

"So he was Ferg's man?"

"Yes. His name was—*is*—Tanner McCade."

Bull chewed on that information in silence. Piece by piece, the puzzle was sliding together.

If Ferg had carried out the so-called theft of his own cattle, why would he have ordered the shooting of one of his own men?

Unless, along with cattle rustling, he'd wanted to pin a murder on the Rimrock.

The murder of an undercover TSCRA ranger.

A ranger named Tanner McCade.

Huddled in the chair, Rose held her tongue, giving Bull time to mull over what she'd told him. She was no mind reader, but she knew she'd done him a favor today. With luck, he might be grateful enough to listen to her request.

But she should have known better.

Bull cleared his throat. "I know what you want, Rose. But let me give you some advice. My father always used to say, 'Trust a skunk before a rattlesnake, and a rattlesnake before a Prescott.' I've held to the same counsel, and so should you. I know Ferg helped you out, buying that old car and having his man drive you to town. But Ferg never did anything out of the goodness of his heart—if the bastard even has a heart. He wants that creek property, and if I turn it over to you, sure as the sun comes up in the morning, he'll find a way to take it for himself."

Rose's smoldering anger flared. "Does that make him any different from you, Bull? You cheated me out of the land my grandpa left me. That property is mine, and I want it back. If you won't give it to me, I'll get it some other way."

"How? By going to Ferg? Hell, girl, he'd destroy you to get that land. Look at what he did today—hiding his cows on the Rimrock so he could frame me for stealing them, and maybe even for shooting your friend, McCade. All that to blackmail me into giving up the creek property. That's the kind of snake you'd be dealing with. His old man killed your granddad for that land. Ferg's just as bad, if not worse. He's capable of anything."

"Maybe so." Rose's voice had gone flat and cold. "But this isn't about the Prescotts. It's about me and what's mine. It's about what's right."

"It's about what's sensible, Rose. The only way to protect that land and the access to the creek is to keep it as part of the Rimrock. I'm willing to pay you a fair price for it, or trade you for a parcel of land somewhere else. But that's as far as I'll go."

"No." Rose jumped out of her chair and stood facing him. "My grandfather meant for me to have that land, and I won't settle for anything else. If that's all you have to offer me, we're done here."

Fighting tears of frustration, she turned away from him and strode down the steps. She'd given Bull every chance to right the wrong he'd done her, and he'd refused. It was time to make a new plan.

It was after midnight when Ferg climbed into the cab of his pickup, which he'd parked down the block from Bonnie Tread-well's house, just like in the old days. He hummed to himself as he settled into the driver's seat and slipped the key into the ignition. Bonnie might be past her prime and putting on a little weight, but when it came to satisfying a man, the old girl hadn't lost her touch.

Back in the day, when she was waiting tables at the Burger Shack, she and Ferg had been hot and heavy. She'd broken off their relationship to have her trucker husband's baby. But now that she was divorced, with her ex sharing custody of the boy, she was hornier than ever. Ferg knew he wasn't the only man who shared her bed—she had a thing for hot, young cowpokes. But as long as he was at the top of her list, Ferg didn't mind. There were worse things than getting what he wanted in bed without the demands of having a wife.

Where Main Street turned onto the two-lane highway, he stomped the gas pedal, enjoying the squeal of rubber on asphalt as the truck picked up speed. He'd had a few drinks at Bonnie's, but what the hell? Traffic was light, and even the cops were asleep at this hour. After rolling down the truck windows, he turned up the radio and blasted Merle Haggard into the night.

Flying bugs splattered a mosaic of wings and guts on the windshield. Ferg made a game of pretending they were people in his life. *Splat!* There you go, Bull Tyler. *Splat!* You, too, Jasper Platt.

*Splat!* And you, Garn, you gutless wonder of a son. Sometimes I want to—

The earsplitting blare of a horn blasted Ferg's ears. A huge semi loomed in his windshield, roaring straight down on him. Seized by panic, Ferg wrenched the steering wheel, hard right— but not far enough or fast enough to pull his pickup out of the oncoming lane. The monster truck was almost on him when the driver swerved hard onto the shoulder of the narrow road. Gravel crunched as the shoulder crumbled under the massive tires. Brakes squealing, the semi shuddered to a stop, resting at an angle, just short of tipping onto its side.

A glance in Ferg's rearview mirror showed the driver's door opening. He floored the gas pedal and sped away without another look. He was grateful to be alive. But the last thing he needed was a confrontation with an angry trucker and maybe a DUI arrest if the man called the highway patrol.

Ferg had broken out in a cold sweat. Shivering, he closed the truck windows and switched off the radio. It was still sinking in how close he'd come to dying back there. What in hell's name was that semi doing on the road at this hour, anyway? Only two things would put a big rig on an isolated highway at this hour—a woman or a bunch of stolen cattle.

The notion of cattle thieving led him to recall the day's events. His foreman had passed on the news that the so-called stolen cattle were safely back. But nobody had mentioned finding Tanner McCade's body. Deke Triplehorn had orders to lie low after the shooting. The fact that he hadn't reported in would suggest that he'd done his job.

But what about McCade? If the TSCRA ranger was dead on Rimrock land, there still had to be some way to pin the crime on Bull. He would think on that. Meanwhile, the romp with Bonnie and his narrow escape on the way home had left him exhausted. Right now, all he wanted was to go to bed. He would take stock of the situation in the morning. Whatever was going on, he would figure out a way to work it to his advantage.

Stifling a yawn, he pulled through the gate and drove up the lane into the yard. The house was dark. Even the porch light was off. It operated on a timer, so the bulb must've burned out.

Ferg parked the pickup, switched off the headlights, and climbed out of the truck. Stumbling up the steps, he made his way onto the porch. His eyes caught a slight movement in the dark. The hair rose on the back of his neck as he realized that he wasn't alone. Somebody was sitting in one of the chairs.

"Hello, Ferg," said Tanner McCade. "Sit down. Let's have a talk."

Tanner had been lying low but keeping an eye on the boss of the Prescott Ranch. Earlier that night, he'd seen Ferg leave in one of the ranch pickups, freshly shaved and wearing a clean change of clothes. A man like Ferg wouldn't have bothered cleaning up at night unless there was a woman waiting somewhere. And he wouldn't have taken one of the work vehicles unless he didn't want to be recognized.

Not that he was breaking any laws. Ferg was a widower, and as long as the women were willing, his sex life was none of Tanner's business. But cattle showing up where they didn't belong and bullets flying out of nowhere were another matter.

Tanner had weighed the wisdom of confronting Ferg. On one hand it might be smart to keep what he'd discovered to himself and try to learn more. On the other hand, his head hurt like hell, he'd come damn close to being killed, and he was sick and tired of being played. This had become personal.

A sliver of a crescent moon rode the peak of the sky. In its faint light, Ferg looked as if he'd seen a ghost. "Hell, McCade, you shouldn't startle a man like that," he muttered. "If I'd had a gun on me, you'd have been dead by now."

"You look surprised to see me, Ferg," Tanner said, deliberately using Prescott's first name. "Any reason why?"

"I don't know what you're talking about," Ferg grumbled, moving toward the door. "Whatever it is, it can wait till morning."

"Fine. But morning will be when I call in to the district office and tell them how your cattle really came to be on the Rimrock and how I came within a gnat's eyelash of getting shot through the head today."

Ferg sank onto a chair. "What is it you want, McCade? Name your price."

"You think I want *money?* I may be a lot of things, but I'm not a blackmailer." Inwardly, Tanner celebrated a small victory. Ferg wouldn't have offered him a bribe if he didn't have something to hide. "I'm not here to get you in trouble," he said. "All I want is the truth. I know that the men who fetched your cattle home were the ones who herded those cows onto the Rimrock in the first place—and that they were acting on your orders. What I don't know is *why.*"

Ferg's silence ended in a nervous laugh. "Why, it was a joke, that's all. A joke on Bull Tyler. We were friends as boys, and we still play pranks on each other."

That was a lie if he'd ever heard one. "So if it was a joke, why did you send me on the trail of those cattle?"

"Don't you get it? That was part of the joke. You were supposed to find the cows and threaten Bull with arrest. Then we'd have a good laugh and it would be over. Trouble was, Bull got wind of it and didn't think it was funny. He ordered me to get my cows off his land."

"You don't see me laughing, either. Was my getting shot part of the joke?"

Ferg's only response was a blank stare.

"I mentioned it earlier. The men who went after the cows knew about it, too. I met them coming back." Tanner raised his hat to show the gauze bandage he'd wrapped around his head. "The bullet grazed me, knocked me out, until . . ." He hesitated. Did he want to bring Rose into this? "I came to and made it back here," he said, deciding against it. Ferg was already lying through his teeth. Nothing he might say about Rose could be counted as truth.

"Well, I'm damned sorry you were shot," Ferg said. "I may have tried to prank Bull with those cows, but I sure as hell had nothing to do with shooting you. It was probably Bull, or one of his men. I wouldn't put it past them to gun down a stranger they caught on Tyler land."

"Your men told me the same thing. I'll have to look into that— assuming there's still work to be done here. I don't like to think you requested an agent here for a joke."

"Lord, no! I'm still losing stock for real. I've shown you the books. We've had at least a dozen prime steers vanish into thin air in the past week."

"Fine. I'll report in and tell Clive I need to stay awhile longer. But no more tricks, Ferg. No more lies or going behind my back. Understand?"

"Understood."

Tanner didn't offer his hand as he turned to go. He hadn't had much respect for Ferg to begin with, and he was learning that the man was a bully and a liar.

As he walked back to the bunkhouse, his head still aching, his thoughts drifted to Rose and the memory of those sunflower eyes looking down at him, that small, firm breast brushing his shoulder, and those tough little hands washing the blood from his skin. She'd smelled like cheap soap and sagebrush, a mix that had stirred his senses and, even now, left him mildly aroused.

Strange that Rose, of all people, had found him lying unconscious and wounded—maybe too strange now that he thought about it. What if she'd already known where to look for him?

What if it had been her finger that pulled the trigger?

Sunday morning, after Bull and Jasper had left to check the stock in the new pastures, Rose made coffee in her duplex, gulped it down, bundled up her scant possessions, and carried them outside to her truck.

Last night she'd given Bull one final chance to make things right with her land. He'd made his position clear. The lines had been drawn. She could no longer take advantage of his hospitality or enjoy the friendship of Jasper, Bernice, and the boys.

This was war.

The previous owner of the pickup had left the camper in good

condition. Rose piled in her clothes, blankets, tools, and her grandfather's shotgun, which she laid gently under the mattress. Then
she climbed into the cab and took the back road to the creek and
the parcel of land that her grandfather had given his life to protect.

Today was Sunday—no day of rest for ranchers and ranch hands
who had animals to feed and care for. Still, as she drove the rutted
dirt road across the scrubby open range, she sensed a serenity that
had settled over the land and over her spirit. What she was about to
do wouldn't be easy. But it had to be done, and she felt right in
doing it.

The roundup had cleared the cattle from this part of their
range. They would likely be moved back when the grass had had
time to grow and the dry summer made the watering tank a vital
necessity. All to the good. With luck, she would have a few months
of peace and quiet before Bull moved his stock back here. She
would consider leasing him rights to the tank, but a lot of things
had to happen first.

She pulled up to the edge of the property and climbed out of
the truck. She no longer feared Ferg Prescott's men. Ferg knew
her and had offered his help. If she was going to get her property
back, she would likely need it.

The narrow strip of land was much as she had left it, the grass
eaten and trampled, the tank untended now that the cattle had
been moved. A few sunflowers were sprouting where she had
once planted her garden—a good omen, she thought.

Looking around, she began to take stock of her needs. First
would be a good, stout fence. The barbed wire and posts that had
surrounded the place in the old days had been trampled into the
ground. Some of the rusty wire might be usable if she could dig it
up. But she would need to buy new posts, or fill in the gaps with
some of the saplings that had sprouted along the creek. She
could sleep in the camper. It had a propane stove but no plumbing. She would have to dig a latrine in a secluded spot until she
could build an outhouse.

The creek water was good for drinking and washing. She would have to bathe with a rag and a basin in the dark, but she'd roughed it before and knew how to get by.

As before, she walked to the massive fallen tree that sheltered her grandfather's grave. Kneeling, she placed her hand on the earth. A lump rose in her throat as she made a silent promise to the old man who had taken her in, protected and educated her. She would make a home here, worthy of the dream he had shared with her.

"Well, look who's here!" A slightly nasal male voice startled her. Rose sprang to her feet, whirling in the same motion. Garn Prescott stood behind her, a grin on his jut-nosed face. That grin widened as he looked her up and down, his manner unmistakable.

Rose's stomach clenched, but she knew better than to show fear. She drew herself up and looked hard into Garn's colorless eyes. His lashes, she forced herself to notice, were so light they were almost transparent, and he had a ripe pimple on his chin. How old was he? Nineteen, maybe?

"You need to get back on your own property," she said, wishing she hadn't left her pistol in the truck.

"Oh? And who's going to make me?" He took a challenging stance, his fists planted on his hip bones.

"You sound like a fourth grader," she said. "You're acting like one, too."

He laughed, but Rose could tell she'd stung him. "I wouldn't be so high and mighty if I were you, Rose Landro. I know a lot about you."

"You don't know me at all."

"I know enough. I know you shot my grandfather. And I know you used to live here, and that you'd do anything to get this place back." He winked. "Anything . . ."

"I think you'd better leave." Rose could feel the adrenaline surging—a wild animal's fight-or-flight response.

"I could do a lot for you," he said. "I've got connections, and my father listens to me and takes my advice. I've got money, too.

And good credit if you need a loan to fix this place up. All I'm asking in return is a little neighborly cooperation."

Sweat beads trickled down the back of Rose's neck. Her first impulse was to make a break for the truck and drive off, but he'd placed himself in her way. He didn't look very strong, but he was young and tall, with long arms and big hands. In a struggle, she wouldn't stand a chance against him.

Heart in her throat, she turned aside, toward the creek. "I'm not that desperate," she said. "Go get yourself another girl, one closer to your own age."

His hand caught her elbow, spun her around, and whipped her against him, pinning her arm behind her back. His face was so close that she could see the pores on his nose and smell the mint on his breath. "A woman like you, the way you've lived, I know you've done it plenty before. And liked it too, I'll bet."

"Let me go." She glared up at him, on the edge of wildness. "Let me go, or so help me I'll scratch your eyes out."

He twisted her arm harder, hurting until she almost cried out. "I'd like to see you try, bitch. You'll thank me when I'm done with—"

"That's enough, Junior. Let her go." Tanner's deep voice came from somewhere behind Garn. With a muttered curse, Garn let go of Rose's arms and shoved her away from him. She stumbled and fell back against the old cottonwood trunk.

Tanner had stepped out of the willows and crossed the creek. He stood facing Garn, so broad-shouldered and muscular that he made Ferg's son look like a scarecrow. The pistol at his hip remained holstered.

"Go home, boy," he said. "If you leave right now, I won't tell your father what you just tried to do to this lady."

Garn's face had turned crimson. "My father doesn't care! He says that a man needs experience to be a real man. And she's no lady. You can tell that just by the look of her. She'd spread her legs for the price of a movie ticket. This is none of your business, cowboy. Back off, or I'll have your ass fired!"

Tanner didn't move, but his mouth twitched in a ghost of a

smile. "I'd like to see you try," he said. "Run along. I don't want to have to hurt you."

Garn glared at him. "You'll pay for this!" He spat out the words as he turned and strode back across the creek, soaking his expensive-looking wing tips in the shallow current. Moments after he disappeared beyond the willows, Rose heard the growl of a light motorbike fading away.

Tanner walked over to where Rose had stumbled against the big cottonwood trunk. She was struggling to stand, her eyes crying angry tears. "Are you all right?" he asked, holding out his hand.

She took it and let Tanner pull her to her feet. Even then she couldn't control her tears. Garn hadn't hurt her physically, but his ugly words had pierced her like an ice pick thrust to the bone. Was that how people saw her, as cheap, common, and available to any man who wanted her? Was that the way she should see herself?

Even Tanner, looking down at her now—was that what he saw, a low-class, pathetic creature with no value except as a toy for men to abuse? Did he feel sorry for her?

It was all she could do to keep from breaking apart like a shattered doll. But she had her pride. She wasn't about to let him see how deeply she'd been hurt. The last thing she wanted was his pity.

Forcing a smile, she drew herself up. "It's a good thing you happened along," she said. "I was just about to beat that poor boy to a bloody pulp."

"I could tell," Tanner said. "I got here just in time to rescue him. And the fool didn't even thank me."

Knees quivering, Rose took a step forward, then stumbled. Tanner reached out to catch her, but she sank back onto the cottonwood trunk, pulling her knees against her and wrapping them with her arms.

"It's all right, Rose," he said. "They were only words. You're not anything like what that little jackass said you were."

"How do you know?" She stared at the ground. "You just met me. You don't know anything about me—and most of it, you wouldn't want to know."

He sat down next to her, their shoulders not quite touching. "I know what I see," he said, turning his head to look at her. "I see a brave, spirited woman, a warrior if you will, fighting against all odds to make something good of her life—a woman who's been knocked down and gotten up again and again. Rose, you're one of the most courageous people I've ever met."

His words had touched her. She sniffed back tears. "And you, Tanner McCade, are full of baloney, as my grandfather used to say. I'll bet you say nice words like that to all the girls, except maybe the pretty ones who don't need to be told how brave they are because, if you're pretty, it doesn't matter."

A mutter of exasperation escaped his lips. Turning, he caught her chin, cupped it lightly with his fingertips, and turned her head to face him. Rose's first impulse was to pull away. But his touch was light, and he made no move to control or force her.

Heart hammering, she met his gentle gray eyes as he studied her face, seeing all the flaws—the salty tear streaks, the little scars from the hard life she'd lived, and the stain that spilled like wine from her temple to her jaw.

He shook his head. "You're not pretty, Rose. You're beautiful. I thought so the first time I saw you—you made me think of a hawk, fierce and wild and strong."

"*Baloney!*" The word emerged as a whisper.

He shook his head again. For the space of a heartbeat, she feared Tanner was going to kiss her. But to his credit, he didn't. She was too raw, too fragile to accept that. Instead he simply released her and put his hand on his knee.

"Rose," he said, "sometimes I don't think you have any idea who you are or what you're worth. That's why it's all too easy to believe jerks like Garn Prescott who see women only as objects to be used. Don't listen to them."

She looked away, not wanting him to see that his words were

getting to her. She could feel herself crumbling, breaking apart inside. As the tears came, she pressed her hands to her face. Her shoulders shook.

"Rose," he muttered, reaching for her. "Oh, damn it, Rose!"

He pulled her close and held her. Only then did she realize how much she'd needed it.

# CHAPTER EIGHT

TANNER HELD HER AS IF HE WERE CRADLING AN INJURED BIRD. HE could feel her womanly warmth, the pounding of her heart, and the gentle pressure of her curves against his body as she breathed. He could hear the little catch of her breath as she struggled to hold back full-blown sobs.

The subtle fragrance of her skin crept into his senses. It would be the most natural thing in the world, he thought, to crush her close against him, even kiss her. But he'd seen enough of Rose to be aware of the barriers she'd thrown up and to know that pushing those barriers could shatter her.

Could this tender, emotionally fragile woman have aimed a long-range rifle and fired a bullet at his head?

Holding her now, it didn't seem possible. Yet the lawman in him couldn't rule it out. Rose was full of surprises, and she was getting to him in more ways than one. His body had already responded to her nearness. He was rock hard and ready inside the prison of his jeans. Much more of this torture and she would become aware of it. Then he'd be in trouble.

He was about to ease her away from him when she spoke. "I don't understand it. Why do the worst men consider me such an easy mark? Is it because I don't look big enough to fight them off? Is it because I'm so ugly that they think I'd be grateful? What is it?"

Tanner cleared his throat, scrambling for the right answer, but it wasn't there. "You're anything but ugly, Rose. As for the rest, hormone-crazy boys like Garn and men like that jerk in the garage are apt to go after any woman in sight. Maybe you've just had the bad luck to be in the wrong place at the wrong time."

"That's a sensible answer. I suppose it will have to do." She smiled up at him, a glint of tears in her eyes. And suddenly Tanner knew the real answer to her question. She was beautiful, vulnerable, and completely alone. That combination would tempt any man. But it might not be wise to tell her that. With his body threatening to betray him, he decided to change the subject.

"Somebody shot me yesterday, Rose. I need to ask this question. Was it you?"

She drew back, a shocked expression on her face. "Of course not! What on earth makes you think I'd want to shoot *you?*"

"Because you're working with Bull Tyler, or at least friends with him, and I was trespassing on his land. And because you knew right where to find me. For all I know, you could've been checking to make sure I was dead. As I remember, you even tried to take my gun."

"That's ridiculous!" Her eyes were practically shooting sparks. "Bull's son found you first. I sent him back down the trail because the boy was upset and because somebody needed to be with his little brother. And I tried to take your gun because I was afraid you might wake up and shoot me with it." She took a deep breath. "As for Bull Tyler, I'm not working with him. He's not even my friend. I'm only trying to get back the land he stole from me—this land that my grandfather died protecting so I could have a home. He's buried right over there, under that big tree trunk."

Either she was the world's greatest actress or she was telling the truth. Looking into her face and feeling the intensity of her emotion, Tanner had no doubt that she stood behind every word. But was she more than what he could see, more than what she had told him? Who was this woman?

"Ferg believes you killed his father," he said.

"Believes it? He *knows* it! And he knows it was self-defense. He was there the night it happened. And as long as you're asking, I also shot the brother of a drug lord in Mexico because he was trying to rape and kill me. If the cartel catches up with me, I'm dead or worse. That's why I had to leave Río Seco and come back here. Is that enough to satisfy your curiosity, *Mr. Lawman?*"

Stunned into silence, he stared at her.

"When you came to my rescue in that garage," she said, "the way you spoke and handled your gun told me you weren't an ordinary cowboy. But I still can't figure out why you'd work for a lying snake like Ferg."

She had him. Telling her the truth might be reckless, but after her own brutal honesty, he owed her the same.

Opening an inner pocket of his vest, he took out his TSCRA ranger badge and handed it to her. Fashioned from a 1947 silver Mexican peso, it was round, with the head of a longhorn steer engraved in its center and lettering around the border.

"I'm working undercover to investigate a report of cattle rustling," he said. "Ferg requested a ranger. I was sent because I was new and not many folks would know me."

"How's that going?" A hint of humor twinkled in her eyes as she returned his badge.

"Knowing Ferg, you can guess. I'm beginning to suspect he's giving me the runaround."

"Bull and Jasper have a saying—I've heard it so many times that I think it must be the Tyler family motto. 'Trust a skunk before a rattlesnake and a rattlesnake before a Prescott.' You'd do well to remember that."

"Thanks, I'll remind myself." He paused, wondering how much he could learn from her without making her feel as if she was being grilled. "Ferg keeps telling me that when it comes to cattle rustling, I should check out Bull Tyler and his foreman."

"Don't waste your time. Jasper Platt is the most honest man I know. And as for Bull, he'd never stoop to stealing cattle. Land grabbing is more his style."

"So you don't think there's any chance one of them took a shot at me?"

"Why should they? They might chase a trespasser off the Rimrock, but they wouldn't shoot him. Anyway, the whole crew was off on the roundup when it happened."

"At least you saved me some time." He looked down at her, taking in her smallness, her delicate features, and the marred beauty of her face with the mark that somehow seemed to suit her. He tried to imagine her shooting a Mexican gangster, the courage it must have taken.

"It seems we know a few of each other's secrets, Rose," he said. "Can I trust you to keep mine?"

"If I can expect the same from you. Friends—for now, at least?" She held out her hand.

"Friends." Tanner accepted the handshake, reining back the urge to gather her into his arms and kiss her. It was more than an urge. It was more like a deep, hungry ache, and right now it was the last damned thing he needed.

"You'd better go," she said.

"You're staying here?"

"I'm going to camp on this land while I work out a way to fight for it legally—with any help I can find."

"Camping here won't be safe," he said.

Her eyes blazed with determination. "Is anything safe—anything worth having?"

He left her standing by the grave, so alone and so vulnerable that he had to tear himself away. Rose was a bundle of spunk and courage. But given the dangers surrounding her, she was like a little bird flying into a tornado. And short of checking on her—dangerous in itself—there was nothing he could do about it.

Was he falling in love? But Tanner knew better than to entertain that notion. He was fascinated by Rose, even infatuated. And he wanted her the way any man would want a woman. But love? He gave a mental shake of his head as he mounted the horse he'd left in the trees beyond the creek. He would never love again. He had buried his heart in the ashes of a simple frame house in a small Wyoming town.

\* \* \*

That afternoon, tired and dirty after unearthing a long line of rusty fence wire, Rose splashed her hands and face in the creek, smoothed her hair, and set out for the Prescott Ranch. She was taking a chance, just showing up without an invitation, but she'd lost her access to a phone when she'd left the Rimrock. She'd lost access to other things, too, including meals.

Out of principle, she'd taken nothing from the Rimrock kitchen. After a morning's hard work with no breakfast, her empty stomach was growling. But hunger would have to wait for a trip to town. And the trip would have to wait until after she'd spoken with Ferg. Right now, her whole plan hinged on getting his help.

Feeling awkward, she drove up to the house and parked below the porch. She'd been here before, but there was something about the place, with its towering gables and gingerbread trim, that made her feel small and unimportant.

Climbing out of the cab, she glimpsed a few of the hands going about their work. Tanner wasn't among them, and she chided herself for looking. He'd been friendly to her, but Rose knew better than to read more into his actions.

As she mounted the porch steps, she saw Garn lounging in the swing. He gave her a slow grin. "Change your mind?" he asked.

"I'm here to see your father," she said.

"Go on in. The king is in his throne room down the hall. Just in case you're wondering, Ferg Prescott may be the boss around here, but I've got a bigger dick."

"If that's the way you talk to women, I'm guessing you don't get much chance to use it." Rose walked through the open front door. Behind her, Garn burst into hoots of laughter.

Rose told herself she should have kept quiet and ignored the overgrown brat, as she walked past the gallery of stuffed trophy heads and made her way down the hall to Ferg's office. She had a smart mouth and a bad habit of using it too freely, especially when somebody needed putting down.

Ferg's office door stood ajar. Rose gave it a light rap. "Who's there?" a voice grumbled from inside the room.

Her heart sank. "It's Rose, Mr. Prescott. Rose Landro."

"Rose!" His tone mellowed and became welcoming. "Come on in."

She stepped into his office. Ferg rose to greet her, extending his hand across the massive desk. Rose accepted the handshake. She didn't trust the man, but right now she needed his help.

He motioned her to a straight-backed chair that faced the desk, then resumed his own seat. "Now what can I do for you, dear girl? Garn mentioned that he saw you on that old creek property your granddad owned. Does that have anything to do with the reason you're here?"

Rose inferred that Garn hadn't told his father all that had happened on the creek. But either way, she couldn't allow that to matter. "You invited me to call on you if I ever needed your help," she said.

"That's right. And I meant what I said. So tell me your story." He gave her a sugary smile. He was making this easy, maybe too easy. But he was her only hope.

"You know that parcel is mine by inheritance, don't you?"

"I do." His light brown eyes were fixed intently on her. "And I know that Bull claims to own it now. I know that because I've tried to buy it from him, for a fair price of course."

"Of course. But Bull can't sell the property because it isn't his. He took it from me illegally by changing the deed. And now that I want it back, he won't budge. He's refused to let me have it."

"Too bad. But that's Bull for you." Ferg was all sympathy. "I take it you need me to twist his arm a little. Not physically, but maybe . . . legally. Yes?"

"Yes. Legally, I mean. I need a lawyer to help me prove my claim. Right now I can't afford to pay anyone. But if I could just get some advice from the person who handles your legal affairs . . ."

"Say no more!" Ferg exclaimed. "I keep an attorney on retainer. I'm sure he'd be glad to advise you. His office is in Lubbock, but he has some court business in Blanco Springs this afternoon. I've already invited him for an early dinner. Why don't you come, too? You can talk to him then, just informally, and he can give you some suggestions."

"And if I need more than suggestions?"

"You mean, if you have to sue Bull to get your land back?"

"Something like that. Bull's dug in his heels. Persuasion isn't going to change his mind."

"In that case, it would be my pleasure to help. And if you need a loan to fix the place up the way you want it, I'll even cosign with the bank. Believe me, I'd rather have you for a neighbor than Bull."

Still smiling, he stood and extended his hand. "Thank you for calling on me, Rose—may I call you that? Dinner will be at six-thirty. I'll see you then."

Rose accepted his handshake and left Ferg's office. Garn was gone from the porch when she went outside, and there was no sign of Tanner. She climbed into her truck and drove away, feeling almost giddy. She was moving forward on her own, finally taking charge of her life. And if a deep inner voice whispered that she was making a deal with the devil, she willed herself to ignore it. Ferg Prescott was not a good person—that was a given. When it came to dealing with him, she would have to watch her back. But she needed all the help she could get, and sometimes the devil was the only help available.

After digging up some more wire, Rose filled a bucket from the creek and took a sponge bath inside the camper. The water was cold, the space cramped. But at least by the time she finished, she felt clean.

The few good clothes she had were folded in the bottom of her duffel. María had made her a *quincianera* dress for her fifteenth birthday party, which was like a coming out for Mexican girls. Rose lifted it from the duffel and held it up for inspection. María had done a beautiful job, but the ruffles and lace were better suited to a fifteen-year-old girl than a grown woman who wanted to be taken seriously. In the end Rose settled for a simple white blouse and a handwoven Mexican skirt, paired with leather sandals and plain silver earrings. There was no mirror in the camper. She would just have to trust that she looked presentable.

Her only working clock was the one on the dashboard of the pickup. When the numbers read 6:20, she started the engine and drove the back road to the Prescott Ranch. She pulled up to the house to find Garn waiting on the front porch. Bracing herself, she climbed out of the cab and mounted the steps.

He met her with a grin. "My, oh my, you clean up right nice, Miz Rose," he said, affecting the mock Texas drawl he'd shed in his everyday speech.

"Don't start with me, Garn," she said. "I've got more important things on my mind than dealing with your silliness."

"I know," he said, dropping the drawl. "Dinner isn't quite ready yet. I was hoping you'd have a minute to hear what I have to say. I guarantee it'll be short and sincere."

She followed as he beckoned her to a corner of the porch. "Well?" she asked as he stopped to face her.

"I wanted to apologize," he said. "As my father reminded me, I was raised to be a gentleman. No gentleman talks to a woman the way I talked to you. Will you forgive me?"

His expression was as earnest as a coonhound's. But this change of heart was a bit too sudden to suit Rose. She gave him a frown. "I might be willing. But you said some awful things to me. It'll take time for me to forget them, and for you to show me that you've changed your ways. But meanwhile, I'll agree to a truce. All right?"

"I guess that's the best I can expect. Thanks." Thrusting his hands into the pockets of his khakis, he turned toward the porch rail and gazed out over the flatland. "I'm my father's only child—the only legal one, at least," he said. "None of my mom's other babies survived, and in the end, neither did she. So I'm all the family he's got. And he can't stand me. He doesn't even try to hide it."

"I'm sorry," Rose said. "But at least you'll inherit this ranch when he's gone. You'll be rich and powerful without having to lift a finger."

His laugh was raw and bitter. "Let me tell you a secret. If and when I inherit this place, I'm going to sell every goddamned acre of it! I hate cattle—the way they bellow, the way they stink, and the way they always seem to shit right where you're about to put your feet. I hate getting my hands dirty, and I get motion sickness on a horse. These days there are big syndicates that buy up ranches and run them like a business. They'll snap this place right up and give me the cash, or make me a silent partner who collects income and never has to show up."

"And what will you do then?" Rose asked, intrigued in spite of herself.

"I'll invest the money and go into politics. I've already got an internship lined up this fall in Washington, DC. Once that's done—"

The clang of the dinner bell ended the conversation. Rose allowed Garn to escort her into the dining room. She still didn't like the young man, but at least she understood him better. He was unhappy and insecure and wanted a different life than the one fate and birth had thrust on him.

Even that didn't excuse the way he'd treated her at the creek, though. If their paths crossed again, she would do her best to tolerate the young man. But she would never feel at ease with Garn Prescott.

Ferg and a thin, graying man in a blue suit were standing by the cabinet in the corner, having a drink. As they took their places at one end of the long table, Ferg introduced the stranger as Cantwell Sutherland, the Prescott family lawyer.

"Miss Landro." Sutherland greeted her with a coldly formal handshake. "Ferg, here, has been telling me your story."

"I'm pleased to meet you, Mr. Sutherland." Rose assumed that Ferg had left out the part where she'd killed his father—which would be tantamount to an admission that he'd lied when he'd accused Bull.

"Sit down. We can talk about it while we eat," Ferg said.

There were just four of them at the table, eating from plain, white china plates on a rumpled cloth. The cook, who walked with a limp and looked like an aging cowboy, brought in a platter of leathery roast beef, along with lumpy mashed potatoes, canned peas, and watered-down gravy. It wasn't the best, but Rose had eaten worse, and she was starved. She made a good show of filling and emptying her plate. Garn watched her in amused silence, smiling as if he'd heard a secret joke.

Between bites, a sanitized version of how she'd lost her property to Bull had emerged. Sutherland had listened with mild interest, maybe because it didn't involve his making a handsome fee.

"So, did you ever see the deed to your grandfather's property, Miss Landro?" he asked.

"No," Rose said. "My grandpa was pretty secretive. He kept it locked away and hidden, even from me. But he told me he'd made out the deed so the land would go to me. All I had to do was sign the transferred deed and register it at the county office. But after he died, Bull got his hands on the deed, altered it somehow, and filed it under his own name. I never even saw it."

"And there's no copy in the recorder's office."

"No. I asked."

"Then it seems to me . . ." Sutherland spoke slowly, as if pondering each phrase. "It seems that what you need to do is get the court to subpoena the original deed from Mr. Tyler and hire an expert to determine how it was altered. With that done, you could take the evidence to court and make your claim."

Rose felt as if she were shrinking in her chair. She was already out of her depth. "How much would that cost?" she asked.

"I'd have to do some checking. But I could make an estimate and get back to you."

Rose knew what that meant. The cost, for her, would amount to a small fortune, more than she could ever hope to pay. And asking Ferg to loan her that amount would surely involve giving him a lien on the land—which would be like bargaining away her soul. She saw the smile on Ferg's face—a smile that fled as soon as he realized she was looking at him. Yes, he was thinking the same thing. This was a trap.

"Can't I base my claim on the fact that I'm my grandfather's only living descendant?" she asked the lawyer.

"Can you prove it, Miss Landro?"

Rose's heart dropped. She'd never given a thought to the question. But her grandfather was dead and buried. So was her mother, who was his estranged daughter. She'd managed to keep her birth certificate, but everything in the way of photos, letters, and other evidence had been lost after her mother's death, when the state had placed Rose in a foster home.

She knew beyond doubt that she was the granddaughter of Cletus McAdoo. But as far as anyone else was concerned, she might as well be nothing more than a runaway orphan who'd found her way to his shack and been taken in by the old hermit.

Just one person had spoken with the old man and could bear witness that he'd believed her to be his granddaughter. Unfortunately, that person was Bull Tyler.

"Can you prove the blood relationship, Miss Landro?" the lawyer asked again.

Rose shook her head. At least she understood her options. But none of them were good. "Let me think about this. If I need your help I'll let Mr. Prescott know."

*Not much chance of that,* she thought as the cook hobbled in with squares of dry-looking yellow cake. Her appetite gone, she washed down bites of dessert with sips of sour lemonade. If she chose to pursue a suit against Bull, she would have to mortgage her land to Ferg Prescott—a mortgage she could never hope to pay off. Looking across the table at Ferg's smug face, she realized that was what he'd had in mind all along.

At the next lull in the conversation, she excused herself, thanked her host and the lawyer, and made her escape.

As she crossed the porch, her eyes probed the darkness, seeking one tall figure, one rugged face. But Tanner was nowhere in sight. *Time to stop playing the fool,* Rose chided herself. Tanner had better things to do than hang around keeping an eye on her. She'd be smart to forget about him and look out for herself.

Still, driving back to her land, where she planned to camp, she couldn't help thinking about him. Every word she'd told him about herself had been true. But had he been as honest with her? She'd seen his badge. She knew he wasn't really working for Ferg. But she'd sensed a wall around him. He had shown her his job— but not the man he was. Giving him her trust would be more than she dared to risk.

Pulling up next to the fallen tree, she took her pistol from under the seat, cocked the hammer, and climbed out of the cab. By now it was almost dark. Across the creek, willows rippled in the night breeze. Crickets chirped in the undergrowth. The babble of the creek was peaceful, the shadows quiet. Still, Rose knew that this wasn't a safe place to spend the night. She would sleep with her pistol beside her and probably lie awake, listening for any sound or motion that might signal danger.

After locking the cab, she went around to the back of the camper and opened the door. The bed was above the cab. She would have to climb over her pile of tools and belongs to get onto it. But right now, that couldn't be helped. She could arrange the place better for living tomorrow.

Getting ready for bed involved stripping off her clothes in the dark and finding a nightgown in her duffel. There were no sheets, and she could only hope the mattress wasn't too dirty. Dragging a quilt behind her, she climbed onto the bed, rolled the comforter around her, and closed her eyes.

She was exhausted. It would have surprised her to know that she had fallen asleep almost at once.

From across the creek, Tanner watched her settle for the night. He had scouted the shadows and satisfied himself that there was no immediate danger. But nothing was going to happen to Rose on his watch.

Her account of killing the drug lord who'd raped her, then going on the run from the cartel, seemed almost too fantastical to be true. But one look into Rose's frightened eyes compelled him to believe her. His instincts told him that she was honest to the bone and unspeakably brave, with little more than grit and courage to protect her. Yet Tanner sensed that in her heart she was afraid.

As far as he knew, this small woman had killed two evil men. Those acts would be burned into her memory. She would carry them with her for the rest of her life. And that was just a glimpse she'd given him into the past that had made her a battered refugee from her own private war. What else was she hiding? What else lay behind the fear he'd seen in those breathtaking sunflower eyes?

As a lawman, he'd had no experience with drug cartels. But he'd heard and read about them. The ones that operated south of the border were ruthless enough to wipe out entire towns, mowing down men, women, and children and shoveling their bodies into mass graves. Even the thought of the things they'd done made him shudder.

If these kinds of monsters were trailing Rose, she was in grave peril. And yet she remained defiant, camping out here alone on the land she'd resolved to claim, stubborn, determined, and so vulnerable that Tanner ached for her. Every instinct in his body cried out to protect her—if not from the cartel, at least from the unseen dangers that lurked in the shadows on a quiet Texas night.

For the space of a long breath, he stood watching the pickup. Then he went back to his horse, untied his bedroll from the back of the saddle, and returned.

Finding a level spot, he laid out the bedroll, checked his pistol, and lay down on his side, facing the creek. He didn't plan to sleep much. All that mattered was making sure she was safe.

# CHAPTER NINE

*T*HE MORNING BIRDS ROUSED TANNER FROM A LIGHT DOZE. HE yawned, stretched, and sat up, eyes and ears probing the pewter dawn. Rose's pickup and camper sat undisturbed in the clearing across the creek. A flock of quail skittered under the wheels and melted into the trees. A good sign, Tanner observed, as he stood, stretched, and fingered the tender bullet wound on the side of his head. The birds would be exploding into the air if anybody was prowling around.

All the same, he kept watch, melting back into the trees as the sky began to lighten. Rose would accuse him of babysitting her if she knew he'd spent the night here. All the same, he would wait until he knew she was awake and safe before he went back to start his work at the ranch. He hadn't slept much, but a good strong cup of bunkhouse coffee should be enough to wake him for the day.

There was no sign of movement in the camper. He was wondering whether he should check more closely to make sure Rose was all right when an older blue pickup appeared in the distance, bouncing over the rutted trail from the direction of the Rimrock.

Tanner slipped back into deep shadows and drew his pistol, waiting as the truck rumbled closer, the driver making no effort to hide or sneak. As the truck pulled next to the camper, Tanner heard the honk of a horn. The driver's side opened, and a man walked around to the camper's back door. Tall and beanpole skinny, he was dressed in faded denims and a battered Stetson.

He appeared unarmed, and he wasn't behaving like an enemy, but Tanner wanted to make sure he was harmless.

The stranger rattled the door of the camper. "Rose! Are you in there, girl? Are you all right?"

A muffled reply came from inside the camper.

Tanner exhaled and holstered his weapon. Evidently Rose was safe and among friends. Time to hit the trail and start his own day.

"Jasper?" Rose climbed over her pile of tools and supplies and flung open the camper door. "How'd you know I'd be here?"

"And where else would you be?" Jasper grinned as he looked Rose up and down. "Lordy, but you're a sight. You look like you spent the night in a loaded cattle car. Why didn't you sleep at the ranch? You had a good bed in the duplex."

"You know why." Rose ran a hand through her tangled hair and tugged the ripped neck of her nightgown onto her shoulder. She'd spent a restless, mosquito-plagued night in the camper, only falling asleep a few hours before dawn. "Bull won't budge on giving my land back. It's war. I've claimed this ground, and I'm not giving it up."

"So what are you fixin' to do, build barricades? Shoot all comers? Blast it, Rose, you always were a stubborn little mite. Maybe it's time you stopped digging yourself deeper and listened to reason."

Rose rubbed at a mosquito bite on her arm. "So, what are you doing here, Jasper? Babysitting me?"

He shook his head. "Miss Rose Landro, I'm here to deliver you a formal invitation to breakfast at the Rimrock—now. So get your duds on and come with me. Bull's orders."

Rose rushed to unscramble her thoughts. Bull could have easily found out she'd gone to Ferg for help last night. He was probably mad enough to spit hot lead. But he didn't own her, and she didn't have to come when he beckoned.

"Now, I know what you're thinking, girl," Jasper said. "But Bull wants to palaver. It appears to me you've got nothing to lose by hearing him out. Besides, I know damn well you're hungry. Now let's get a move on."

With a grumble of acquiescence, Rose climbed back inside the camper and pulled on her work clothes. Jasper was right. At this point she had nothing to lose. After all, Bull could only get so mad.

Minutes later, she'd dressed, swept back her hair, and splashed her face in the creek. That would have to do. At least it would be good enough for facing Bull.

Jasper opened the door of his pickup for Rose to climb in. "Don't worry," she said. "I'm not packing a gun."

"I didn't expect you to. You may be a stubborn little hothead, but you're not crazy—although I'm beginning to have my doubts." Jasper started the truck. The engine roared as the heavy tires bounced over the ruts and hollows. "Lord, girl, you can't stay out here alone. It isn't safe."

"I've survived worse than this, Jasper." *Much worse,* Rose thought. And if the cartel ever tracked her down . . .

Her thoughts shifted as the heart of the Rimrock Ranch came into view—the house and barn, the corrals and outbuildings that provided a home for people she cared about, in spite of her differences with Bull. Could she count on them to protect her if *Don Refugio's* thugs showed up? She thought about Bull and his sons, about Bernice and Jasper and the hands who'd treated her with respect and kindness. No, she couldn't risk these precious people. If the enemy came after her, she would face them alone—on the land that was her heritage.

Jasper pulled the truck up to the house. Only the dogs rose from the porch and came down the steps to greet them. Rose patted their shaggy heads. The boys would be off to school by now, and Bernice was probably busy in the kitchen. As for Bull . . .

But that remained to be seen.

Jasper accompanied her up the steps and across the porch but paused at the door. "Aren't you coming in with me?" Rose asked, uneasy at the prospect of losing her ally.

He shook his head. "Not this time. It's to be just you and the big boss. You're on your own."

"At least wish me luck."

"You're going to need more than luck." He nudged her shoulder, giving her a push through the open doorway. "You go for it, girl."

Chin up, Rose walked through the shadowed great room toward the light in the dining room. The table was set like a feast for royalty with platters of ham and sausage, fresh biscuits, fried potatoes, and Bernice's airy scrambled eggs with cheese. Some subtle rustlings from beyond the closed kitchen door told her Bernice was there, but Rose guessed that the woman had orders not to disturb her boss.

Bull sat like a king at the head of the table, his face a study in stone. "Sit down, Rose." His deep, gravelly voice revealed nothing. "Have some breakfast."

Rose's appetite had fled, but she filled her plate with a respectable amount of food, then glanced up at Bull. "Is this supposed to be my last meal?" she asked.

Her joke didn't draw so much as a flicker of a smile. "Just eat," he said.

"You didn't answer my question," Rose said.

"We're not here to answer your questions." His scowl deepened. "Eat. Your food's getting cold."

She took a bite of biscuit, which melted in her mouth. "Well," she persisted. "I still want to know—"

"Damn it, Rose!" Bull's fist crashed onto the table, jingling glasses and cutlery. "I swear you could irritate the spines off a prickly pear! Just shut up, eat your breakfast, and listen to me, all right?"

"Go ahead." Rose nibbled a forkful of scrambled egg. "I'm listening."

Bull refilled his coffee mug from the carafe on the table, took a sip, and set the mug down with a thud. "For starters, I know you went to see Ferg last night and that his sleazy lawyer was there. And I'm pretty sure I know what you talked about."

"Nothing was decided," Rose said. "We just talked. I wanted to know what my options were. If you're so upset, why are you feeding me?"

"Rose—"

"Never mind, go on."

"You said nothing was decided. But if you're as sharp as I think you are, I'm betting you learned a thing or two? Am I right?"

Rose nodded, seizing on the question, wherever it might lead. "I did. I learned that I should trust a skunk before a rattlesnake, and a rattlesnake before a Prescott. Is that the right answer?"

Bull's left eyebrow slid upward. "Not bad. And can you tell me why?"

"Because if I were to accept Ferg's terms, take him up on his offer to lend me money for a lawsuit against you, he could steal my land right out from under me."

"A lawsuit? Good God, Rose, would you really have taken me to court?" Bull seemed more amused than angry.

"I still plan to. Whatever you did to alter that deed and get it recorded in your name, it couldn't have been legal. When I subpoena the original deed, I should be able to prove it!"

"You can't do that on your own. And a lawyer won't be cheap. Where will you get the money?"

"I told Ferg I'd think about it. It wasn't a no. I just have to figure out a way to protect myself before I agree to anything."

Bull took a long, slow sip of his coffee. His arresting blue eyes were surprisingly calm. "Rose, why do you think I asked you to this nice breakfast this morning?"

Rose stared at him. "I don't really know, do I? Suppose you tell me."

"I have a business proposition for you."

"What do you want from me?" Red flags of suspicion sprang up in Rose's mind. This man had already stolen her land. How could she trust him now?

"Right now, I want you to fill your plate again and eat your breakfast while I talk. And no interrupting. Understand?"

"All right." Rose was still cautious, but what did she have to lose by listening? Taking her time, she added more eggs and potatoes to her plate, along with a couple of sausages and another buttered biscuit with homemade jam. If Bull could wait, so could she. Besides, she really was hungry. And if things didn't go well here, who could say when she'd have another chance to feast on Bernice's cooking?

Bull finished his coffee and leaned back in his chair. "Here's what I'm thinking, Rose," he said. "There are two reasons I've hung on to that parcel—two things I insist on keeping. First, I must have access to the creek water for Rimrock cattle. Second, I need an ironclad guarantee that no Prescott can ever get his filthy hands on that property. If I allow you to deal with Ferg Prescott, I could end up losing both. Whatever it takes, I can't allow that to happen."

His words ignited a spark of interest in Rose. But she willed herself to keep silent and focus on her breakfast. When it came to dealing with Bull, the less she appeared to care, the better.

But what if he was about to offer her a compromise—one that could solve everything? The thought quickened her pulse. But she swiftly dismissed the idea as too good to be true.

"I admit to knowing that your grandpa meant to leave you the land," Bull said. "But if I hadn't stepped in and taken it over when I did, the Prescotts would have found a way to steal it, and you'd have no hope of ever getting it back."

*So do I have any hope now?* Rose's pulse was racing. She willed her expression to freeze to a mask of indifference.

"I always meant for you to have that land, Rose," he said.

*Sure you did, liar. Come on, what's the catch?*

"Here's what I'm proposing," he said. "I would be willing to deed you back your grandfather's land, but with conditions attached."

He paused, his riveting blue eyes pinning Rose to her chair. "First, I want your written, signed promise that the Rimrock will never be denied access to the creek water, for any reason."

Rose suppressed the urge to nod. So far, so good. She could live with letting Bull fill the water basin from the creek, as long as she didn't have his livestock trampling her yard.

"The second condition is that if you ever decide to sell the property, you will sell it to me and only to me or my boys. Your heirs, if any, will be bound by the same conditions. If you pass away without heirs, the property will revert to the Rimrock."

"Anything else?" Rose could hear her heart pounding over the sound of her voice. This agreement could give her all she wanted. It was almost too good to be true. But she'd be a fool not to think it over carefully.

"That's the gist of it," he said. "But each of those conditions is a deal-breaker. It's all or nothing."

"And if we can't come to an agreement?" Rose asked.

"Then we'll be no worse off than we are now."

Rose laid her fork on her empty plate and pushed her chair back from the table. "I'll need time to think about this, of course."

"Take all the time you need," Bull said. "But you're not leaving this room until you give me an answer."

The set of his jaw told Rose that Bull meant what he said. She decided not to test him by trying to walk out.

"All right." She took her seat again, realizing there was no need to stall for time. The answer had already come to her. "I might be able to live with your conditions," she said, "but I have one of my own."

He looked surprised, as if she'd caught him off guard, not an easy thing to do when it came to crossing swords with Bull Tyler.

"I want a written, signed promise from you that I can develop and use my land any way I choose—build anything and raise anything. And you won't interfere unless I ask for your help."

"Fine, as long as it doesn't compromise my access to the water."

"And what about the neighbors? What if they want a say in what I do?"

"That goes without saying. Anybody who bothers you will have me to deal with."

Rose stared at him over the remains of her breakfast, amazed at how easily they'd come to an agreement. Was it because she'd threatened to get help from the Prescotts? Or had Bull simply decided to do the right thing?

Only Bull knew the answer to that question, and Rose knew better than to ask him. Why look a gift horse in the mouth?

"So, do we have a deal?" he asked.

"It appears . . . we do," Rose said. "Now what?"

"Now we get in the truck and head for town to visit my lawyer and get the papers drawn up and signed. Then, after we file the new deed at the courthouse, what do you say to my buying you a Corona at the Blue Coyote? As I recall, you're of age and then some."

"I'd say thanks for the offer, but what I really want is to come home and get to work on my land."

"Suit yourself." Bull stood, reaching for his hat and the keys to his pickup. "I already told my lawyer to expect us. Come on. Let's go to town before one of us gets cold feet."

Rose followed him out the front door. Bull had planned this, she realized. He'd even spoken with his lawyer about it. And here she was, walking like an innocent lamb into a situation she barely understood. Was she doing the right thing? The smart thing?

But what choice did she have? She wanted her land and she needed protection. Maybe this was the best she could do.

As for trusting Bull—the man had lied to her, stolen her land, and left her stranded in Mexico. But he had also saved her life and absolved her of guilt in the shooting of Ham Prescott. So what now? Would he turn out to be her friend or just one more enemy plotting against her?

Only time would tell.

After the legal papers were signed and the new deed recorded, Bull drove Rose back to the land that was now hers and stopped next to her truck.

"So, what's next for you?" he asked her.

She forced a grin, still half afraid to believe she wasn't dreaming. "I'm going to unload the camper. Put up a fence. Start planning the cabin and laying out the garden. The sooner I can get seeds in the ground, the sooner I'll have vegetables to eat. And I'm hoping, once I get a coop built, that you'll sell me a few of those chickens."

"They're yours. Call it a housewarming gift. But blast it, Rose, you can't live out here alone. At least not until you have a solid house. It isn't safe. Come on back to the ranch and stay in the duplex while you work on your property. Jasper will be glad for the company. And the boys like having you around, too. They've both told me so."

He was making sense, Rose knew. But impractical as it might seem, she wanted to be on her land—to wake up to birdsong and the whispering babble of the creek, to work the ground and fall asleep with the rich, dark earth still embedded under her fingernails. She wanted to touch everything with love and make it truly hers.

But if she tried to explain that to Bull, he would only argue with her, or worse, laugh. "I'll think about it," was all she said.

"Well then, all I can do is wish you luck," Bull said. "But know that if you need help—and you're bound to—you can come to me anytime. It's to my advantage, as well as yours, for us to be good neighbors."

The old suspicions were already rising to the surface. It wasn't like Bull to be so generous. He always had an agenda, and this time would be no different.

Rose was about to climb out of the truck when she realized she wasn't ready. She needed to ask some questions and get some honest answers.

Could she trust Bull to tell her the truth? She turned back in the seat to face him. "Why are you doing this after you told me no?" she demanded. "What changed your mind? And what's the bottom line—what's in it for you?"

"You ask tough questions, lady."

"I need tough answers, not pretty words."

For the space of a long breath he was silent, emotions flickering like passing clouds across a face aged beyond its years. He hadn't become a powerful rancher by being nice or playing by the rules, Rose reminded herself.

"Why did I change my mind? After thinking it all over, I realized that whether I liked it or not, you wouldn't rest until the land was yours again. I could settle things peacefully, with the hope of our remaining friends, or I could let you declare war, call in the Prescotts and their legal dogs, and create a situation that could end in a literal bloodbath. At the very least, I could lose access to the creek. Does that make sense?"

"Are you saying I actually won? Come on, nobody beats Bull Tyler at his own game—not unless he lets them."

Bull's frown deepened. "Call it whatever you want. But this was never a contest, Rose. I never meant to deprive you of your land.

I only wanted to keep it safe, not only for you but for the Rimrock. We can't survive long, dry summers without that water. And there's nothing Ferg would like better than to cut us off without a drop.

"As for what's in it for me, I'm getting a buffer against the Prescotts, with an ally who's determined to live on the land and protect it. I'm getting a guarantee of access to the creek and legal assurance that the property will never pass into Prescott hands. Is that good enough for you, Rose?"

Rose took a moment to weigh his words. She knew better than to trust Bull. He'd lied to her before, and would do so again if it served his purpose. But she'd seen what the Prescotts had done to her grandfather, and she knew that she could never hold out against them on her own. Taking on Bull as partner and protector would be the only way to keep herself, and her property, safe. For now, at least, she would have to accept that.

"Friends?" Bull extended his hand.

"Friends." Rose accepted the handshake. Maybe this new arrangement would work out. Maybe time would test the friendship and prove it real and solid. But she had already learned that she could never take Bull for granted.

After opening the door of the pickup, she slid to the ground. "Now, if you'll excuse me, I've got work to do."

"Don't go taking chances out here alone, Rose," Bull said. "If you need help, ask. And the duplex is yours for as long as you need a place to stay."

"I'll keep that in mind." Turning away, Rose fished her keys out of her hip pocket and strode around her truck to unlock the camper. It was time to unload her tools and start making a home for herself.

Bull waited until Rose had vanished behind the camper before he gunned the engine and swung his truck toward home. The legal arrangements had taken much of the day. Now the late-afternoon sun was low in the sky. Clouds were drifting in above the escarpment, carrying the faint hope of spring rain.

He had done the right thing, he told himself. But only time

would tell whether he'd done the smart thing. Rose was a small bundle of grit, determination, and courage. But she was also rash and impulsive, and she attracted trouble like a magnet attracts nails. He'd have to be crazy to just turn her loose on the land. She was going to need help getting safely settled—and plenty of supervision to keep her in line.

Rolling down the side window, Bull filled his lungs with the sage-scented air. Rose was bound to hate his interference. But that was too bad. Whether she liked it or not, he was still the one in charge. He was the boss, and even on her small parcel of land, that wasn't about to change.

Tanner had stolen a few hours of sleep around midday, but even that was more time than he could spare. Now, as the sun sank low above the escarpment, he was driving one of the older pickups around the perimeter of the ranch, looking for any sign of the mysterious rustlers that were still spiriting away Ferg Prescott's prime beef.

After Ferg's attempt to frame his neighbor for the cattle theft, Tanner had almost thrown up his hands and left the ranch. But this time Ferg's frustration over the lost animals seemed genuine. The numbers showed on the books, and the cowhands, all men with clean records, confirmed that some of the cattle—all prime, mature beef stock—were indeed missing.

So Tanner had put in a call to Clive, and they'd agreed that he should stay on. Still, Tanner couldn't help questioning his own motives. How much did the need to protect Rose weigh on his decision?

He'd done his best to put her out of his mind as he drove the fence line. Earlier, he'd inspected every inch of the pasture where most of the stolen animals had been kept. Leading through the main gate, which was securely fastened with a combination padlock, were the faint tracks of a vehicle with heavy tires. Tanner had sketched the tread pattern in his notebook, but the tracks weren't fresh, and the vehicle could just as easily have been delivering winter hay. There was no sign that the heavy padlock on the steel gate had been tampered with, no mended spots anywhere in the fence. The cattle had been taken either at a different time and place or by someone with the means to unlock the gate—which left Tanner exactly nowhere. He could only conclude that he was dealing with very clever thieves, most likely with inside knowledge of the ranch and the movement of the cattle.

He'd almost dismissed the idea that Rose could be in league with the rustlers. But what if he was wrong? Now that she knew he was a TSCRA ranger, she could easily warn her cohorts to avoid him, or even set traps to mislead him.

He wanted to believe she was innocent. But he'd be derelict in his duty as a ranger if he didn't keep her under close surveillance.

Or was he just making excuses because he wanted to see her again?

Swearing under his breath, he paused to check one of the tanks that was fed by the lower part of the creek, downstream from the Rimrock property on the Prescott side. He could understand why Ferg Prescott wanted that land and why Bull Tyler was so determined to keep it. The thirty-acre parcel was the key to the water from the west, where it flowed from an artesian spring under the caprock. And now Rose was insisting that the land was hers. The whole situation smelled like trouble.

With the sun sinking low, and clouds thickening above the escarpment, Tanner headed upstream to the place where he'd last seen Rose that morning.

He was nearing the creek when a puzzling sound reached his ears—a series of metallic clanks, like heavy tools being flung about. Danger senses prickling, he dismounted and tethered the horse in the shelter of a willow thicket. Drawing his pistol, he stole forward on foot until he could see the clearing on the creek's far side.

Rose stood alone in the doorway of the camper. She was dragging tools, ropes, a big canvas tarp, and other gear into the open and laying everything on the ground.

"Rose! What the devil are you up to?" Holstering his pistol, he strode across the creek.

A startled look flashed across her face. Then she recognized him and smiled. "Hey, Tanner, you're just in time to help!"

"Help with what?" He reached her side and stomped the wetness off his boots.

"Help me unpack my gear. I'm trying to clear out enough space in the camper to make it livable—and organize everything out here so I can start work in the morning."

"Start work on what? Are you out of your mind?"

"No!" The grin that lit her face was pure radiance. "I'm going to build a cabin, and a garden, and a chicken coop. This is my land! Bull signed it back to me today!"

According to what he'd already heard, Rose's news didn't make sense. But Tanner knew better than to imply that it wasn't true.

"Don't just stand there with your mouth open!" she said, half-laughing. "Help me get these things out of the camper and covered with the tarp before it starts to rain!"

Tanner glanced at the sky. In the west, the setting sun glowed like a faded ember through the black clouds that were spilling across the sky. Sheet lightning flickered above the horizon.

Ducking into the camper, he picked up a heavy block and tackle and carried it outside. "Where did you get all this stuff?" he asked.

"I brought it from Mexico. Figured I was going to need it here." Rose's laughter echoed the joy that lit her face. It was the first time Tanner had seen her truly happy. She was more than beautiful, he thought. She was magnificent.

She was a woman he could almost love—if he were capable and worthy of loving.

"Are you going to sleep *here*, in this ratty old camper?"

"That's the idea. This is my land, and I mean to live on it."

"But you don't even have a bathroom here, Rose. Don't you have anywhere else to go?"

"I have an open invitation to stay in a duplex on the Rimrock. But this camper is my home now—until I can build something better."

Tanner dragged what looked like a tow chain out onto the

ground, leaving the camper emptied of gear. "For what it's worth, I think you're out of your mind, Rose Landro."

"And for what it's worth, I don't give a hang what you think. Here, grab that tarp and help me anchor down the corners. A few of those rocks should do the job."

By the time they'd dragged the canvas tarpaulin over the tools, the rain had begun to fall. Tanner had just dropped the last heavy rock in place when lightning forked across the sky, splitting the heavens with a deafening boom. Rain poured down, soaking them both to the skin.

"Come on!" Rose grabbed his arm and dragged him behind her through the back door of the camper. Out of breath, they sank onto the narrow bench that ran along one side. The camper was dark inside and warm from the afternoon sun. Rain beat a heavy tattoo on the shell and streamed down the windows.

*The rain won't last long,* Tanner told himself. But as the seconds passed he felt a growing awareness of the tantalizing woman beside him. He was a man with a man's built-in responses. Something told him he was already headed for trouble.

# CHAPTER TEN

S ITTING A HAND'S BREADTH APART, THEY HUDDLED ON THE BENCH in the camper, with the rain drumming outside. Rose was shivering in her damp clothes. Tanner ached to touch her wet hair, to curl it around his fingers as he cupped the back of her head and brought her close enough to brush her lips with his. He yearned to taste her, to warm her as a woman needed to be warmed. But knowing Rose as he did, he knew better than to try.

"I'm still trying to figure out why Bull Tyler gave you this land," he said, looking for any topic to ease the tension.

"He didn't give it to me. It was already mine. It just took time for him to figure that out."

"So what do you plan to do with it—not just now, but in the years ahead?"

"Find ways to make the place pay—maybe some kind of small farming operation. My Mexican foster mother taught me how to make wonderful goat cheese. I could raise some goats, sell the cheese, or maybe some eggs as well. Whatever people would buy."

"What does Bull have to say about that?"

"Not a thing. I made sure that was in our contract. I could raise alligators if I wanted to, and he'd have no legal power to stop me."

Tanner chuckled. "Alligators. Now that would be something to see. But what about your life? It's bound to get lonely out here alone. Don't you want to get married and have a family someday?"

"I'm twenty-six years old. I think *someday* has come and gone—especially for a freak like me."

"You're not a freak."

"In Mexico, some people, especially men, called me a witch. They said I had the devil's mark on my face. And before that—" She broke off as if facing a closed door that she didn't want to open.

"You're beautiful, Rose." Tanner couldn't help saying it. "A man would have to be out of his mind not to want you."

"Oh, some of them wanted me. Just not in the right way." She fell silent, her delicate profile outlined against the rain-specked window. "I was raped, along with other women and girls, when the cartel took over the town. And long before that, there was my mother's boyfriend, and the caretaker in the group home where I was sent after she died . . ."

"Rose—" Tanner checked the impulse to pull her close and cradle her in his arms. Right now, he sensed, the last thing she'd want was to have a man's arms around her.

"I tell myself I've been luckier than most, because I've known some decent men who never touched me. There was my grandfather, and *Don* Ramón in Mexico, who treated me like his own daughter. And my friend, Jasper Platt—and even Bull."

*But never a man who loved you the way a woman should be loved?* Tanner knew better than to ask that question.

"There are other good men, Rose."

"None that I'd care to trust. I'm better off on my own." Pausing, she glanced in his direction and changed the subject. "What about you? Do you have a family back where you came from?"

"A brother. He lives on our family ranch in Wyoming, with his wife and kids."

"And you? Do you have a wife, or maybe a sweetheart waiting for you back in Wyoming?"

"No." Tanner felt the familiar tightening of the knot in his stomach. "But that's a story for another time," he added.

"We all have stories for another time." Rose fell silent. In the warm darkness, Tanner could hear the low sound of her breathing. He imagined how it would feel, reaching out to her, pulling her close and holding her trembling body against his. He imagined laying her on the bed and loving her, kissing those small, perfect breasts, stroking her with gentle fingers until she opened to him like a moist flower in the rain . . .

But what was he thinking? Tanner's arousal was threatening to push through his jeans, proving to Rose that he was one more man she couldn't trust.

He stood, his head brushing the ceiling of the camper. "I need to go," he said.

"Fine. The rain seems to be letting up."

"Will you be all right? Promise you'll lock the door after I leave. You can't tell what—or who—might happen along."

"Don't worry. I've got a gun, and I know how to use it."

"The idea of locking the door is that you won't have to use your gun."

"Stop mothering me, Tanner. That's not your job."

"Somebody needs to do it." *And somebody needed to snatch her up and kiss her smart little mouth. But that wasn't going to happen tonight.*

"Just go," she said. "If I see any rustlers prowling around, I'll be sure to let you know."

"You be careful. Promise?"

"I promise."

"Fine. I'll stop by later and check on you." He stepped out the door, closing it behind him.

He heard the *snick* of the door bolt as he strode away. At least the little hellion was taking his advice. But he couldn't help being worried about her. A lone woman like Rose, so independent, so damnably sure of herself, and yet so vulnerable, would be easy prey for any man who set eyes on her—transients, roving cowhands, and even that sissified son of Ferg Prescott who'd already tried to cross the line with her.

It wasn't his job to protect her, Tanner reminded himself as he climbed into his truck. But whether he liked it or not, Rose had become important to him. The thought of her coming to harm was more than he could stand.

But he wasn't Rose's only friend. Others would be concerned about her, too. He would keep an eye on her for the night. In the morning, it would be time for a visit to the Rimrock.

Turning on her flashlight, Rose opened the cheese and crackers she'd bought in town, fashioned bite-sized sandwiches, and washed them down with a swig of cranberry juice. Tanner had left her less than fifteen minutes ago, but she was already feeling his absence. She'd tried to convince herself that she could manage entirely on her own. But she'd felt protected while he was here. His strong, male presence had given her a feeling of safety. When he'd warned her to keep the door locked, she'd pretended to be annoyed. But it had felt good, knowing that he cared enough to worry. Did she like him? Maybe, Rose conceded. But she couldn't afford to trust his motives—or to trust the warm, tingling sensations that his nearness had awakened.

The rain was already letting up—a good thing, because she really needed to pee, and there were no facilities inside the camper. Tomorrow she would make it a top priority to find a secluded spot and dig a latrine, with plans to build an outhouse. For now she would just have to make do.

Gripping the flashlight, she opened the door and stepped out into the misting rain. Wet grass brushed the legs of her jeans as she headed for a nearby clump of alder saplings. Nobody would be able to see her through the rainy darkness, but Rose's innate sense of modesty would not allow her to squat in the open.

She had her jeans down and was nearly finished when the underbrush began to sway and crackle. Rose froze in terror as a huge shape loomed out of the night and came lumbering toward her, swinging its massive head.

Rose swallowed a scream, almost tumbling backward as the startled cow shied, wheeled, and trotted off in the opposite direction. Shaking, Rose picked up the flashlight she'd dropped, pulled up her jeans, and raced back to the camper. Safely inside, she dissolved in hysterical laughter. She'd been so scared—of a silly cow. If she was going to live out here, she would have to get used to such things. But she was going to need a good, stout fence to keep her planned garden safe.

Leaning out of the door, she brushed her teeth, then locked herself in, undressed, and climbed into bed. The day had been exhausting, but it had ended fine, she told herself. And tomorrow would be better.

Lulled by the light patter of rain, she pulled the quilt around her and began to drift. As she sank into sleep, the last image to fill her mind was the memory of Tanner's gentle gray eyes.

At dawn, Tanner returned to the Prescott bunkhouse, cleaned up, and drove the back road to the Rimrock. With luck, he would find Bull Tyler at breakfast or chores and willing to talk. He had never met Bull, but he wanted to. He was curious about the man who'd already become a legend for his toughness and near-ruthless determination.

At least Rose hadn't spoken too badly of him. And Bull had thought enough of her to return the title to her land. Tanner only hoped he could convince Bull how much she still needed his help.

The Rimrock was smaller and less impressive than the Prescott spread. But the heart of the ranch had a clean, efficient look about it, the outbuildings solid and in good repair, the rambling wood and stone house designed to blend with the sweeping landscape. To the west, the towering escarpment rose against the sky. It was the kind of place a man could love and fight for, Tanner thought, a place that reflected its formidable owner.

As he pulled up to the house, two men came out onto the porch. The taller, older one Tanner recognized from the morning before, when the man came to the camper to call on Rose. He could only be Jasper Platt, the Rimrock's longtime foreman. The other man, broad-chested and rock-solid, with dark hair showing gray and a challenging gaze, would be Bull Tyler.

They watched Tanner's every move as he climbed out of the truck and approached the porch steps. Tanner had left his pistol in the truck—a wise decision, he decided. When facing this pair, any suggestion of a threat would be a bad idea.

"Good morning, gentlemen." Tanner paused, waiting for an invitation to join them. "I'm hoping you can spare me a few minutes. My name is—"

"I know who you are." Bull's voice and manner matched his nickname. "You're Tanner McCade. You're a TSCRA ranger, working undercover on the Prescott ranch. And I'm guessing that the two of us won't need an introduction, either. So suppose you come on up and tell us your business. If Ferg is losing cattle for real this time, I'm all ears."

"Evidently, he is losing cattle, and I'd appreciate your passing on anything you see or hear." Tanner mounted the steps to the porch. "But that's not why I've come this morning. I need to talk with you about Rose."

"Is she all right?" Jasper Platt's voice was sharp with concern.

"She's fine, so far. But I'm worried about her, and you should be, too."

Jasper stepped directly into his path. "If you don't mind my asking, mister, what business do you have with our girl?"

"I'm her friend, that's all," Tanner said. "I helped her buy her truck, and I've stopped by the creek to check on her a couple of times. It strikes me that she's taken on more than she can handle alone. That's why I'm here."

"We're all concerned about Rose," Bull said, opening the front door. "We were about to have breakfast. You're welcome to join us."

"Thanks, I'll take you up on that." Tanner followed the two men inside, through an impressive great room with a tall stone fireplace and into a cozy kitchen with mismatched chairs around a well-used plank table. A plump, brunette woman gave Tanner a smile as she added an extra place setting and went back to cooking French toast. Jasper took a moment to introduce her as his sister, Bernice. "She's the real boss of this place," he said. "Get crosswise with her, and you don't eat."

Tanner took the seat he was offered and helped himself to some fresh coffee. "Thanks again," he said. "It's right neighborly of you to invite me in."

"Just good timing." Bull took his seat at the head of the table. "How much do you know about Rose?"

"Only what she's told me. And what I've observed for myself. She's pretty independent, isn't she?"

"Independent?" Jasper snorted as he forked sausage onto his plate. "Rose Landro is the most mule-headed female on God's green earth!"

"Maybe so," Tanner said. "But stubbornness and grit won't build her a cabin. And that rickety camper isn't fit for a doghouse."

"Rose is family to us," Bull said. "We've offered her a place to stay. But she wants to live on her land. We're hoping, when she sees how hard it is, that she'll come to her senses and ask us for help."

"And if she's too proud to ask?" Tanner filled his plate with sausage, French toast, and potatoes.

"Rose is a grown woman," Bull said. "I can't force her to accept our help."

"But you know, Tanner's right," Jasper said. "Rose could be in danger, out there alone in that old camper. What if she gets sick or hurt? What if some horny bastard takes a notion to go after her? If anything were to happen to that girl, I'd never forgive myself. And neither would you, Bull."

Bull swigged his coffee, saying nothing. But Tanner could imagine his mind working.

"She might not have any more common sense than a prairie chicken," Jasper continued, "but that doesn't mean we can just throw her out there and hope for the best. Like you say, Bull, Rose is family."

Bull put down his coffee mug. His narrowed gaze was fixed on Tanner. "What about you, McCade? Have you got designs on her?"

"If you mean that the way I think you do, the answer is no," Tanner said. "I've got a job to do. When I've caught the rustlers that are taking Ferg Prescott's cattle, my work will be done here and I'll be leaving. But I like Rose, and I'm concerned about her. I want to know that she'll be all right."

"Have you got a wife and family anywhere?" Jasper asked. "Just wondering, mind you."

"I'm a widower," Tanner said. "And I'm not looking to change that anytime soon."

In the brief silence that followed, Bernice ushered two young boys into the kitchen. It hadn't occurred to Tanner that Bull would have children, but the older child was a carbon copy of his father. The younger one was fair and slender, but with something of the Tyler look about him.

"We're off to the bus stop," Bernice said.

"Homework done?" Bull asked.

"Yes, sir," the older boy replied.

"Fine. You boys behave, now, and mind your teachers."

"We always behave." The younger boy spoke with a smile, as if harboring a secret joke.

"They're fine-looking boys," Tanner said as the pair left by the front door. "You must be very proud of them."

"I am," Bull said. "Everything you see on this ranch, and the work that goes into it, none of it's for me. It's all for them and their families to come. If you don't already know, you'll learn that only two things matter in this life—family and the land. At least that's what I believe."

Tanner knew better than to ask about Bull's wife. Bernice's presence and the hauntingly beautiful portrait he'd noticed in the great room were sure signs that somehow Bull had lost her.

"As long as I'm here, I might as well do my job," Tanner said. "When I spoke with Clive earlier, he mentioned that you were missing some cattle, too."

"We were," Jasper said. "But we found 'em on the last day of the roundup. Seems they'd just wandered off looking for something to eat."

"So all your cattle are accounted for?"

"That's right," Bull said.

"Did you notice any suspicious activity? Any strangers or unfamiliar vehicles."

"Nothing except for that fool stunt Ferg tried to pull. If he was trying to get me in trouble, he picked a stupid way of going about it. Come to think of it, it was Rose who told me about those so-called stolen animals. She said she was out riding with the boys, and Will found you lying shot next to your horse. The boy thought you were dead. He was pretty upset about that."

"Maybe it's just as well he didn't recognize me this morning," Tanner said. "I never did find out who fired the shot. Ferg's cowhands tried to convince me it was you—or one of your men."

"Not likely," Jasper said. "We were all on the roundup. And we don't go around taking potshots at strangers. There are laws against that sort of thing."

"Ferg's been known to hire some shady characters to do his dirty work," Bull said. "But even if he'd be crazy enough to order the shooting of a TSCRA agent, you'd have a tough time proving it. He's careful not to get his hands dirty. You did say that Ferg was missing cattle, right?"

"Only the best prime animals, gone without a trace," Tanner said. "Whoever's taking them knows exactly what he's doing."

"Sounds like an inside job," Jasper said.

"That makes sense, but I've checked out all the Prescott cowboys, and their records are clean. And there's no reason for Ferg to be stealing his own cattle. If you notice anything suspicious, like tracks cutting through your property, let me know. Or if you can't reach me, give Clive a call."

"Will do." Bull had finished his breakfast. He stood. "I've enjoyed this visit, but it's time to get back to work. Stop by anytime, McCade. You'll be welcome."

Tanner and Jasper had risen with him. "And don't you worry about Rose," Jasper said. "We'll see that she's safe and has what she needs."

Tanner sensed that Jasper Platt was a man of his word. But it wouldn't hurt to check on Rose, anyway, just to make certain she was all right.

Bull walked Tanner outside and stood watching from the porch as he climbed in his truck and drove away. As Tanner glanced in his rearview mirror, one thought struck him. Bull Tyler was everything that Ferg Prescott had ever wanted to be—and that he never would.

"So it's true." Ferg's fist clenched on the desk top. "Bull really gave her that property."

"Checked it out myself," Garn said. "That kid at the recorder's office thinks I'm his best buddy. Buy him a beer after work, and he'll tell me anything I want to know."

"But that's one of the most valuable pieces of ground on the Rimrock. What the hell was Bull thinking?"

"Maybe that giving the land back to Rose was the only way to keep us from getting our hands on it. There's a clause in the deed forbidding her to sell it to anyone but the Tylers. And if she dies without an heir, the parcel goes back to the Rimrock. All tied up in a neat little package with a bow." Garn grinned, as if he were enjoying his father's frustration. "So I guess that leaves us up the proverbial creek without a paddle."

"You're saying we should give up?" Ferg cast a contemptuous glance at the son he'd never wanted. "Prescotts don't give up. Haven't you learned that by now?"

"Are you about to tell me you have a plan?" Garn's eyebrow tilted, giving him that cynical expression Ferg had always hated.

"One plan, at least. You seem to like the little bitch well enough. You could marry her—maybe even knock her up."

"What?" Garn's jaw went slack. "No! I mean, she's a sexy little piece, and I'd sleep with her at the drop of a hat. But marry her? Hell, the woman's too old for me. And with that mark on her face . . ."

"There are remedies for things like that. Besides, you wouldn't have to stay married forever—only long enough to become her legal heir."

"I'm going to pretend I didn't hear that," Garn said. "But for your information, Dad, I'm planning a future in politics. When I get married, it'll be to a proper girl with the family name and money to advance my career. If you're so all-fired anxious to have the woman and the property in the family, you can damn well marry her yourself!"

With that, Garn stalked out of Ferg's office and slammed the door behind him. Ferg shook his head, a bitter smile teasing a corner of his mouth. He'd been only half-serious about Garn marrying Rose. At least he'd had the satisfaction of seeing his son truly rattled—a rare thing these days. But damn Bull Tyler to hell for the way he'd tied up that creek property. This time there seemed to be no way around it.

He was pouring himself a shot of bourbon when the door opened again, this time without a knock. The man who slipped into the room, closing the door behind him, was muscular and weasel-eyed, with a military tattoo on his shaved head.

"I told you not to come here, Deke," Ferg said.

"Then you should've brought me the cash at the Blue Coyote, like we agreed." Deke Triplehorn spoke with a slight lisp.

"If you wanted to be paid, you should've done the job right."

"I hit the bastard. I saw him fall off his horse and go down before I lit out."

"You winged him. He's fine, and madder than hell. In my book that's not worth a nickel. I thought you were a dead shot."

"Sun was in my eyes. But my time's worth something."

Swearing under his breath, Ferg opened a drawer, took $500 out of petty cash, and handed it to the man. The scheme to frame Bull for the cattle theft and the ranger's murder had seemed like a good idea at the time. But too many things had gone wrong. He needed a simpler, better idea.

"You want I should try again?" Triplehorn asked.

"Not now. It's too late for that. But there might be something else down the road. I'll be in touch."

"Fine." Triplehorn pocketed the cash. "You know where to reach me."

"I do. And don't show up here again. It isn't safe."

After Triplehorn had left, Ferg downed the shot of bourbon and poured himself another. He didn't enjoy working with half-crazy scumbags like Triplehorn, who'd blackmail his own mother if there was anything to gain by it. But he had enough dirt on the man to protect himself. And when certain matters needed arranging, it helped to know the kind of people who'd do anything for money.

Now what was he going to do about Bull, the woman, and that creek property?

From the shade of the porch, Garn watched Triplehorn drive off in his army surplus Jeep. The bastard had some nerve, coming to the house. But as far as Garn was concerned, he'd never been here.

Garn knew his father was a crook and that he hired scumbags like Deke Triplehorn to do his dirty work. But Garn's only concern was his future in politics, and that meant keeping his own reputation spotless. That meant making like the three little monkeys—see no evil, hear no evil, and speak no evil. Someday the father he hated would be dead and gone. When that day came, Garn planned to put the ranch up for sale and use the money to advance his career, complete with a beautiful, blue-blooded wife and connections to powerful people.

But meanwhile, he'd promised to spend the summer here. It was like serving a sentence in hell. He hated the noise and odors of the animals and the crude manners of the hands who took care of them. He hated the sweat, the dust, and the hot sun. But most of all, he hated the boredom.

Maybe that was why he'd devised small rebellions, little acts of mischief that would have driven his father apoplectic had he known about them. This morning he'd relished giving Ferg the news about the transfer of the creek property. He knew his father had been expecting Rose to fall into his hands—to lend her money for legal fees and demand repayment as soon as she won her case. Now he was out of luck.

It had done Garn's heart good to see his old man squirm. But boredom was already setting in again, and the thought of Rose roused fresh notions in his mind. As he'd told his father, she wasn't wife material, but she was one sexy little package. He wouldn't mind getting to know her better.

Garn whistled a tune as he walked down the steps. He would think on that and come up with a plan.

# CHAPTER ELEVEN

*T*HE NEXT MORNING, ROSE PULLED ON HER OLDEST WORK CLOTHES, breakfasted on the last of the cheese and crackers, and went outside to organize her day.

The storm had passed in the night, leaving behind the freshness of rain-scented earth. Rose took deep breaths, filling her lungs with the scented air. *Petrichor*, that was what her grandfather had called the wonderful smell she'd always loved. Maybe it was a good omen for a day that held so much promise.

The canvas tarpaulin had kept her gear dry. Rose studied the heap of tools, wondering what to start first. She'd planned to dig a latrine back in the trees, but last night's visit from the wandering cow had brought home the need for a secure fence. Enclosing the entire thirty acres would take more time and materials than she could spare right now. But at least she could fence off the area around her planned house and garden.

Crouching beside the creek, she splashed her hands and face and slicked back her hair. Unbidden, her eyes scanned the willows on the opposite bank and the trees beyond. She couldn't help hoping that Tanner might show up, but she saw no sign of him. Tanner had his own work to do, she reminded herself. And it wasn't as if she needed his protection. She had her pistol in the truck in case she needed it. But so far, her most dangerous intruder had been that silly cow.

Since she'd already made some progress on digging up the old fence, she took up the task again. The rusty barbed wire from her grandfather's fence line had long since been trampled into the ground. But much of it came free as she dug under it with her shovel. Unfortunately, she was going to need new fence posts. Either she would have to cut them from the small trees that were growing on the property or she would have to dig into her precious cash reserves and buy some in town.

She would need to buy other things as well—lumber, hardware, pipe fittings, windows and doors for her cabin . . . and she couldn't work without food.

How did one go about building a cabin, anyway? To start with, she would need to draw up some kind of plan and make some decisions about materials. She'd always loved the idea of logs. But where would she get logs around here? And how would she move them by herself? Logs were heavy. Maybe she should think about something easier to move. Bricks were at least small. Or rocks—at least rocks were free if she could find enough. Or maybe adobes. She'd learned how to make adobe bricks out of mud and straw in Mexico. But would adobe hold up in heavy rain?

Once she had her materials, she would have to start by laying a foundation. That would mean digging a trench and filling it with cement to anchor the supports for the walls. And after that . . .

Rose sighed. What had she been thinking?

She gazed at her rig in dismay. She had no idea how to build a cabin. She hadn't even figured out how to get the camper off the bed of the pickup so she could haul her supplies. Even living in the camper was harder than she'd imagined, with no plumbing, no electricity, and barely room inside to stand up and turn around.

But never mind, she'd work it out as she went along. Maybe Jasper could give her some advice.

As if the thought could conjure him up, she heard the familiar growl of Jasper's truck coming around the bend in the rough road. Leaning on her shovel, she gave him a wave of greeting.

He pulled up beside Rose and climbed out of his truck. One hand carried a covered metal baking pan. "Figured you might be hungry, so I brought you some breakfast," he said.

Out of pride, Rose was about to protest that she'd already eaten breakfast. But when he raised the cover, the aromas wafting from beneath almost made her knees melt. French toast with maple syrup, sausages, and fried potatoes.

"Eat up," he said, handing her a fork and pouring coffee from a thermos.

"You just saved my life." Stripping off her gloves, Rose sank onto a stump and began eating. She was ravenous.

Jasper chuckled. "A friend of yours stopped by to see us this morning."

"A friend?"

"Nice fellow named Tanner McCade. He seemed pretty worried about you, roughing it out here on your own."

"No need for that." Rose spoke between bites. "As you see, I'm doing just fine. Somebody should tell Tanner to mind his own business."

"Blast it, Rose, look at you! You're half starved, living like a homeless tramp in a box with no electricity, no bathroom, and nobody here if you get sick or hurt. Come to your senses, girl. How long do you think you can hold out here without help?"

"Things will get better. You'll see." Rose drained her coffee cup and held it out for more. "Actually, I could use some help with getting the camper off the pickup so I can haul supplies. Do I need a hoist or something?"

Jasper mouthed a curse. "What you need is a dose of common sense! Bull and I have talked it over. We care too much about you to let you live like this. Bull's gone to check out an ad for a nice used travel trailer that we found in the paper. If it looks good, he's going to buy it, have it towed here, and set up with water, propane, waste tanks, and a generator. Once you learn to do the maintenance, you'll be fine, and we won't lie awake nights worrying about you."

Rose sighed. She'd wanted to manage without Bull's interference. But for all her pride, she had to concede that Jasper was making sense.

"You know I wanted to do this on my own," she said. "I wanted to build my own cabin."

"With what, girl?" Jasper exploded. "Look around you. Are you going to chop down trees like the pioneers? Or spend a fortune on building supplies you don't know how to use? Rose, if you want to live on your land, this is the best solution."

She sighed again. "I know. But don't you see? It'll be Bull's trailer, not mine. I'll be living off his charity."

"If that bothers you, you can figure out a way to pay him back."

Rose handed him the empty pan, from which she'd scraped every last crumb. "All right, we'll see how it goes. But I'm still going to need a fence. If you're not busy, you're welcome to help me salvage the wire and figure out where the post holes go."

Jasper gave her a grin. "My pleasure," he said. "Let's get started."

The trailer arrived late that afternoon. Just eight feet wide by nineteen feet long, it was small. But compared to the camper, it was a palace.

It was solidly built, the outside finished in shiny aluminum. The inside was a wonder of efficient design. From the double bed and built-in closet in the rear to the tiny bathroom, the compact but functional kitchen, and the cozy sitting area in the front, it was as charming as it was practical. In spite of her misgivings, Rose fell in love with it on sight.

Bull and Jasper exchanged knowing smiles as she dashed back and forth, opening the cabinets and drawers, checking out the miniature fridge and stove, trying out the bed.

"Now, Rose, the trailer isn't livable yet," Bull cautioned her. "The tanks and connections won't be set up until sometime tomorrow. So you can plan to stay in the duplex tonight."

"But why?" Rose demanded. "I slept in the camper without lights and water. Surely I can sleep here. I'll be fine."

Jasper threw up his hands. "Don't look at me," he said to Bull. "It took me most of the day to talk her into this."

"All right, Rose," Bull said. "But you're to show up for supper tonight and for breakfast in the morning. I want to know you're all right."

He was bossing her again. Rose didn't like it, but since he'd just done her a great kindness, maybe he thought he was entitled. She *did* mean to pay him back somehow. She hated being beholden to anyone, especially Bull.

While the two men were there, they helped Rose remove the camper from the pickup bed and stow it at the edge of the clearing. "It's a piece of junk," Bull said. "I can call somebody to pick it up."

"Let's wait on that," Rose said. "It might come in handy as a storage shed, or I could even turn it into a chicken coop. Right now, I can't afford to throw anything away."

Bull grumbled but at least he didn't argue. Rose could tell that it was going to be an uphill battle to keep him from taking charge.

"Now, don't you worry about stuff like dishes and towels," Jasper said. "Bernice has a box of things she was planning to donate to the church rummage sale. You can pick them up when you come to supper tonight."

"And make sure you show up," Bull said. "If you don't, I'll come over here and get you."

Rose sighed as the two men drove away. Bull was already trying to take over her life. She would have to do something about that. But for now she could only be grateful for his help.

With darkness setting in, she rushed to move her few personal things to the trailer. In one of the bedroom's built-in drawers, she found a set of sheets, washed and folded. She hummed a little tune as she put them on the bed. It would be pure heaven to sleep between clean sheets tonight.

Supper on the Rimrock was a simple meal of beef stew and fresh sourdough bread. The boys took up much of the conversation, talking about a school track meet. Beau had won in his age group and brought home a blue ribbon. Will had finished third in the older group but was gracious enough to let his little brother take the spotlight.

Rose had excused herself after the meal, thanking Bernice for the box of supplies. "You're welcome to bring your laundry here, Rose," Bernice had told her as she was leaving. "We can always visit while your things are in the wash."

"Thanks for the offer. I'll see how it goes." Rose had noticed a

Laundromat in town. Using it would mean one less obligation to the Rimrock. But she could think about that later.

Driving home over the rough road, Rose dodged the jackrabbits that seemed to make a sport of leaping through her headlights. She looked forward to spending the first night in her cozy new home, even without lights and water.

She parked next to the trailer and climbed out of the truck with the box Bernice had given her. The night air was mild, the peace and quiet broken only by the babble of the creek and the musical chirp of crickets in the undergrowth.

Rose had unlocked the trailer and set the box on the kitchen counter when a thought struck her. She hadn't bathed since her last night in the duplex, and she'd just spent a long day digging up fence wire in the hot sun. Her skin was salty with the dried residue of her sweat. The clean sheets on the bed would be wasted if she didn't wash.

There was no water in the trailer except in the small bottle she'd saved for drinking. But it was dark outside. A splash in the creek would refresh her and rinse off the sweat, and shouldn't take more than a minute or two.

In the bathroom, she peeled off her dirty clothes. There were a couple of bath towels in Bernice's box. After wrapping one around her and tucking it at the top, she tiptoed outside, raced barefoot to the creek, and waded in up to her knees. The water was cold, but Rose, who'd taken plenty of cold baths in Mexico, was braced for the chill. Draping the towel on an overhanging tree limb, she dipped her hands in the water and began splashing herself.

The cool wetness felt delicious on her skin. Rose crouched, lowered her head, and let the water flow through her dusty hair. Clean, refreshed, and safe, she would sleep well tonight.

She'd nearly finished bathing when, from the far side of the creek, she heard the rustle of bushes and the unmistakable mutter of angry voices.

With a gasp of horror, she snatched the towel off the limb, flung it around her body, and dashed for the trailer.

* * *

Tanner had been patrolling the perimeter of the Prescott ranch, with plans to stop by and check on Rose, when he'd recognized Garn Prescott's sleek black Porsche parked in the trees, twenty yards this side of the creek. The sight of the empty car had set off alarms in his head. If Ferg's half-baked son had come to press his attentions on Rose, it wouldn't be the first time. But damn it, it would be the last.

After dousing the lights and parking the ranch pickup at an angle to block the Porsche, Tanner had climbed out of the truck, closed the door with a quiet click, and walked forward in the direction of the creek.

Through the willows, he'd seen the outline of Garn Prescott. Garn's back was toward him, his attention riveted on something in the creek.

Tanner's mouth had gone dry as he realized what it was. Rose stood in the water. Her body, just visible in the first light of the rising moon was gloriously naked, her wet hair streaming down her back. Garn's hands were in front of him. No question what he was doing.

"Turn around and zip your pants, boy." Tanner's voice was a low, menacing growl.

Garn flinched and turned around, fumbling with his fly. "You've got no business here, McCade. One word to my father and your job is toast."

Out of the corner of his eye, Tanner saw a pale flash as Rose grabbed a towel and raced out of sight. At least she was safe for now.

"And what would your father say if I told him what I found you doing here?" Tanner demanded.

"He'd laugh in your face. The woman's fair game. He already gave me the go-ahead. Said I could even marry her if I wanted. Not that I would. She's as common as dirt. Not much better than a whore. You think she didn't know I was watching her? Hell, she was showing off."

Tanner loomed over him, battling the urge to grab Garn by the scruff of the neck and slam his head against the hood of his fancy Porsche. Much as it would have given him pleasure, he was here to do a job, not beat up the boss's son. "Is this what you do in your spare time? Sneak around and spy on women?" he growled. "Hell, you deserve to be tarred and feathered."

"I didn't plan this," Garn said. "I just stopped by to see how she was doing, and this is what I found. You can't blame me for enjoying the sight. You'd do the same, I'll bet. And I'll bet you want her, too."

Tanner took a deep breath, mentally counting to ten. "I'm going to move the truck," he said. "After I do, I want you to drive out of here. If I catch you bothering Rose again, so help me, I'll—"

Tanner didn't bother to finish the sentence. Garn's grin said it all. As long as he was on his own property and not breaking the law, Ferg's son could—and would—do whatever he damn well pleased.

Still fuming, Tanner backed the truck out long enough for Garn to roar away in his fancy-ass car. Then he parked again, climbed out of the truck, and headed across the creek.

Only then did he see the trailer. Nice, he thought. Bull hadn't wasted any time getting Rose into a decent place to live. But right now his first concern was making sure she was all right.

He rapped lightly on the door and waited. There was no answer. After a moment he tried again. "Rose," he called softly. "It's me. It's Tanner."

He heard a footstep and the sound of a bolt sliding back. Slowly Rose opened the door. She was dressed in an old-fashioned flannel nightgown. Her hair hung around her shoulders in damp strings. Tears glimmered on her cheeks.

Something broke inside him. She was so hurt, so vulnerable.

"Oh, Rose . . ." he murmured, and gathered her into his arms.

He half expected her to resist him, but she stood quietly, trembling, as he stepped inside, pulled the door shut, and locked it with one hand. Standing in the darkness he simply held her, letting her tears soak into his shirt as he waited for her to speak.

"Was it Garn?"

"Who else? I don't think he'll be back anytime soon. But you'll need to be careful."

She nodded. "I'm all right now," she said.

"I don't think you are, Rose. Let me stay awhile."

When she didn't answer, he led her into the front part of the trailer, which had built-in upholstered seating along the sides, and sat down, holding her on his lap. She nestled close, like a child seeking comfort.

"I really will be all right," she said. "So you can go if you need to."

"I don't need to." His mouth nuzzled her damp hair. He could feel the curves of her body and her sharp little bones through the thin nightgown. The hunger that warmed and stirred inside him was both familiar and forbidden. But right now the last thing he wanted was to leave her.

"I'm a big girl," she said. "I don't need protecting."

"Maybe you do. If anything had happened to you tonight, I would never have forgiven myself."

"What makes you think you're responsible for my safety?" She looked up at him, her eyes wide in the moonlit darkness. Tanner didn't reply. The question had triggered memories that would haunt him forever.

"Something's bothering you, I can tell," she said. "What is it, Tanner? I want to understand."

He took a sharp breath and let it out in a long, slow exhalation. He never talked about what had happened two years ago in Wyoming. But maybe it was time.

"I was a deputy sheriff back in Wyoming," he said. "It was a good life, helping my brother run the family ranch and working as a part-time lawman to help out in the lean times."

Rose nestled closer, like a child about to hear a bedtime story. *Maybe I should stop*, Tanner thought. But now he'd started, so it was too late for that.

"My brother and I both had families. He and his wife, Ruth, had four youngsters, and now they're now expecting a fifth. My wife . . . Annie." Even the name was painful to speak. "We'd been married just three years. We had a young son and another baby on the way . . ."

Tanner bit back a surge of emotion and continued. "My work as a deputy was pretty routine—a few burglaries, some stolen cattle, some domestics. But all that changed when a wanted serial killer named Cletus Murchison, who'd murdered a woman in the next county over, was tracked to a mountain cabin above our town. To make a long story short, there was a standoff, with half a dozen local lawmen pinned down on the slope below the cabin. I volunteered to circle around the back way and try to take him from the rear."

"And did it work?" Rose asked.

"It did, mostly because I was too dumb and inexperienced to know any better. I shot the bastard through the window, from behind. He was dead before he even knew he'd been hit.

"The news media called me a hero, and I guess it went to my head some. The county folks decided to hold a ceremony and give me a medal. My wife was proud and wanted to be part of it, but on the night of the celebration, our boy got the flu, and Annie wasn't feeling so great herself. There was nothing to do but leave them home and go by myself."

The memories were raging now, ripping into him and through him like claws. Tanner wanted to stop, but this was a story he knew he had to finish.

"I drove home to find our house in flames. I tried, almost died trying, before the firemen dragged me out—but it was too late to save my wife and son."

"Oh, Tanner," Rose whispered.

"Murchison had a brother. He set the fire. I was still in the hospital when the feds caught him the next day. He died last year in a prison stabbing . . ."

Tanner was quivering with emotion. Rose wrapped her arms around him. He was broken, as she was, but more painfully than she could even imagine.

"It was my own fault. If I hadn't been so damned full of myself, I'd have turned down the award, canceled the ceremony, and been there to protect my family."

"You couldn't have known," Rose said.

"I should've at least been worried about leaving them alone, with no one watching the place. But it didn't enter my damn fool head." Tanner took a long, painful breath. His hand stroked Rose's hair. "I went back to the ranch and tried to move on. But everything I saw and heard reminded me of what I'd lost. When I read about this job opening, I knew I had to apply. I was hoping it would help me make a new start, but all I've done is bring my old baggage with me."

Rose's arms tightened around him. Was this why he seemed so protective of her, because he'd once failed to protect the people he loved?

Tilting her face upward, she brushed his lips with hers. She'd never made such a move with a man before, but he was so wounded, so much in need of comfort that she forgot to be afraid.

The low sound in his throat could have been a growl or a sob as he responded to her kiss, his lips caressing hers so gently that she wanted to weep with the sweetness of it. Wanting more, she arched upward against him, inviting his hands to graze her body through the fabric of her nightgown. She had been forced, raped, and violated by men, but she had never been loved—and only now did Tanner's tenderness give her the courage to want what every woman deserved.

"Take me, Tanner," she whispered. "Make love to me."

Without a word, he rose, lifting her in his arms. His long strides carried her back to the bedroom, where he lowered her to the bed, kicked off his boots, lay down beside her, and took her in his arms. His hands found their way under her nightgown, gliding up her body, cupping her breasts, triggering whorls of sheer pleasure.

"I want you, Rose." His lips brushed her ear. "But I don't want to hurt you or frighten you. Anytime you want me to stop—"

Her kiss blocked the rest of his words. Her hands tugged at his belt buckle. He helped her, then paused to roll away, drop his jeans and briefs, and fumble with something in his wallet. It took a moment before Rose realized he was protecting her.

Lying back, she opened her arms. A memory flashed through her mind—the pain, the sweat, the awful grunting and thrusting, and the shame that never went away; but it vanished as he held her close. Her hand felt his arousal, like velvet-cloaked steel, and suddenly she was no longer afraid. Her legs parted. She waited for him.

"Lie still, Rose." He surprised her by moving down in the bed until his head was between her legs. She gasped at the sudden, intimate contact. Exquisite sensations poured through her body. Her womb pulsed and contracted. She cried out. Never in her life had she known that anything could feel like this.

With a low chuckle, he slid forward and entered her in one smooth glide. She was ready, more than ready. Her legs wrapped around his hips as he pushed deeper, heightening the waves of ecstasy that his mouth had ignited. It was . . . heaven.

Afterward, he held her gently, kissing her face, her eyes, her throat. "You know I mustn't stay," he whispered.

"I know. But hold me just a little longer. You make me feel safe, Tanner, for the first time in my life."

He left her, after checking to make sure the door was locked and that her pistol was loaded and handy. "I'll see you soon," he said. "Be careful."

"I'll be fine," she said. "Thanks to you, Jasper and Bull have become like old mother hens. They'll take good care of me, and probably drive me crazy."

"Good for them." After a final kiss he crossed the creek and walked back to the pickup he'd left at the edge of the trees. There was no sign that Garn Prescott had come back, but Tanner's instincts were prickling. Since he was far from sleepy, it wouldn't hurt to spend more time checking the pastures and the entrances and exits to the ranch. Maybe tonight he'd find a clue to the mystery of Ferg's missing cattle.

# CHAPTER TWELVE

*T*ANNER HEADED THE TRUCK BACK THE WAY HE HAD COME. IT WAS still too early for cattle-rustling activity. He would go back to the bunkhouse and put in a call to his brother, then lay out a plan for the rest of the night.

Rose would be safe in her sturdy trailer, he told himself. Still, he planned to circle back that way later just to make sure. He knew that past guilt was working on his mind. He'd lost his loved ones because he'd taken their safety for granted. He was probably being overcautious, but Rose had become precious to him. Their lovemaking had been sweet and healing—though he could never be completely healed from the loss of his family.

Was he falling in love with her?

Falling, at least. But love was a word Tanner didn't use lightly. He and Annie had been childhood sweethearts. They'd known each other all their lives. That was love. Feisty, sensual little Rose had come into his life only days ago. She fascinated him. She'd filled his dreams with erotic fantasies—fantasies that had become real in her bed tonight.

But *love?*

Maybe he'd be smart to nip the relationship in the bud. He didn't want to hurt Rose. She deserved far better than that. She deserved a man who'd treat her like a queen, a man who'd stay by her side and never leave her. Even if he wanted to be that man,

Tanner knew he didn't have it in him. His heart would never be whole again.

Getting Rose's expectations up, then letting her down, would be cruel—and Lord knows, she'd known enough cruelty from men in her life. The last thing he wanted was to become one more.

A coyote streaked into his headlights. Tanner touched the brake to let the animal bound off into the darkness. He had no quarrel with coyotes, especially tonight when he was still feeling the afterglow from making love to Rose. But the ranch lights in the distance ahead reminded him that he had serious work to do.

A couple of days ago, he had zeroed in on a small herd of mature steers. They were prime quality, market ready, perfect targets for theft. Acting on a hunch, he'd kept a close eye on their pasture. So far he'd seen nothing, but he planned to watch again tonight. It might be a waste of time, but maybe the rustlers would show up and he'd be lucky enough to catch them in the act.

It was coming up on nine-thirty. He'd have time to call his brother from the bunkhouse, grab a sandwich and some coffee, and catch a couple hours of shut-eye before getting back to work.

Driving past the house, he noticed that Garn's black Porsche was missing from the lineup of parked vehicles. Maybe Ferg's son had gone to town for some Blanco Springs–style excitement. That was fine, as long as he wasn't hanging around Rose's place. But Tanner planned to check later on, just to make sure.

In the bunkhouse, most of the cowhands were either sleeping or watching TV in the common room. The hall, where the pay phones were set up, was quiet. Tanner deposited the handful of change he'd saved up and called his brother. With luck, Clint would be indoors at this hour and able to talk with him.

"Is that you, Tanner?" Clint had a way of shouting into the phone when he knew it was long distance. "Lord, it's been tough, here. Ruth's in danger of delivering early, so the doc's ordered bed rest. I hired a woman from town to help her out with the house and kids, but that costs money."

"I'll send more, Clint. I get paid tomorrow. There'll be another five hundred in the mail."

"It's not just the money, Tanner. It's you. I need you to come and help me run this ranch. The high school kid I hired wasn't worth spit. I let him go yesterday. And the calving season's on."

"We need the income from this job," Tanner said. "But maybe when I wrap up this case I can take unpaid leave for a couple of weeks to help you with the calving. I'll see what I can do."

It was a mercy to run out of phone change. Tanner ended the call writhing with guilt. He had deep roots in the family ranch, and he knew his brother needed help. But he would have drowned in despair if he hadn't left to take this job. He would send his brother every cent he could spare. Maybe someday he would be strong enough to return to Wyoming and take up his life without Annie and Ethan. But he wasn't ready to go back. Not yet.

He made himself a sandwich in the kitchen and washed it down with stale coffee. Then he went down the hall to his small private room, set the radio alarm, stretched out on the bunk, and closed his eyes. He'd had it with the Prescott family drama and with not finding any answers to the cattle theft. One way or another, he needed to wrap up this frustrating case and move on.

But as he drifted off to sleep, it was the memory of Rose's beautifully flawed face that haunted him.

Ferg splashed his cheeks and jaw with Old Spice before going out the door. He might not have bothered, but Bonnie had mentioned that the scent turned her on, and he wanted her turned on tonight.

As he drove his new Cadillac to town he whistled along with the radio. It hadn't been a great day—hell, it hadn't been a great week with the missing cattle and all. But hot sex with Bonnie was like a tonic. She made him feel like a young stud again. He would almost marry the woman—if only he could expect her to be faithful.

He'd thought about marrying again—in the hope of getting a more promising son than Garn, if nothing else. But he hadn't done so well the first time. And wives were trouble. They wanted constant attention. They wanted money. And if they weren't happy, they'd leave you and take a chunk of everything you owned. Marriage, for what you got out of it, wasn't worth the risk.

So why bother, when there were women like Bonnie?

The hour was late—it was almost midnight. But Bonnie always saved late nights for him in case he wanted to stay for an encore, or just to have a few drinks. He knew he wasn't her only lover, but he was the only one who mattered. Most of the time he left cash on her dresser, and he wasn't stingy. But when he didn't, he knew it was all right with her. Their relationship was about more than money. She was his girl, and he was her special man.

Ferg's buoyant mood evaporated as he pulled up to Bonnie's house, parked discreetly down the street as he usually did, and climbed out of his car. There, parked at the curb right in front, for all to see, was an all-too-familiar black Porsche.

There was only one car like that in the whole county. What the devil was Garn doing here?

Stupid question. As if he didn't know.

As Ferg stood fuming by the curb, Bonnie's front door opened. Garn stepped out, then strutted down the sidewalk as if knowing he had an audience.

Livid, Ferg stepped into his path, blocking his way. "You've got some explaining to do, boy," he said.

Garn laughed. "I don't owe you an explanation, or anything else, Daddy-O," he said. "Bonnie's in there now, making herself fresh and pretty for you. Nothing else that happened in the past hour is any of your business."

It was all Ferg could do to keep from ramming his son's front teeth down his throat. "Are you trying to make me a laughingstock? Find your own damn woman!"

"Why bother? Bonnie's available, and she knows the score. By now, you should know it, too. No complications, just good, clean fun." Garn smirked. "Fun for all! When you do her tonight, remember that I was in that sweet spot before you. As they say in some circles, I buttered your bun."

Ferg slapped his son. His big hand struck with a force that he felt all the way up his arm. Garn reeled and staggered, but the smug smile Ferg hated never left his face.

"You watch your mouth with your father, you namby-pamby little punk. Show some respect."

"I lost my respect for you years ago." Hatred glimmered in Garn's eyes as he faced his father. "That's the last time you'll ever lay a hand on me, old man," he said. Then, still smiling, he walked around Ferg and out to his car.

Ferg hesitated, wondering whether he should ring the doorbell or turn around and leave. He knew better than to ask Bonnie for an explanation. She didn't owe him one. He knew what she was and what she did. But why now? And why did it have to be with his son?

Garn was still sitting in his car, waiting to see what his father would do—turn and walk away or ring the doorbell and go in. With Garn watching, either way would be a humiliation. But what the hell. Sex was sex, and Bonnie was damned good at it. As long as he was here, he might as well get some. Swallowing his pride, he pushed the doorbell button and waited for Bonnie to come and let him in.

Garn pulled away from the curb. One hand massaged his swelling jaw. His father's slap had done some damage, but the blow to the old man's ego had been worth the pain. It had been damned sweet, seeing the almighty Ferguson Prescott squirm. It would serve him right if he couldn't get it up with Bonnie tonight.

Garn had enjoyed Bonnie, and he'd paid her generously—not only for the good time in bed but for her services as a liaison between Garn and the mob-owned steakhouse chain that was buying the ranch's prime beef at a substantial savings over what they'd pay on the open market.

It was a nice little operation, and relatively safe. When Ferg was due to spend time with Bonnie, she'd send out an "all clear" signal by phone. If the timing was right, Garn would call in the location of the cattle and show up to open the gate for the truck. After that, all he needed to do was hold out his hand for the cash, which would go into a secret account, earmarked for the brilliant future he planned—or as a safety net in case he found himself out on the doorstep.

Ferg's visit tonight had been unplanned until he'd called Bonnie at the last minute. But as it turned out, the timing was good. The truckers would be there at one-thirty, cash in hand.

As for the run-in with his father at Bonnie's house, that had been an accident. But Garn had no regrets. Even with his sore jaw, the memory of Ferg's outraged expression would keep him laughing for weeks to come.

Tanner had stationed himself on the ground behind the crest of a grassy hill, overlooking the small pasture that confined eighteen head of prime Hereford beef. He'd been there for more than an hour without seeing any activity. His legs were getting cramped, and the night air was chilly through his thin jacket. The temptation to give up and go back to the warmth of his bunk was becoming more real by the minute. But he'd resolved to watch until the crack of dawn. He would see this through.

By now the moon had crossed the sky and was settling in the west. Its light cast cedars, animals, and fence lines into long shadows. An owl called out in the darkness. A coyote trotted into sight, spotted Tanner, and turned tail.

He'd fallen into a light doze when the faint, distant crunch of tires on gravel startled him to full alertness. On the far side of the small pasture, a dark shape was moving without lights along the rough road. It was too small to be a truck, but even by moonlight its outline was unmistakable.

It was a black Porsche.

Tanner had brought along a pair of night vision binoculars. Now, as the car stopped short of the pasture gate, he focused them on the windows to make a positive ID of the driver. No surprise there. Even in silhouette there was no mistaking Garn Prescott's high nose and receding chin.

Tanner whispered a string of curses. Why hadn't he suspected Garn all along? Ferg's son had an insider's knowledge of the ranch and its cattle. He would know how to open the pasture gates. And it was no secret that the young man resented his father. Stealing Ferg's prize steers would be like a game to him. But now it was time for the game to end.

A larger vehicle—a truck pulling a stock trailer—rumbled around the bend in the road, its headlights off. Garn climbed out of the Porsche with a flashlight and shone it on the lock while he worked the combination. The gate swung open, allowing the truck to drive into the pasture. The two men who climbed out of the truck selected three steers and herded them up a ramp, into the back of the trailer. The time it took allowed Tanner to memorize the license number and general description of the rig.

One man locked the trailer and climbed into the driver's seat of the truck. The other man handed Garn a fat manila envelope. Garn used the flashlight to peer inside and check the contents, then nodded his acceptance.

With the truck and trailer back on the gravel road, Garn swung the gate shut, closed the padlock, and used a handkerchief to wipe it clean of prints. Then he tossed the envelope into the Porsche, climbed in, and drove off without lights in the direction of the ranch house.

And that was that.

Once Garn was safely out of sight, Tanner stood, stretched his legs, put away the binoculars, and hiked back to where he'd left the pickup.

From the bunkhouse he would call the dispatcher at TSCRA headquarters and have them put out an APB on the truck and trailer. With any luck at all, the cattle buyers would be picked up within the hour.

The real question was what to do about Garn, whose only crime, any good lawyer would argue, was aiding in the theft of his own family's livestock. Would Ferg be angry enough to press charges? That question would have to wait until tomorrow.

In the bunkhouse, Tanner made the call to headquarters. His

job was done for now, but he had one duty left. He wouldn't go to sleep until he'd made sure Rose was all right.

He went back outside, then climbed in the pickup and drove back along the west border of the ranch to the creek. Switching off the headlights, he parked in the trees and walked to where he could see the trailer, dark and peaceful in the moonlight.

He didn't want to disturb her sleep. But as the memory of their loving swept over him, a hard reality struck. Now that he'd solved the mystery of the stolen cattle, his time here, with her, would be over.

Tomorrow he would come by the trailer to say good-bye. After that, he could be transferred anywhere in the region. Or maybe he should at least ask for time off to go back to Wyoming and help his brother on the ranch. Either choice would mean a parting from Rose. And given the nature of time and fate, he could be seeing her for the last time. From now on, it would be up to Bull and Jasper to look after her and make sure she was safe.

He stood for a moment, remembering her sweet passion and the feel of her body in his arms. Then he forced himself to turn around and walk back to the truck.

Rose thrashed and moaned, caught in the grip of a nightmare. The agents of the cartel had captured her and dragged her back to Refugio. He had staked her to the ground for his men to torture with red-hot brands. The first one would put out one of her eyes. She writhed and screamed as the glowing iron, fashioned in the shape of an elaborately curled "C," moved closer . . . closer . . .

She woke with a convulsive jerk. Her eyes shot open, seeing only darkness. Slowly she began to breathe again. She was alone in the trailer, safe and secure within its walls. The sheets that wrapped her still held the masculine scent of Tanner's body. She turned over and pressed her face into the pillow, breathing in the aroma of his hair. Even now, she knew better that to expect him back again. But for once in her life he had made her feel safe, almost loved, in a man's arms. He had given her the gift of hope—

the hope that someday she might know that wonderful feeling again.

But nothing, it seemed, could banish the dreams or the fear that they would come true. She had a home now. She had friends to help and protect her. But Refugio would never stop looking for the woman who'd killed his brother. And when he found her, his revenge would be a death of unspeakable pain and horror.

Reflexively, she reached down to where she'd stashed her Smith and Wesson .44, under the edge of the mattress. Drawing it out, she laid it next to her pillow, with her fingers touching the grip. The 12-gauge double-barreled shotgun that had been her grandfather's was wrapped in a blanket and stashed behind the seat in her pickup—not a safe place. If anybody broke into the truck, that gun would be the first thing they'd find and steal. She would need to find a safer place for it.

Tanner had been worried about Garn Prescott. But Garn was little more than a silly boy. She knew who the real enemy was, and she knew that one day Refugio or his men would come for her. When that day arrived, she would have to be ready to fight for her life.

Closing her eyes, she tried to go back to sleep. But she was wide awake now—free, at least, from another nightmare. Through the window she watched the moon vanish behind the escarpment. Then she lay back to wait for dawn, listening to cricket songs and to the soft babble of the creek. This was her life now. Until the terror closed in on her, she would savor every precious moment of it.

"Sorry." Ferg rolled to one side of Bonnie's bed and lay staring up at the ceiling. "I'm afraid this isn't my best night," he said.

"Well, there's always the next time," Bonnie soothed. "Most nights you're a real stallion. Don't worry, you'll get it back."

"I know," Ferg said. He'd never had this problem before. But tonight had been a fiasco. Every time he got close, the memory of Garn's insolent, laughing face would hit him like a dash of cold water. *Garn.* He'd never liked his son. Right now he just plain hated him.

He knew better than to talk about Garn with Bonnie. She never mentioned her other clientele, and even if she did, the subject of Garn would only sour their relationship. The best thing he could do now was get up, go home, and forget tonight had ever happened.

He sat up, swung his legs off the bed, and reached for his clothes. His wallet was in his jeans. Pulling it out, he laid a wad of bills on the pillow. "Here, you worked hard enough to earn it."

"Forget it." She pushed the money back at him. "Save it for next time. It'll be better, I know."

Ferg took the money, even though it was one more blow to his manly pride. *She's right,* he told himself. Next time would be better. But wherever Garn was right now, he fervently wished his son in hell.

Later that same morning, Tanner's call to Clive Barlow at headquarters confirmed that the truck and trailer, with the stolen cattle, had been stopped by a patrol. The driver and the man who'd paid the money were in jail, and the steers were in a holding corral, waiting to be hauled back to the Prescott Ranch.

"Have the two men said much?" Tanner asked.

"They're claiming it was a legitimate purchase, but they've both got known mob connections," Clive said. "I'm guessing they'll be out on bail before lunchtime."

"So they fessed up that Garn Prescott was selling them his father's prime beef at a bargain price?"

"It looks that way. How do you want to handle that?"

"You're asking me?"

"It's your case," Clive said. "We know Garn's guilty, but if Ferg chooses not to press charges, Garn's off the hook. And even if it went to court, my money would be on a good lawyer getting him off. Ferg would be better off slapping the kid's hands and cutting off his allowance."

"Garn's an adult."

"In this case it won't make much difference. The Prescotts are the most powerful family in the county. I'm guessing Ferg will want to keep this out of the press."

"I'll keep that in mind." Tanner hung up the phone and walked outside. He'd solved the mystery of Ferg's stolen cattle, but not to anyone's satisfaction. All he could do was wrap it up and move on.

After breakfast he found Ferg in his office. "I've discovered the truth behind your stolen cattle," he said. "You're not going to like it."

"I'm a big boy. I can take bad news." Ferg had been about to light a Havana, but he laid it down on the onyx ashtray. "Go ahead."

Still on his feet, Tanner told him what he'd seen last night and what Clive had reported this morning. Ferg didn't speak, but a dark red color crept up his neck and rose like a conflagration into his face. His fist smashed down on the bell that he used to summon the cook. Moments later the old man shuffled into the room.

"Get Garn down here!" Ferg thundered. "I don't care what he's doing. I want him in here *now!*"

Tanner waited as Ferg lit the cigar and puffed furiously. "How we handle this is up to you, Ferg," he said. "If you want to press charges, I can arrest Garn here and now, or you can choose to deal with the situation yourself. Clive said he'd go along with whatever you decide."

Ferg's face was so deeply flushed that Tanner feared he might have a stroke. He didn't speak until his son stumbled into the room wearing a maroon silk robe over blue silk pajamas. Garn's blond hair was mussed, his eyes still bleary from sleep. He made a move toward the empty chair that faced his father's desk.

"Stand up like a man, if that's even what you are!" Ferg growled. "Garn, I'd like to introduce you to Tanner McCade, a TSCRA special ranger assigned to track down the cattle thievery on this ranch. It seems he's tracked it down to you!"

The sidelong glance that Garn cast at Tanner simmered with pure hatred.

"Tell him, McCade," Ferg said. "Tell my so-called son what you saw last night."

Tanner summed up what he'd witnessed as briefly as possible. "The men in the truck were arrested. They named you as an accomplice."

Garn glanced around the room like a caged animal seeking escape. There was none.

"It wasn't stealing!" he blurted. "Those steers were as much mine as yours! I had every right to sell them!"

Ferg laid the cigar in the ashtray. "Then why do it in the middle of the night? Damn it, you're my only son, Garn. I've tried to raise you right. I've tolerated your laziness, your fancy-pants manners, and your total lack of interest in the ranch that our family has worked to build over generations. I've tried to tell myself that you'd come around and take responsibility for your inheritance. But now you've crossed the line. You've sullied the family honor by stealing from your own flesh and blood! What've you got to say for yourself?"

"What've I got to say?" Garn drew himself up. "All my life you've been trying to make me into another you! But I'm not you! And I don't give a damn about this ranch or the so-called family honor. Honor? Coming from a man like you, that's a joke!"

Ferg's anger had turned cold. He glanced at Tanner. "This man has the authority to arrest you and take you to jail. All I have to do is say the word. Is that what you want?"

Garn didn't answer. For the first time, he looked nervous.

"*Is it?*" Ferg thundered. Garn gave a slight shake of his head.

"All right," Ferg said. "Since I don't want this stain on our family to become public record, I don't plan to press charges. But I want you gone by the end of the day. I don't care where you go or what you do. I just don't want to look at your ugly face again."

Garn flinched but held his ground. "Fine. I won't miss this hell-hole of a ranch, and I won't miss you. If I ever set foot here again, it'll be because you're dead and gone!" He turned to go, a ludicrous figure in flowing silk nightwear. "Oh, one more thing. If you wonder how I made contact with those buyers, you can ask your girlfriend, Bonnie!"

With that he walked out the door and closed it behind him with an abrupt click. Ferg had gone pale. Evidently he hadn't known about his lady friend's involvement.

"Come here, McCade." His voice was hoarse with strain. Tanner walked to the desk. "Listen. I want you to swear that you'll forget everything you heard in this room."

"Done," Tanner said. "I'll tell Clive that you decided not to press charges. The rest never happened."

"And Bonnie—you never heard her name."

"Got it. I'll be going now." Tanner turned away and left the house. He'd already stashed his personal things from the bunkhouse in his own truck. It felt good to see the Prescott ranch growing smaller in his rearview mirror. The whole experience here had left him with a bad taste in his mouth.

Before he drove back to headquarters, just one thing remained to be done. It would be the most painful thing of all—saying good-bye to Rose.

Rose was stringing out the salvaged wire for her fence when Tanner pulled up in his truck. Even before he switched off the engine, she knew that he'd come to say good-bye. The pickup he was driving had a Wyoming license plate, which meant it was his own. And he hadn't come the usual way, from the Prescott side of the creek. He'd driven through the Rimrock to get here. She could only conclude that he'd solved his case and was on his way out of Blanco County—and out of her life.

She stood, pulling off her gloves and putting on a brave face as he climbed out of the truck and walked toward her. She'd known this moment would come. The only surprise was that it had come so soon.

"So your work here is finished," she said, before he could speak. "Thank you for coming to say good-bye."

Something like pain flashed across his face, but he managed to return her smile. "We've got a little time, Rose," he said. "Let's go for a walk."

As if it were a natural thing, he took her hand. She let him lead her down through the trees, along the creek. Her pounding heart felt as if it were about to break, but she was too proud to let that show. "I've known this time would come," she said. "Where are you off to next?"

"Back to headquarters for now," he said. "From there I could be sent off on another case—unless I get leave to go back to Wyoming and help my brother. I'll be requesting time off, but since I'm new at my job, I'm not expecting a yes."

"How long would you be in Wyoming?" she asked, not that it would make any difference. Gone was gone.

"A couple of weeks, maybe. My brother's in a bad way. His wife is expecting their fifth baby, and the doctor's ordered her to bed. And the calving season is on. The ranch isn't a big one, but Clint can't afford to hire much help, even with the money I send him."

"Would you be all right, going back?" She knew about the memories waiting for him there.

"It wouldn't be easy. But family is family."

"You could write me in care of the Rimrock," she said, and immediately wished she'd kept her mouth shut. "But you'll be busy either way. And why bother? I know this is good-bye."

They had stopped by a spot where the creek formed a dark pool, overhung with willows. It seemed the right place. She turned to face him.

"You did a good thing for me last night, Tanner McCade. And I hope I did a good thing for you. No regrets. So shall we leave it at that?"

"Rose—"

"No, not another word," she said. "Kiss me good-bye and leave me right here. At least we'll be ending this with a good memory."

Without another word he gathered her in his arms. His lips were gentle, sweetly caressing, shattering her heart like hammer blows. "You're the best, Rose," he whispered. "You're solid gold. Remember that."

Rose blinked back a tear. "Be safe, Tanner," she said.

"You too." He released her and walked away. Just once he turned and looked back. She gave him a smile before he disappeared from sight. A moment later she heard the sound of his truck driving off.

Rose stood for a moment, looking down at the water. Then she wiped her eyes, pulled on her worn-out leather gloves, and went back to digging fence wire. At least she'd known enough to expect this. People left—they died, they went away, or they let her down, and in the end she could count on no one but herself. No expectations, no disappointments, and no regrets.

Tanner hadn't hurt her. Showing her that sex could be tender, even thrilling, wasn't at all a bad thing. And she'd certainly given him a good time. So call it an even exchange and move on.

She thrust her shovel into the dirt, but the next length of barbed wire wouldn't come up. It was caught on something, probably a tree root. She pushed the blade deeper, then put her weight on the handle to pry it up. When she still couldn't free it, she scraped the dirt away with her gloved hands, hooked the wire with her fingers, and pulled hard. The wire came loose, pitching her backward onto her rump. Her finger was bleeding where a barb had gouged her through a hole in her glove.

Sitting in the dirt, she pulled off her bloodstained glove. At least Ramón had taken her to a government clinic a few years ago and had her properly immunized, including a tetanus shot. But here she didn't even have a bandage.

As her grandfather might have said, this was a metaphor for life. It kicked you onto your behind and made you bleed, and when it happened, all you could do was get up and keep going.

But sometimes it hurt. Sometimes it hurt a lot.

The drive from the Texas panhandle to Wyoming's Wind River Mountains was long and grueling. But Tanner had learned that if he started early, paced himself, and took occasional rest breaks, he could make it in a single day. He drove with the windows down and the radio blaring whatever country music station he could tune in. Sometimes, when he felt himself flagging, he even sang along, loud and off-key.

But mostly he thought about Rose. In his mind, he could still see her, standing by the creek, alone and proud, trying to prove to him that she didn't care. But he knew that she did care. He cared, too. And it wasn't just because he'd made love to her or even that it had been wonderful. It was her honesty that got to him. She was truth, courage, tenderness, and compassion wrapped up in one feisty little package—and she deserved so much better than the hand that life had dealt her.

In two weeks he'd be going back to his job in Texas. He didn't plan to see Rose—no future there except pain and regret. But he already wanted to. He wanted to see her, to touch her, and to sleep with her—so much it hurt.

At dusk he stopped for drive-up coffee, switched on his head-lights, and turned the radio up full volume to keep him awake. It was after eleven when he took the freeway exit and almost mid-night by the time he turned onto the dirt road by the sign that said McCADE RANCH, 4 MILES. A doe and her fawn crossed the road in his headlights. Tanner braked to let them pass. A few minutes later he pulled up to his brother's two-story log house.

The lights were off in the house, but Tanner had already planned to sleep in the small, empty bunkhouse that stood nearby. He shouldered his duffel and stepped out of the truck, his legs stiff from the long drive. The air that met his face and filled his lungs was cold and sweet, smelling of sagebrush, grass, and cattle. Wyoming air. It smelled like home.

The bunkhouse was unlocked, the bed made up and waiting for him. Exhausted, Tanner flung down his duffel, stripped off his clothes, and crawled between the sheets.

In the morning he would greet his brother's big, noisy family and join them around the breakfast table. He would be cheerful, uncomplaining, and willing to shoulder more than his share of the work. With the calving season on, there would be plenty to do—tending the cows and calves, making sure the new little ones were healthy, warm, and nursing as they should be, along with taking care of the other animals.

He would visit the two lonely graves on the hilltop and try, again, to make peace with what had happened, or at least try to make some sense of it.

And he would try not to think about Rose.

But as he sank into sleep, the face he saw in his dreams had a striking crimson blaze down its left border.

# CHAPTER THIRTEEN

*Two weeks later*

APRIL HAD RIPENED INTO EARLY MAY. SPRING RAINS HAD KISSED THE Rimrock with blazing color. The bluebonnets had faded, but patches of firewheel, Indian paintbrush, black foot daisies, and buttercups dotted the foothills and open flatlands. Bees hummed in the sunshine. Where horses and cattle stepped in the lush spring grass, butterflies rose in clouds.

Rose's vegetable garden had sprouted. She guarded the small green plants as if they were her children, watering them each day inside the low border she'd covered with netting to keep out hungry birds and animals.

Jasper had helped her finish the fence, using salvaged metal posts to support the barbed wire. They'd even found the old iron gate her grandfather had erected years ago and put it in place.

Jasper was busy with his duties on the ranch, but he enjoyed coming by to visit when he could spare the time. Today he was helping Rose build a chicken coop. When it was finished, Bernice had promised her three young laying hens and a rooster.

"I was remembering that other coop we built on the Rimrock, when you were just a sprout," Jasper said. "Let's hope this one is just as sturdy and lasts just as long."

"I plan to be here the whole time." Rose held a nail for him to pound. "This is my home, and I'm putting down deep roots."

"That's all well and good," Jasper said. "But you're still a young woman. You could find yourself a good man, have a family to raise and carry on after you."

"Some people were meant to be alone. Like you." Rose placed another nail.

"Now me, that's another story," Jasper said. "If my Sally hadn't died before our wedding, we'd have taken over her parents' farm in the hill country, and I'd have had a whole different life. But she was my one true love, and I've never found another."

"Well, since I'm not expecting my one true love to show up anytime soon, I'll just soldier on. I don't need a man to give me a good life. I can do that for myself."

"Now, I don't know about that," Jasper said. "That nice TSCRA ranger who came by to make sure you'd be looked after seemed to have taken quite a shine to you."

Rose felt the stab of memory like a deep pain, but she willed herself not to show it. "Tanner's gone," she said. "And anyway, he was still mourning his wife. He told me how she died in a fire with their little boy and unborn baby. Maybe he'll be like you. Maybe she was his one true love."

"Maybe. But I could tell he liked you a lot." Jasper unfolded his lanky frame and went to fetch the roll of fine-gauge wire he'd stashed in the back of his truck. "Here, hold this at the end while I staple it to the posts. I can't stay much longer today, but we should be able to finish this coop the next time I come by."

After Jasper had left, Rose stood back to survey her small kingdom. The coop, when finished, would be strong enough to keep out any predator. It would be wonderful, waking up to the crow of the rooster and gathering fresh eggs for breakfast.

She was glad she'd kept the old camper. It would be useful for storing tools and chicken feed. As for the trailer, now that the generator and tanks had been hooked up, it had become the perfect little home. She could even shower and cook in it. Bull had hired a man in town to come by and service the tanks, freeing her from the worry of maintenance.

To repay a small part of what Bull had done for her, she had given him her most valuable possession, the double-barreled shotgun that had belonged to her grandfather. She knew Bull had long admired the weapon that had killed Hamilton Prescott. For a time in Mexico, it had belonged to *Don* Ramón, given to him as a gift for taking Rose into his care. After Ramón's death, Rose had hidden it from the cartel and brought it back to Texas. Now the powerful gun belonged to Bull. He had accepted it as his due, without protest. It seemed right, somehow, that he should have it.

Even so, the thought of all that Bull had done, and continued to do for her, raised a troubling concern. Her dwindling cash reserves were bound to run out in the next few months. She couldn't be dependent on Bull. She needed her own income—either a job or something she could sell.

Eggs? That was a nonstarter. Three hens wouldn't lay enough eggs to sell. And people around here already had places to buy eggs. She'd thought about goat cheese, too. María had taught her how to make the wonderful cheese she'd sold on market days back in Río Seco, before the cartel took over. But this wasn't Río Seco. There were government health and packaging regulations, and the matter of a business license. And of course, she had no goats and no place to set up a cheese-making operation.

On her last trip to town she'd picked up a local newspaper, in the hope of finding a job. But there was nothing suitable for a woman. Nobody was going to hire her as a truck mechanic or a ranch hand.

But one ad in the For Sale section had caught her interest. A farmer in the area was selling off surplus lambs.

Rose knew a lot about sheep. The Ortega family had raised a small flock of sheep in Mexico. The days she'd spent in the saddle, herding sheep in the desert with Don Ramón's nephews, Raul and Joaquin, had given her some of the happiest memories of her life. She often thought about the two young men who had been like her older brothers. They'd gone off to work and she'd never heard from them again. Had they crossed the border and taken refuge in the United States? Had they gone over to the cartel? Were they even alive?

But back to the lambs. Rose had cared for her share of orphaned and abandoned lambs, teaching them to drink from a bottle, getting up every four hours to feed them at night, snuggling them under a blanket to keep them warm. How much would it cost her to buy several lambs and raise them to sell in the fall?

What would it take? Rose could almost feel her brain whirring into action. She would need a strong, sheltered pen to keep them safe, with plenty of straw for warm bedding. If the lambs weren't weaned, she would need bottles, nipples, and formula mix. And she would need to pay a veterinarian for services like vaccinations. Could she manage all that and still sell them at a profit at the end of the season? It was a scary prospect but one that excited her.

When the lambs were big enough to graze on their own, she could run them on the federally owned open rangeland that bordered one end of her property. Keeping them safe and getting them in at night would be a full-time job. Maybe that would be the time to get herself a good herding dog. If the plan worked out this year, she could raise even more sheep in the future.

She was surveying her yard, thinking about the best spot for a sheep pen, when another thought slammed her like a cold fist.

Bull.

He wasn't going to like this. Bull was a cattleman to the bone, and Rose remembered hearing him talk. Like most cattlemen, he had no love for sheep. "Range maggots," he called them, claiming that they tended to bite grass off all the way to the root, leaving the land barren where they'd grazed. Bull didn't just dislike sheep. He hated them.

Her agreement on the property transfer gave her the right to use her land any way she wanted. That included raising sheep. But if she chose to do this, she couldn't expect any more help from Bull, and probably none from Jasper, either. She would be on her own.

It was a heavy decision. But after thinking it over, Rose decided that, before she made up her mind, the least she could do was learn more about the sheep-raising option.

The next morning, she drove into Blanco Springs and used a

pay phone to call the number in the newspaper ad. The man who answered her call and gave her directions to the farm sounded elderly and was slightly deaf, but his friendly manner put her at ease.

The farm was on the far side of town, an immaculate place with a pretty white cottage, a big red barn, and spring hay fields waving in the breeze. The aging farmer, who introduced himself as Ezra Perkins, was waiting in the yard when Rose drove in.

"My wife's not doing so well, so we're moving to a senior facility next week," he said. "It's a nice-enough place, and Merle will have the care she needs, but I'll never stop missing my farm. Come on, young lady. I'll show you the lambs."

Limping slightly, he led her around to the far side of the barn. There, in a metal pen with a built-in shade roof, were four lambs. They appeared to be about six weeks old, an age when they'd still be taking milk but would soon be ready to wean. Their tails and their testicles, if any, were already docked.

"Every year I've enjoyed raising a few orphan lambs and selling them in the fall," the farmer said. "But I won't be around to finish with these, and the man who bought my farm doesn't want them. I'll give you a good price just to get them off my hands. I'll even throw in their pen. It comes apart, so it's easy to move. You could haul it in your truck."

Rose had been prepared to give the lambs a quick look and go her way. But Ezra Perkins's offer was pure temptation. Four healthy, adorable lambs and a stout pen to put them in. The farmer would probably throw in the milk bottles and a supply of milk replacer, too. She sighed. "Let's talk price," she said. "And maybe you can give me an idea of what they'd sell for at the end of the season."

The numbers made enough sense to convince her. Rose walked away with a deposit paid and a promise to come back tomorrow with the rest of the cash. After the final payment, she would take the pen, along with a box of milk bottles and supplies and some hay and straw, in her truck. Perkins, who had a comfortable trailer for hauling the lambs, would follow her home and help her set up the pen.

As she climbed into her truck and started the engine, she could feel herself shaking. She'd actually done it. She'd committed the money and taken the risk. Tomorrow, come what may, she would be a sheep owner.

What would Bull say? What would Jasper say? She couldn't imagine they'd be pleased. But she'd taken a step toward real independence, and she couldn't help feeling proud of herself.

Would Tanner be proud of her, too, if he knew what she'd done? But why wonder? He was out of her life, their lovemaking nothing more than a bittersweet memory.

By the time Tanner had finished pitching hay for the cows with newborn calves, it was almost suppertime. He washed his hands and face at the outside pump, glad that the long day of work was coming to an end. It had been the right thing to do, taking two weeks off work to help his brother; and it had been decent of Clive to let him go. But he couldn't help worrying about how the time off would affect his job. And he couldn't help worrying about Rose and how she was getting along.

Wiping his wet hands on his jeans, he stood for a moment, gazing out across the pastures of long, waving grass toward the snow-capped Wind River Mountains beyond. Was there a more beautiful place in the world than this ranch, with its broad meadows, aspen forests, and pine-carpeted slopes? Yet this land could be harsh and unforgiving, with its deep winter snows and frigid winds. It took a special breed to survive here, he thought. The McCades belonged to that breed—a close-knit family of strong, hardworking people. He had been part of their world until grief had driven him out of it. Now he felt almost like a stranger.

At supper, he sat at the long plank table with his family—Clint; Ruth, who'd given birth to a healthy boy; and the four towheaded youngsters—two older boys and two girls—arranged like steps along one side of the table. They bowed their heads while Clint said grace, then passed around bowls of beef stew with potatoes and carrots. It was a simple meal, but as always there was plenty of food for everybody.

"Are the new calves doing all right? Any trouble nursing?" Clint was four years older than Tanner, a half-inch taller, raw-boned, and unsmiling, his dark hair already streaked with gray.

"I checked them all," Tanner said. "They're doing fine, and the cows have plenty of hay and water. Anything else?"

"That paint mare's been favoring her left forefoot. I think she might have a loose shoe," Clint said.

"I'll take care of it first thing in the morning." With no farrier available, Tanner had become an expert at keeping their horses well shod. Over time, with no professional help available, the brothers had also become expert plumbers, electricians, and mechanics. Given the parts, or even having to improvise, they could fix almost anything.

"Have some more stew, Tanner." Ruth was the perfect ranch wife. Four days after giving birth she was already on her feet, taking care of her family. Despite the ravages of time, hard work, and bearing five children, she was still an attractive woman with cornflower blue eyes and short blond hair. She'd had a stressful confinement, but now that her baby boy had arrived safely, Ruth had regained her cheerful nature.

How would Rose fit in with this big, outgoing family? But why even ask such a question? His time with Rose had been a sweet, healing interlude. But he'd walked away and put her behind him. She had her own life to live. So did he.

After supper, he stood on the front porch, watching clouds drift past the moon. In two more days he'd be leaving this place. In a way he found himself looking forward to being back in Texas again. He enjoyed his new job and was anxious to prove his worth on some serious cases. But Texas was not his home. He felt like even more of an outsider there than he did here, on the ranch where he'd grown up.

Only in Rose's arms had he felt he was where he belonged.

Clint had come out to stand beside him. "You don't have to leave," he said. "You could call your boss in Texas and quit your job. That's all it would take."

Tanner shook his head. "I understand that you could use me here, but I'm not ready. When I leave Texas, I want it to be with a job well done behind me. Otherwise I'll feel like a quitter."

"Is that all?" Clint asked. "I know you had a hard time here, after losing Annie and Ethan. But you can't mourn them forever. You can't let the memories and the guilt keep you from coming home where you belong."

"I can tell myself that. But I'm just not ready. Yesterday I went to the hill where we buried them. It was peaceful there, with wild violets blooming on the graves. I stood there and waited, as if I were hoping for some sign of forgiveness, or at least a feeling that all was well with them. But nothing came. I only felt sadness, barely dulled by time. They're gone. Just gone. And I'm to blame. Some things will never change."

"I never questioned the rightness of choosing this life," Clint said. "You were always the restless one. Even when you were married, I could tell you were dreaming of something more exciting—maybe that's why you took that deputy job."

"We needed the money," Tanner said. But Clint was right. He'd taken the job because he wanted a change—and that change had cost him everything.

He didn't have all the answers. He only knew that, much as he loved Wyoming's wild beauty, he wasn't ready to come back here for good.

Two days later he finished packing his truck, said good-bye to his brother's family, and took the highway south. Clive was expecting him first thing in the morning. He would be there, ready to go wherever he was assigned.

Would he see Rose again? But he couldn't think about that now. To go back to her, love her, and then say good-bye again wouldn't be fair. It would only leave her hurt and bitter.

Turning the radio volume all the way up, he focused on the road ahead and the job that awaited him in Texas.

Rose had set up the lamb pen in a grassy clearing, on the far side of the new chicken coop. She'd covered the open area with netting to discourage the big hawks and golden eagles that were known to prey on young animals. So far, after a few days, the four lambs were thriving. She was still bottle-feeding them twice a day, but they were beginning to nibble the grass and hay in their pen.

Over the next few weeks she would wean them. Then they would be ready to venture out of their pen and explore their new home.

On the morning of the fourth day, Jasper showed up to help her finish the chicken coop. Rose was weeding her vegetable garden when his truck stopped outside the fence. He climbed out of the truck, came into the yard through the gate, and stopped as if he'd just walked into a brick wall.

"Lord save us, girl!" His face had gone slightly pale. "What do you think you're doing with *those*?"

Rose sighed. She'd hoped Jasper, at least, would understand. But she should have known better. "I'm raising them to sell in the fall—hopefully for enough profit to help me through the winter. I got a great deal on these animals, including the pen. If I can make good money, I plan to raise more sheep next year."

He stared at the lambs, shaking his head. "I wouldn't mind them myself. My Sally raised some lambs on her farm in the hill country. But Bull hates sheep. He'll have a stroke when he hears about this!"

"Bull doesn't have any say in this. The agreement we signed gives me the right to use my land any way I want. That includes raising sheep. When they're bigger, I can graze them on that open range to the north. He won't have any say in that, either."

"But why spit in his face, Rose? Bull's been good to you. You could buy a calf from him, raise it, and sell it for about as much as you'll be getting for these lambs."

"Maybe," Rose said. "But I know about sheep. The Ortegas raised them in Mexico. I've herded them, birthed them, fed them, nursed them when they were sick. I can handle sheep. And I *like* them!"

Jasper walked over to the pen and stuck a finger through the steel mesh. A lamb latched onto it, sucking with its little pink mouth. He chuckled as he pulled his finger away. "They're cute little critters, all right. But that won't make any difference to Bull."

"Do you have to tell him? He doesn't come around much."

"Bull is my boss and my friend," Jasper said. "I can't keep this from him. I'll be telling him today. He's going to be madder than hell. And it won't just be Bull. Every rancher in the county hates sheep on the rangeland. Once words gets around, you'll make enemies—enemies you don't need right now."

"You're saying I could be in danger? I can't believe that, Jasper. This is the twentieth century, not the Old West."

"All I'm saying is that the sooner you get rid of these lambs— any way you can—the better off you'll be. If you need to earn money, talk to Bull. He can find some work for you on the Rim- rock." He scowled down at the lambs for a long moment, then turned away. "Come on, let's get the coop finished so I can bring the chickens over for you."

They finished the work in tense silence. Fortunately there wasn't much left to do on the coop, just stapling the mesh to the frame- work, securing it in the ground, and attaching the door.

Was Jasper right? Rose wondered. Could she really be in dan- ger? Ezra Perkins had mentioned that he'd been raising lambs for years, but he'd done it on his farm, not between the boundaries of two ranches and open rangeland. Maybe the lambs hadn't been such a good idea after all. But never mind. Come hell or high water, she was determined to make her plan work.

They finished the coop, and Jasper put his tools in the truck.

"When are you going to tell Bull?" Rose asked.

"As soon as I see him," Jasper said. "I'm hoping you'll take my advice. I'd hate for things to go bad between you and Bull, or for you to come to any harm."

Rose watched him drive away. Jasper meant well, she told her- self. But as he'd made clear, his first loyalty was to Bull. If she clashed with the boss of the Rimrock, she could expect no help from the man she considered her most steadfast friend.

By the time she'd finished weeding the garden, it was time to give the lambs their late-day feeding. Rose was inside the trailer preparing four bottles of milk replacement formula when she heard the sound of Jasper's truck pulling up outside the gate. Leaving the bottles on the counter, she went outside to meet him.

This time Jasper hadn't come alone. The back of his truck held baskets and crates, containing the promised hens and rooster.

And that wasn't all. When the passenger door of the truck opened, two small figures tumbled out and raced across the yard.

"Jasper says you've got baby lambs!" Beau was breathless with excitement.

"We want to see them," said Will.

As Jasper came around the truck, his gaze met Rose's. "I may have gotten myself into a peck of trouble," he said.

"Did you tell Bull about the lambs?" Rose asked.

He shook his head. "Bull's gone to Lubbock on business. He won't be back till tonight. But these two rascals heard me telling Bernice about the lambs, and they wouldn't give me any peace until I brought them over here."

The boys had found the lambs. They were standing outside the pen, poking their fingers through the mesh, giggling as the lambs tried to suckle them.

*This development could be in my favor,* Rose thought. But she couldn't count on it. Bull was still going to be upset, maybe more so than ever, now that his sons had been allowed to see the lambs.

"Would you like to give the lambs their bottles?" she asked the boys.

"You bet!" they chorused.

Rose got the four bottles out of the trailer, gave one of them to each of the boys, and let them into the pen. The hungry lambs crowded around them, almost pushing them over. "Now, be careful," Rose said, showing them what to do. "You have to make sure the lamb's head is up, the way it would be if it was drinking milk from its mother. After you've fed the first two, I'll give you the other bottles."

The boys laughed with delight as the lambs drank from the bottles. Watching them, Jasper shook his head. "Now we've done it, Rose," he said. "I'll never hear the end of this."

Rose gave him a grin. "Come on, let's get these chickens in the coop. I'll sprinkle some grain on the ground so they'll feel at home."

Twenty minutes later, the visit ended with the lambs fed, the chickens in their coop, and everyone at least on friendly terms. But as Jasper drove away with the boys, Rose had to ask herself one question. Had she won a small victory, or simply escalated the war?

She wouldn't know the answer to that question until Bull showed up at her door.

The next morning, while she was feeding the chickens and checking for eggs, Bull drove up in his truck. She came out of the coop to see him swinging through the gate.

She closed the door behind her, then turned to face him. "I've been expecting you, Bull," she said.

"I can imagine." His expression was dark, his manner coldly restrained. "You could have asked me before you decided to raise *sheep*." Hatred punctuated the last word.

"I didn't know I needed your permission," Rose said. "According to our contract, I can raise anything on my land."

"Blast it, I'm not talking about permission," he said. "I'm talking about common sense. If you'd asked me, I'd have told you that sheep are a sure way to make enemies—right when you need to make friends."

"I don't need friends as much as I need money. I helped the Ortegas raise sheep in Mexico. I know how to take care of them. You've been good to me, Bull, and I'm grateful. But sooner or later I have to strike out on my own. I hope Jasper isn't in trouble for bringing the boys over."

His mouth tightened. "Jasper's fine. But all my sons can talk about are those damned sheep of yours."

"So what now?" Rose asked.

"I've already come up with a solution. There's a farmer in the next county who's willing to take your lambs and raise them with his on private, fenced land. I've already called him. As long as they're healthy, he'll even pick them up and repay what you paid for them. You can't get a better deal than that."

"And then what?"

"We can work out some other way for you to have an income—something we can both live with."

Bull was trying to be fair, Rose told herself. But he was doing it again—taking over her life. The lambs were hers. She had every right to keep and raise them. And, so help her, that was what she intended to do.

"Sorry, Bull, no deal," she said. "I'm keeping the lambs."

His expression hardened. "Fine. Do what you want. But those lambs won't always be little. The first one that wanders off your property is going to become target practice."

Rose stifled a gasp. "You're saying you'd shoot them?"

"I'm not talking about me."

Without another word, Bull turned away, strode to his truck, and climbed inside. Frozen in shock, Rose watched him drive off. The lines had been drawn, firm and clear. But what had Bull meant? Would someone really shoot her precious sheep?

Never mind, it was just an empty threat, Rose told herself. And right now she had work to do.

Finding a rake, she stepped into the lamb pen and began raking the droppings out of the scattered bedding straw. She glanced up, her eye catching a movement in the willows on the far side of the creek. For a moment she stood still, watching, then went back to work. It had been nothing, she told herself. Only a bird or animal, or maybe the wind. But it was hard to believe she wasn't being spied on.


Ferg Prescott sat on the front porch, sipping a bourbon and enjoying the spring sunshine. He'd felt a growing sense of contentment now that Garn was gone. No more listening to that annoying nasal whine. No more stolen cattle. No more stealing time with Bonnie. And no more frustration over a son who wouldn't lift a finger to meet his father's expectations.

Garn would get along fine, wherever he was. The boy had all the instincts of a bottom-feeder. For all Ferg knew, he could be president of the friggin' United States one day. But Garn's welfare was no longer his concern, and Ferg was damned glad of it.

Last night he'd enjoyed a rip-roaring time in Bonnie's bed. It had been an easy decision, not mentioning her part in the cattle theft. The woman was a survivor, doing her best to make a few extra dollars. Why punish her for that? And why spoil a relationship that worked so well for him?

The only thing that still troubled him, like a sharp stone in his boot, was the way Bull Tyler had bested him on sewing up that creek property. Putting it in the Landro woman's name, with ironclad conditions attached, had been a smart move. As long as Bull controlled Rose, he controlled the property. And there was no way Ferg could get his hands on it.

Ferg had been keeping a close eye on the place. One of his new hires, a homely eighteen-year-old named Reuben Potter, had a talent for sneaking around without being noticed. Ferg had assigned him to watch the creek property and report back on everything he saw and heard there.

Thanks to Reuben, Ferg knew about the trailer on the property. He knew about Rose's garden and the chicken coop. He even knew about the four lambs she'd brought home and set up in a pen. And now, here was Reuben, coming around the corner of the house with that expectant look on his face that told Ferg he'd learned something new.

Ferg got up, gave him a nod, and went into the house. It wouldn't do to have a hired hand sitting on the porch with him, like a buddy. As was customary, he would see Reuben in his office.

Ferg sat down at his desk and waited. Reuben usually gave him a few minutes before wandering in. By the time he showed up, Ferg was getting impatient.

"Well?" he demanded, as Reuben stepped into the office and closed the door behind him.

Reuben cleared his throat. "It looks like Rose and Bull Tyler had an argument over the lambs. Bull wanted her to get rid of 'em. He'd even found somebody to take 'em off her hands. But Rose said she wouldn't let 'em go. Bull was pretty mad. I even heard him say that if any of those sheep left her property, they'd be shot."

"You don't say . . ." Ferg leaned back in his leather chair. "Anything else?"

Reuben shook his head. "After that, Bull drove off, and Rose went to work cleaning the lamb pen. I figured that was a good time to go."

"Very interesting," Ferg said. "Thanks for the update. You can get back to your regular work, but keep your eyes and ears open."

"I will. Thanks, Mr. Prescott." Reuben's slithery way of walking carried him out of the office. Seconds later, Ferg heard the front door open and close.

"Interesting," he said aloud, thinking of what he could do with what he'd learned. Maybe he couldn't get his hands on the property. But what if there was a way to widen the breach between Bull and Rose? If the two were to become bitter enemies, that might leave an opening for him to step in and befriend her. Who knew where that might lead?

With his mind made up, Ferg reached for the phone and punched in the number for the Blue Coyote Bar in Blanco Springs. "I'd like to leave a message," he said when the bartender answered. "Whenever Deke Triplehorn shows up, tell him Mr. Prescott wants to talk to him."

# CHAPTER FOURTEEN

*T*ANNER WAS BACK IN TEXAS, WORKING FOR THE TSCRA. HIS FIRST assignment had taken him to a ranch outside Rock Springs, where he'd caught the pair of bungling teenage cattle rustlers within a couple of days, recovered the calves they'd stolen, and turned the boys over to the juvenile court system.

He'd hoped Clive would be impressed enough to assign him something more challenging, but he was in for a surprise when he walked into the TSCRA regional headquarters the next day.

"Come into my office." Clive Barlow was stocky and middle-aged, with horn-rimmed glasses and wispy gray hair. His exploits over his years as a special ranger had become the stuff of legend.

"Have a seat." Clive took the chair behind his desk. "I've got a proposition for you, McCade. Hear me out. Then you can say yes or no."

Tanner took a chair and waited while Clive cleared a space on his cluttered desk. "Over the past few months, there've been growing reports of cattle rustlers hiding stock in the canyons below the caprock. My supervisors have decided to open a post in Blanco Springs to deal with them. Since you're one of the few rangers who's familiar with the area, and the people, we'd like to put you in charge."

"You're sure?" Tanner was momentarily stunned. "But I'm just barely familiar with the area. I've only been on the job a few months, and most of that was training. Hell, I'm not even a Texan."

"Let's just say we've checked out your background, and we think you've got what it takes to grow into the job. You've gotten to know the big ranches and the important people. That's a good start. And before you make up your mind, I don't suppose it would hurt to mention that it comes with a nice raise in salary."

Tanner thought of the extra cash he could send his brother's family. The money would help. But there were other things to consider. "Like you say, I can at least hear you out," he said.

"We've had a realtor looking for the right place to set up," Clive said. "She's found us a two-bedroom house outside Blanco Springs. You'd stay there, mostly with another ranger on rotation. We'd set up your office with connections to our dispatcher and everything else you'd need. There's a stable out back with a tack room and space for a couple of horses. We'd furnish those, along with a truck and horse trailer." Clive chuckled. "Don't look so surprised, McCade. A lot of planning's gone into this. That includes finding the right man for the job. However, there is a catch. It's not likely to be permanent. Once the rustlers are cleaned out, you'll be shut down and transferred."

"In other words I'd be working myself out of a job."

"That's the idea. Are you still interested?"

Tanner answered without hesitation. "Absolutely."

"Fine. Get some lunch and we'll start the move this afternoon."

Tanner walked out into the sunlit parking lot and climbed into his truck. From the moment Clive had mentioned the post in Blanco Springs, he'd been fighting back thoughts of Rose. But now the prospect of seeing her again, holding her again, slammed him like a flash flood roaring down a canyon.

*Rose.* She'd been on his mind the whole time—on the road, in Wyoming, and in his dreams. His mind remembered every detail of her face. His body remembered loving her and the wonder of her response.

*Rose.* Bless her. Curse her. He'd tried to walk away for good, but it was as if she were branded on his skin—branded, even, on his soul.

His job had to come first. But he would see her. There was no way he could not see her. It was only a question of when and under what conditions. He could only hope she was safe and still willing to welcome him.

But what if she'd had enough of his walking away? What if she wasn't ready to trust him with her heart again? He would understand. But could he accept her decision?

Two days later, he had settled his meager belongings into the small frame house on the outskirts of Blanco Springs. The technicians were still installing the radio, phones, and other communication devices, as well as beds, desks, and chairs for two rangers, and a filing cabinet. A trailer had delivered two sturdy horses to the stable, along with their tack and enough feed for several weeks. On the far side of the stable was a paddock where the animals could be turned out to graze.

For the first few days, at least, Tanner would be alone here. He would use the time to review the files and study the aerial maps of the escarpment, which was a maze of cliffs, gullies, and deep, broad canyons. Small ranches were scattered among these canyons. It would be Tanner's job to remember their locations and get to know their owners, especially the ones who might have reported missing stock.

He was going to have plenty of work. But he'd have some time to himself tomorrow. He would drive out to Rose's place first thing in the morning. What happened after that would be up to her. She could welcome him with open arms, or she could slam the door in his face.

When it came to Rose, Tanner knew better than to assume anything. He only knew that he had to see her, and he wouldn't rest easy until he knew where they stood.

Rose hadn't seen Bull, Jasper, or the boys for the past three days. Fine, she told herself. If Bull didn't like the idea of her raising sheep and was keeping the others away, that was his problem. But she missed their company. The days were longer, the work less like fun in their absence.

Her little farm was thriving. The chickens had settled down and begun to lay again. The lambs were putting on weight. By now, they were down to one bottle feeding a day and eating plenty of grass and hay. Soon they'd be big enough to leave the pen and roam around the property—but not until she could build more protection around her precious vegetables.

Rose had warned herself not to make pets of animals that she planned to sell for food. But the lambs were so adorable, it was hard to keep from loving them. When she was in their pen, they would crowd around her, butting their wooly heads against her legs, wanting to be scratched. She'd even been tempted to give them names—but no, she told herself. That would only make the parting more painful when the time came to give them up.

Today she'd started on a higher fence around her garden, driving sharpened stakes into the ground with a heavy wooden mallet. Would the new fence be strong enough to keep out the hungry lambs and save her carrots, potatoes, lettuce, and peas? All she could do was build it and hope.

By the time the sun set behind the escarpment, she was too tired to eat supper. With the new fence less than half finished, she stowed her tools in the camper, rinsed off the sweat and dirt in the shower, pulled on her nightgown, and tumbled into bed.

Her sleep that night was deep but fitful, plagued by formless dreams with swirling shapes and strange animal cries that seemed almost human.

The rooster woke her at dawn. Still half asleep, she lay gazing into the shadows, vaguely aware that the morning was quiet, maybe too quiet. Something familiar was missing.

Realizing what it was, she jerked bolt upright in the bed. The lambs weren't bleating to be fed, as they usually did.

Rose threw back the covers, flung herself out of bed, and stumbled to the door of the trailer. But even before she opened it, she knew what she would see.

Her lambs would be dead.

\*　　\*　　\*

Tanner knew Rose to be an early riser. And even if he were to wake her, the idea of pulling her sleepy body into his arms and carrying her back to the bed made for an appealing fantasy. Either way, he'd been sleepless for hours, restless with the need to see her again. It was still early, but now that sunrise was streaking the sky, he couldn't wait any longer.

Anxiety stirring, he drove the familiar road that skirted the edge of the Rimrock Ranch and ended at Rose's property. What if she had gone? What if she didn't want to see him? He had to be prepared for that.

A few minutes later, he spotted the trees that grew around Rose's property. He could see her truck parked outside the new gate, and the back of her trailer, which faced the creek.

He parked his truck, climbed out, walked through the gate and around the trailer, and stopped cold.

Rose, still in her nightgown, was huddled on the steps of the trailer, crying her heart out.

"Rose!" Two strides took him to her side. He sank onto the step and wrapped her in his arms. She pressed her face against his shirt, her body heaving with sobs. "What is it, girl? What's happened?"

Rose didn't speak. She only turned her head toward a grassy clearing on the far side of a new chicken coop. Following the line of her gaze, he saw the metal pen with four lifeless, bloodstained, white forms lying inside. They were lambs, barely old enough to wean. His first thought was that some animal, like a coyote, had gotten into the pen and savaged them. But then he realized that their throats had been cut.

Rose was a tough little woman. But she must have loved those fool animals, because she was devastated. He cradled her close, kissing her hair and rocking her like a child.

"Who could've done this? Did you see anything?" he asked.

She shook her head. "I was asleep. But Bull hates sheep. He threatened to kill them if I didn't get rid of them. I know it was him."

\* \* \*

Tanner sent Rose inside the trailer and ordered her to stay while he got a shovel and started digging a pit beyond the fence. Could Bull Tyler really have killed those lambs? Tanner had heard that Bull had a ruthless side, but the man he'd met a few weeks ago had struck him as a gentleman and a caring friend to Rose. It didn't make sense that he would commit such a brutal act.

He would finish burying the lambs. Then he would go and talk to Bull. There had to be some explanation for what had happened here.

Tanner had dug the pit about a third of the way down when Rose joined him, dressed in her old clothes and carrying a short-handled shovel. Without a word, she stepped in beside him and began to dig.

"You don't have to do this, Rose," Tanner said. "Go sit down, or go back to the trailer."

She looked at him, her bloodshot eyes blazing with silent rage. "If you hadn't come by, I'd be doing this by myself," she said. "Let's finish this together. Then you can take me to talk to Bull."

"Are you sure he did this?" Tanner thrust his shovel into the sandy earth. "Could it have been somebody else?"

Rose shook her head. "Bull said that if the lambs wandered off the property they'd be target practice. He must've decided not to wait. As for it being somebody else, look at the chickens. They weren't touched. Bernice gave me those chickens. Bull would've known better than to hurt them. Anybody just wanting to harass me would have killed the chickens, too."

"Let me go alone and talk to him, Rose. You're upset. You'll only make things worse."

Rose hefted a shovelful of earth and dumped it over the rim of the pit. "This isn't your fight, Tanner."

"It's become my fight. Anybody who hurts you will have to deal with me. Even if it's Bull Tyler."

When the pit was deep enough, Tanner dragged the dead lambs into it. Rose, who'd begun to cry again, insisted on helping cover them. When the grave was done, Tanner shoveled away the bloodstains in the lamb pen, rinsed off the tools in the creek, and put them away. It occurred to him then that he should have looked for footprints before he disturbed the ground. But it was too late for that now.

Rose had washed her face and hands in the trailer. "Let's go find Bull," she said.

"You're sure you don't want to wait?"

She shook her head.

"Fine," Tanner said. "We'll take my truck."

Sitting next to Tanner in the truck, Rose was silent. She was grateful that Tanner had come back, but right now the slaughter of her lambs overshadowed everything. How could Bull have done such a terrible thing? She had come to trust him. She'd believed he was her friend.

But this was the man who'd dumped her in Mexico for twelve years and taken over her land, she reminded herself. Bull Tyler was capable of anything.

"Are you all right?" Tanner laid a light hand on her knee.

"I will be," she said. "And thanks for being here. It would've been a lot harder on my own."

"Coming from an independent little firebrand like you, that's saying a lot," he said. "When we get through this mess, you and I will have some serious talking to do."

Rose didn't reply. They were pulling into the ranch yard of the Rimrock. Bull had just come out of the house. He walked toward the truck as they drove up. Without waiting for Tanner, Rose flung herself out of the passenger side and strode up to confront him.

His friendly expression faded as he saw her face. "You look like you're on the warpath. What's the matter, Rose?" he asked. "What's happened?"

"You should know!" she sputtered, almost in tears again. "I thought you were my friend. I know you hated those lambs, but how could you do this monstrous thing?"

"Do what?" He looked more angry than innocent. "For God's sake, tell me!"

Tanner had joined her. "Somebody killed her lambs in the night, cut their throats," he said. "She thinks it was you."

"What?" He swore as the news sank in. "Rose, I don't know who killed your lambs, but I swear to God it wasn't me."

"How do I know that?" Rose faced him toe-to-toe. "You've lied to me before. You lied when you took my land!"

"But I wouldn't lie about this—not even if I'd killed those lambs. I'd tell you right up front because I'd want you to know it."

"But you knew I had the lambs," Rose said. "You told me to get rid of them. You even said they'd be shot if I didn't."

"Yes, I did. But I didn't sneak over to your place in the night and slit their throats. Listen, Rose, my sons loved those damn fool animals. They've been begging to go back to your place and see them again."

"And you wouldn't let them."

"They were in school," Bull said. "I told them that if they did all their homework, they could go back and see the lambs on Saturday. Damn it, Rose, I knew those lambs would be nothing but trouble, but I wouldn't have killed them."

For the first time, Rose began to believe him. "But if not you, who else knew I had those lambs? I can't believe it was Jasper."

"Of course it wasn't," Bull said. "But word gets around in cattle country like this. Anybody could've heard about those lambs and decided to send you a message. That's what I was trying to warn you about when I came over the other day. That's why I even offered you a way to get rid of them. You were asking for trouble, Rose. Whoever killed those lambs, you're damned lucky they didn't hurt you, too."

"I can look into it if you want," Tanner offered. "The TSCRA is posting me in Blanco Springs for a while. Catching sheep killers isn't in my job description, but at least I can keep my eyes and ears open."

"It wouldn't hurt," Bull said. "The important thing is making sure that whoever did this doesn't come back with more mischief in mind. Rose, you're welcome to stay in the duplex until we know more."

"Thanks," Rose said, "but I don't want to leave my property un-protected. I've got a gun, and I know how to use it."

Bull and Tanner exchanged glances. They were clearly worried about her. At least it was a relief, knowing she'd been wrong about Bull.

After promising Bull that she'd be careful, Rose joined Tanner in the truck. "Better?" Tanner asked her as they headed back toward her property.

Rose nodded. "But I feel like a fool. I'm glad it wasn't Bull who killed my lambs. But the idea that the monster who did it is still out there, and might be coming back . . ." She let the words trail off. The truth was, she was nervous about being alone, even with a gun.

"I've got work today," Tanner said. "But do you want me to come back tonight?"

"I was hoping you'd ask." As Rose laid her head against his shoulder, she felt her world slip back into place.

Tanner would be coming by around eight o'clock. Rose, in a reckless moment, had promised him a home-cooked meal. Her tiny kitchen didn't allow for elaborate cooking, and Rose had never fancied herself much of a cook, but María had taught her to make a few good Mexican dishes. She decided on enchiladas, with a fresh salad from her garden. Once she'd settled on a menu, it was time to make a run to the grocery store.

María had made everything from scratch with ingredients she'd bought in the village market. She'd made the sauce, grinding dried *chiles* and spices in her stone *metate* and hand-shaping thin, uniformly round tortillas, which she laid out on a *comal*, a large clay griddle that let the air bubbles in the center rise up and form layers, cooking the tortillas to perfection.

Rose had never mastered the art of perfect tortilla making, but she had loved watching María cook. Now the memory brought tears to her eyes. Overcome by rage and the need to flee from danger, she had never taken time to grieve for the good couple who'd taken her in and treated her as one of their own. She remembered how María had taught her to cook and sew and even made her a pretty dress for her fifteenth birthday celebration, and how Ramón had taught her how to drive and maintain a car. Waves of grief swept over her as she realized how much she missed them. She had killed Lucho Cabrera for causing their deaths. If she could, she would kill Refugio and the rest of the cartel, too, and free the sad little village that would never be the same again.

Rose splashed her face to dry her tears. Some things could never be. And right now she had a meal to prepare for a man she had thought she'd lost for good. Now he was back in her life, but would he stay? In case the answer turned out to be no, she would be wise to hold back her heart to keep him from breaking it.

In town, she picked up dressing for the salad, a six-pack of beer, a can of prepared enchilada sauce, a block of cheese, a half-pound of cooked chicken, and a packet of tortillas that looked like cardboard and would probably taste like it, too. She would do her best to make everything taste good. Maybe someday she would have a real kitchen where she could at least try to cook like María.

By the time Tanner was due to arrive, Rose had the table set and the salad made with fresh lettuce and baby vegetables from her garden. The enchiladas had turned out all right, though they couldn't compare to the made-from-scratch version.

But this wasn't about the enchiladas. It was about the man who'd walked out of her life and come back—and what she would do if he didn't stay.

Just when she was wondering whether she'd been forgotten, Tanner showed up in his truck—late, but barely. "Smells good," he said, stepping in through the open door and locking it behind him. "You've gone to a lot of trouble." He paused a moment, studying her face. "Are you all right, Rose? If you had a phone, I'd have called you."

"I'm fine. Just one more loop on the roller coaster." Rose showed him to a chair. "I'm still trying to convince myself you're really back in town. After the last time, I thought we'd said good-bye for good."

"So did I," Tanner said. "I'm glad we were both wrong. But according to my boss, I won't be here forever—just until we clear the rustlers out of the canyons."

"I see." At least he was being up front, letting her know he wouldn't be around long. She could look forward to more fun in bed and another good-bye. Did she think so little of herself that she was willing to settle for that?

"Have some enchiladas." She dished two of them onto his plate, added some salad, and opened two beers. "They're nothing like the ones my Mexican foster mother used to make, but I did my best with what I could find."

"They're good." He ate with enthusiasm. "I haven't eaten all day." He took another bite. "Where's your foster mother now?"

"The Cabrera cartel shot her and her husband. I lived with them for twelve years. They were family. It's a long story."

"I'd like to hear it all sometime."

"But not tonight. It's much too sad. It's just that making enchiladas brought the memories back, that's all." Rose forced herself to eat. Why couldn't she be chatty and charming, hiding her feelings like some women could? Tonight, it was all she could do to smile.

"Sorry to be so gloomy," she said. "I'm not good at pretending. Didn't you say we needed to talk?"

"I did. But it can wait."

"If you're planning to tell me we're just having a little fun before you leave again, I already got the message."

"That's not what I was planning to tell you, Rose." He'd cleaned his plate. "Will you listen to me and try not to read anything into what I say until I've finished?"

"All right." She put down her fork and put her hands in her lap. "Talk."

He gave a slight shake of his head. "Damn it, woman, you're not making this easy. When I left you before, I thought it was for good. I had feelings for you, but I knew I couldn't stay, and I didn't want to hurt you.

"My brother needed me on the ranch, so I went to Wyoming for two weeks. I thought about you every day—in fact, I couldn't get you out of my mind. And driving back to Texas, you were with me all the way. Even so, I tried to keep my distance. I was still getting over the loss of my wife and son—and I didn't want to be unfair to you. I made every excuse in the book, Rose. But then my boss told me I was being sent back here, and I knew I had to see you."

"Against your better judgment."

"Don't, Rose." He reached across the table and captured her hand. "The moment I saw you this morning, and then held you in my arms while you cried, I knew I couldn't just walk away again. I know I can't be here forever, and I can't plan ahead. But I want to follow this path and see where it leads us. Maybe it'll be somewhere good, for us both. All right?"

His fingers tightened around hers. Tears welled in Rose's eyes. "All right," she whispered. "Wherever it leads. And if it doesn't work out—"

"We'll deal with that only when we have to." He rose from his place, walked around the table, and drew her to her feet for a long, deep kiss. "I want to know you, Rose," he murmured. "I want to know everything about you—your body, your life, the thoughts in your head . . . and I'm hoping it will take a long, long time."

He lifted her in his arms and carried her to the bed for a night of loving and snuggling and whispered conversations under the covers, and then more loving until Rose ached with the need to keep him and make him hers. She knew it was too much to ask. There were so many dangers, so many uncertainties. For now, all she could do was hold on to every moment and hope it would last.


Tanner replaced a file in the stack on his desk, rubbed his eyes, and refilled his coffee cup. After three days on the job, he had plenty to do at his new post. His first case and his first rotating partner had yet to be assigned, but the hours of the day were spent reading through the files and memorizing the aerial maps of the canyons. When he could get away, he would take the truck and drive the back roads, visiting each small ranch, introducing himself to the owners, and taking a look at the cattle. Maybe one of these times Rose would enjoy going with him—surely that would be allowed. The nights in her bed—which he made sure to leave before dawn—had restored him in body and spirit. But they needed time just to be together, relaxing and talking.

There'd been no more sign of Rose's nighttime intruder. But Tanner could tell she was nervous, and he was worried for her. Neither of them would rest easy until they knew who'd killed her lambs.

But it wasn't just the lambs. "I get the feeling I'm being watched," she'd told him the night before. "I never see anybody. It's just this creepy feeling I get, that I'm not alone. What if it's somebody from the cartel? What if they've tracked me down? I've started taking my gun when I go outside. But even that doesn't seem to make a difference."

Tanner knew better than to dismiss Rose's fears. She was tough enough to have shot and killed two men in self-defense. Her survival instincts were razor sharp. If she said somebody was watching her, she was more than likely right.

He'd urged her to move to the duplex on the Rimrock, as Bull had invited her to do. Rose had refused. "I'd never forgive myself if I came back to find the chickens butchered and the trailer burned," she said. "This is my land, my home. I'm staying put."

Tanner knew enough about the cartel to be concerned. But he was more suspicious of Ferg Prescott. He'd found fresh boot prints among the willows on the far side of the creek. It would be like Ferg to have somebody spying on Rose, or even to have her lambs killed. But he had yet to find a shred of evidence.

Between files, he checked his watch. It was after six, too early to show up at Rose's but time for a break. He'd drunk the last beer in the fridge yesterday. A shopping trip was in order, but he could do that tomorrow. Right now, a cold one at the Blue Coyote sounded like a good idea.

The parking lot of the town's only saloon was crowded at this hour with people getting off work. Inside, an old Hank Williams song was blaring from the speakers on the wall. The booths and tables were almost full. The only available seat Tanner could see was a stool at the bar. He took it and ordered a Corona.

He paid with a five. The bartender shoved his change across the bar. Before Tanner could pick up the coins, the man on his right, who looked like a military veteran, an eagle tattoo on his shaved head, turned on the stool, swung his forearm to one side, and swept the coins onto the floor.

"Sorry," he mumbled, speaking with a slight lisp.

"Accidents happen." Tanner wasn't going to start an argument over less than a dollar, and he wasn't about to get down on his knees and pick up the coins off the crowded, dirty floor.

"Aren't you going to pick them up?" The stranger, who appeared drunk, reached into his pocket. "Here, man, I'll pay you back."

"Keep your money. It's fine," Tanner said.

"What's the matter, man, isn't my money good enough for you? Okay, fine then, pick up yours."

Tanner usually knew how to handle himself in a brawl. But he was unprepared for the sudden chop of a hand to his neck and the slam of an iron fist to his groin. With a gasp of surprise and pain, he crumpled and dropped to the floor. Anger flooded his body as he struggled to rise. Then he noticed the stranger's boots—weathered brown military boots, liberally spattered with blood. The blood appeared to have been wiped off, but the vivid stains had soaked into the leather. Those stains couldn't have been more than a few days old.

By the time Tanner recovered and struggled to his feet, the stranger had gotten up and left. But that was all right, he told himself. He had seen what he'd needed to see.

The bartender was watching him, a worried look on his young face. "You all right, man?" he asked.

"I'll be fine." Tanner fished two twenty-dollar bills out of his wallet. He held one toward the bartender. "Can you tell me the name of that man with the tattoo on his head?"

"Sure. His name's Deke Triplehorn. He hangs out here a lot."

"Thanks." Tanner handed him one bill and held out the other one. "And do you know who he works for?"

The bartender hesitated. "I don't know for sure. He's kind of like a freelancer. But I know he gets phone calls here from Ferg Prescott."

"Thanks. You just made my day." Tanner handed over the other bill and left the bar. He made it out to the parking lot in time to catch up with Triplehorn, who was climbing into his Jeep. He didn't appear to be armed, but neither was Tanner.

"What the hell do you want now," the man growled. "If it's a fight, bring it on."

"No fight. Just a message for your boss, Ferg Prescott. Tell him I'm onto you, and you're through doing his dirty work. If I hear of you making more trouble, both you and he are going to jail."

Triplehorn didn't reply, but his expression went rigid. "You don't scare me, Mister. I got a medal for gunning down twenty-six Viet Cong in 'Nam. The next time I catch you alone, you might not be as lucky as you were the last time."

The words rocked Tanner, but he knew better than to show it. It made perfect sense that Triplehorn had been the one to shoot him from the escarpment that day in the desert. But if the man had been acting on orders from Ferg, the implications were staggering.

Triplehorn got into his Jeep and roared out of the parking lot. Tanner gave him a head start, then drove off the way the Jeep was headed. If the vet was going to the Prescott Ranch, there was no need to hurry. If not, it didn't matter. Triplehorn was small potatoes. Tanner's business was with the man's boss.

He was mad as hell, but he kept his pickup below the speed limit. There was little doubt in his mind that Triplehorn had been sent to kill Rose's lambs. Maybe the bastard had been paid to spy on Rose, too, or at least somebody had. As for the shot that had nearly killed him that day in the canyon . . . but that would have to wait until he had proof.

For now, he knew better than to think he could pin anything on Ferg legally. Ferg was too slippery for that. But if he could put some fear into the Prescott boss, at least it might stop him from harassing Rose.

Ferg wouldn't be glad to see him, Tanner knew. Twice he'd

been the bearer of bad news—the first time after Ferg had faked
the theft of his cattle, and the second time when Ferg's own son
had been caught rustling the family's prime steers. His .38 pistol
and gun belt were under the seat of the truck. He might be smart
to strap them on, in case anybody had ideas about taking him by
surprise.

It was twilight by the time he reached the Prescott Ranch. Acting on a hunch, Tanner parked next to the barn, strapped on the
gun belt, and, keeping to the shadows, made his way toward the
house.

His hunch paid off. Triplehorn's Jeep was parked at the foot of
the front steps. Tanner was keeping low, behind the shrubbery,
when the front door opened. Triplehorn, clearly in a sour mood,
came outside, stomped down the steps, and roared away in his
Jeep.

Tanner gave him a few minutes, then walked into the open.

Ferg's office was dark, but Tanner could see light and movement in the windows of the dining room. With luck he'd caught
Ferg at dinner. He could only hope his visit would give the bastard indigestion.

His anger mounted as he climbed the front steps, crossed the
porch, and rang the front doorbell. When the aging cook opened
the door, Tanner pushed past him without a word and strode into
the dining room, with its ghastly array of mounted trophies around
the walls.

Ferg was about to cut into a thick rib eye steak. His jaw dropped
as Tanner walked in to face him across the table, but he recovered
swiftly, arranging his features into a crocodile smile.

"I don't recall inviting you to dinner, McCade. Sorry I can't
share this steak with you. I trust you'll forgive me if I eat it before
it gets cold."

He cut himself a bite. "Was there something you wanted?"

"Only to tell you that the next time you send Deke Triplehorn
to do your dirty work, even if it's just killing lambs, it's going to be
on you."

"Triplehorn?" Ferg feigned ignorance. "I'd remember that
name. But I've never met the man."

"That's not what I heard at the Blue Coyote. And unless I need glasses, I saw him leaving here a few minutes ago."

Ferg's gaze flickered to the pistol at Tanner's hip. "You can't prove a damned thing, McCade. Hell, you're not even a lawman. You're a TSCRA ranger, a friggin' cowcatcher. So get out of here and let me finish my dinner."

"Not until I tell you that if you or your goons ever go near Rose again, and that includes spying on her . . ."

A smile slid across Ferg's face. "So it's you. I heard the little lady had a gentleman caller. Congratulations. She's a nice piece of ass—in the dark, at least."

Tanner battled the urge to hurl himself across the table and smash the man's ugly face. "So you *are* spying on her!"

Ferg laughed. "That's my right, to keep an eye on the neighbors as long as I don't go on their property. The young man I've assigned to the job has orders not to disturb her. So it's perfectly legal, and there's nothing—"

He broke off as the front door burst open. A gangly young man with a big nose and a bumper crop of pimples burst in, wild-eyed and out of breath.

"Something's up!" he gasped. "I saw two men, sneaking around her trailer! I couldn't see their faces in the dark, but I could hear them talking. They were talking *Mexican!*"

# CHAPTER FIFTEEN

THE CHICKENS WERE STIRRING IN THEIR COOP, CLUCKING, SQUAWK-ing, and ruffling their feathers. Rose, who had a long history with chickens, knew the signs. Something was spooking them.

It was most likely a coyote nosing around, she thought. Or maybe a weasel, or even an owl. The coop had been built to keep out predators, but it wouldn't hurt to chase the creature away, in the hope that it wouldn't come back.

But what if the intruder wasn't an animal?

She rose from her seat on the step of the trailer and went in-side, locking the door behind her. Her loaded gun was under the pillow, where she kept it. Her hand closed around the weapon's cold, reassuring weight. It was too bad the batteries had burned out on her flashlight. She could have used it now. But she wasn't about to cower inside the trailer and leave her chickens unpro-tected. Thumbing back the pistol's hammer, she opened the door of the trailer and stepped outside again.

It was early yet. She'd been expecting Tanner, but sometimes he didn't show up until nine or ten. And she understood that due to the demands of his job, he might not come at all. When he did come, it was always in his truck. There was no truck tonight.

The darkness was silent except for the babbling flow of the creek and the fussing of the chickens. There was no visible sign of danger. But Rose could feel the familiar prickling on the back of her neck that told her something wasn't right.

Her gaze probed the deep shadows on the far side of the creek. There was no movement. No sound, not even the wind.

She walked over to the coop. Behind the wire mesh, the chickens were restless and alert. "What is it?" she whispered to them. "What are you trying to tell me? I know you're worried, but don't be scared. I'll protect you."

"*Rosa.*"

Her whispered Mexican name sent a chill up her spine. Had the cartel tracked her down?

"*Rosa. No tengas miedo. Estamos aquí.*"

She turned as two men stepped out of the trees. They were strangers—but only for an instant. Recognizing them, Rose lowered her gun and ran to embrace the pair who'd been like her older brothers back in Río Seco.

She hadn't seen Ramón's nephews, Raul and Joaquin, for more than three years. She'd long since begun to believe they were dead. But here they were, and she had a world of questions to ask them.

"Where have you been? How did you find me?" She spoke with them in Spanish, which came as naturally to her as her mother tongue.

"That's a very long story." Joaquin was the better looking and more talkative of the brothers. "Invite us into your little home, and we will tell it to you."

Overjoyed to see them again, Rose led the two men inside her trailer, opened the last two bottles of Tecate in her miniature fridge, and made them tuna sandwiches, which they wolfed down, telling her their story between bites.

"Last winter, we were working on that big sheep ranch outside Sabinas when the Cabreras came by," Raul said.

"The cartel?" Even the name sent a chill through Rose's body.

"They were looking for runners who knew the border and how to cross. They promised good money and that our family would be safe if we went to work for them."

Rose suppressed a shudder. She didn't like what she was hearing. But these two men were all that was left of the Mexican fam-

ily she'd loved. And surely they hadn't known what they were getting into. How could she presume to judge them?

"Your family was already dead," she said. "When the Cabreras
came to Río Seco, they shot the people who stood up to them.
Ramón and María died against a wall, along with many of the
young men. Only the younger women were spared. I don't have
to tell you why."

"We know, little sister." Raul put a comforting hand on her
shoulder. "When we learned the awful truth, we decided to leave
the country. But you don't just walk away from the Cabrera cartel."

"It took time and planning," Joaquin said. "But we finally did
it—crossed the river on foot and caught rides all the way here.
*Señor* Bull Tyler helped us years ago, after our father died. We are
hoping he will have work for us again."

"I can't speak for Bull," Rose said. "He's a good man, but the
laws are stricter now. I can take you to see him, but you'll have to
ask him yourselves."

Did they know that she'd killed Lucho Cabrera and that the
cartel was after her? For now, she might be wise to keep that information to herself.

"I understand how you knew where to find Bull," she said. "But
how did you know where to find me?"

Joaquin smiled, showing his beautiful white teeth. "The neighbors in Río Seco told us you'd left and taken our father's old car.
Since it was Bull Tyler who brought you to our family, we guessed
that you would go back to him."

"When we didn't see the car on the Rimrock, we asked around,"
Raul said. "Other Mexican workers on the ranches, some of them
had seen you. Word spreads. They told us where you lived."

So it had been that easy. If Raul and Joaquin had been able to
track her down, how difficult would it be for the cartel?

Refugio Cabrera wouldn't have known anything about Bull or
where he lived, Rose reminded herself. All the same, she felt cold
with fear.

It came as a relief when bright headlights shining through the window of her trailer announced Tanner's arrival. "My friend is here," she said, and rushed outside.

As he doused the headlights and climbed out of his truck, she flew into his arms. "Hold me," she whispered.

He clasped her fiercely. "Thank God," he muttered. "When I heard somebody was here . . ." He let the words trail off. Thrusting her a little away from him, he looked into her eyes. "Are you all right? I was worried about you."

"I have visitors inside—my Mexican brothers. I've told you about them. Until tonight I wasn't even sure they were alive. But they just showed up. They know Bull, and they're hoping he'll take them in. I—don't know what to do about them."

"It's all right. I'm here." He took her hand and walked with her to the trailer. She stopped him just outside.

"There's more, Tanner. They say they were forced to work for the cartel and that they've run away. I haven't told them that I'm hiding from the cartel, too, or about the man I killed. Bull doesn't know about that, either."

"Don't worry, I won't mention it."

"I'm scared, Tanner. I don't know what's going to happen."

"Rose, I'm here for you. Take me in and introduce me to your visitors."

His presence reassured Rose, for now at least. She ushered him into the trailer's crowded sitting room and made the introductions. Joaquin and Raul spoke fair English, so they had little trouble communicating.

"Rose tells me that you already know Bull," Tanner said, making conversation. "There must be a story behind that."

"There is," Joaquin said. "Our father worked as a cook on the Rimrock. Some bad men murdered him for his beautiful old car."

"Where is that car, Rose?" Raul asked. "They said you took it when you left Río Seco."

"Sadly, I had to sell it," Rose said. "I suppose it was really yours. I'm sorry."

"*Que lástima.*" Raul shrugged. "Too bad."

"I remember that car," Tanner said. "It was beautiful. But I want to hear the rest of the story."

"Before he died, my father asked for his body to go back to Río Seco to bury next to our mother," Raul said. "Bull drove him back. Joaquin and I, we were living with his brother, *Don* Ramón. We had to find the men who killed our father and make them pay. So Bull took us back to Texas and gave us jobs."

"And did you find the men?"

"*Sí*, we did. It was easy because they had the car. Our father saw them before he died, so he could tell Bull what they looked like."

"And you made them pay?" Tanner asked.

"They died in a very bad way, and we took the car back to Mexico," Joaquin said. "So you see, Bull is a good friend. He will help us for sure."

"In that case," Tanner said, "why don't we go see him now? Come on. You can ride in the back of my truck. Rose, do you want to come?"

"I think I'd better. I just hope we don't wake everybody up."

Raul and Joaquin grabbed the backpacks they'd left by the chicken coop and climbed into the bed of Tanner's pickup. Tanner opened the passenger door for Rose, then went around to the driver's seat.

"Thank you." She laid a hand on his knee as he started the engine. "I just hope this ends happily."

"Well, there's no room for them to sleep in your trailer," Tanner said. "Besides, I still have plans to get you all to myself tonight."

"I love you, Tanner." Rose hadn't meant to say it—especially since she'd never said those words to any man. But somehow it seemed to fit the moment.

He touched her hand. "You know what? I love you, too, Rose." He laughed. "I'm glad we got that settled."

As was his habit, Bull stepped outside before bedtime to get a breath of fresh air and calm his mind. The sky was clear, the moon bright enough to cast long shadows across the yard. Two nighthawks, with white-tipped wings, zigzagged through the darkness, their gaping beaks catching insects in midair. A single light glowed in the upstairs window of the bunkhouse—that would be young Fred Bushman, who kept a stack of books by his bed and dreamed of traveling the world with his earnings as a cowhand.

Everything was peaceful, Bull assured himself. So how to explain the tension in his gut—the baseless sense that something was about to happen—something apt to turn out badly?

He was about to forget his premonition and go back inside when a pair of truck headlights, coming from the direction of Rose's place, swung into the yard. At first he thought maybe Rose had decided to stay in the duplex after all. But the truck wasn't Rose's. As it pulled up to the house, he recognized Tanner Mc-Cade at the wheel.

And Tanner wasn't alone. Rose opened the passenger door, jumped to the ground, and came racing up the porch steps. Now Bull could see two more men in the back of the truck. They appeared to be Mexicans, but even though they looked familiar, he couldn't place them.

Rose had reached him. He read excitement and worry in her face. "What the devil's going on, Rose?" Bull demanded.

Her manner was apologetic, almost embarrassed. "Raul and Joaquin—they showed up at my trailer. They need work and a place to stay."

*Raul and Joaquin.* A memory flashed through Bull's mind—Carlos's old Buick vanishing down the dusty back road, headed for Mexico—leaving behind the bodies of the murderers the boys had captured and dragged almost to death.

Bull had finished off the killers with two pistol shots and walked away. It had been his twenty-first birthday, he recalled. And he had never expected to see Carlos's sons again.

Now here they were, on his doorstep. And he couldn't expect Rose to take them in. They were about to become his problem.

The two brothers had climbed out of the truck. Bull came down off the porch and shook their hands. Smooth hands. Whatever they'd been doing, it hadn't been ranch work.

"I'd invite you in, but my sons are asleep and I don't want to disturb them," Bull said. "Have you eaten?"

"Yes, Rose made sandwiches." Joaquin was the taller one, Bull remembered now. The last time he'd seen them, they were barely out of their teens. Now they were men, their faces hardened by time and experience.

"Now that the roundup's done, there's some vacant space in the bunkhouse. Downstairs hallway, last door on your right. You can bunk there tonight, and we'll talk in the morning. Keep quiet. All right?"

"Yes. *Gracias.* We know the way." They lifted their backpacks out of the truck bed and headed across the yard to the bunkhouse.

Rose hovered by the truck, as if she had more to say. Tanner had climbed out to stand beside her.

"Sit down." Bull sank onto the top step, leaving room next to him. Rose took a seat. Tanner moved to stand beside her.

"So tell me what this is all about," Bull said.

"They just showed up, out of nowhere," Rose said. "I was happy to see them at first, because they were like brothers to me, and I hadn't even been sure they were alive. But now that I've brought you into this, I'm worried."

"You didn't have much choice about bringing me into it," Bull said. "With you or without you, they'd have come to me. But what is it you're worried about?"

"They told me they'd been forced to work as drug runners for the Cabrera cartel. According to them, they ran away and hitched rides to get here."

*That explains their soft hands,* Bull thought. But what he'd heard so far didn't sound good. "Do you think they're telling the truth?" he asked her.

"I don't know why they'd make up a story like that. But what if there's more to it? What if the cartel comes looking for them?"

"It could happen. But why would the cartel go to so much trouble for a couple of flunkies? They can always get more hired help."

Rose's gaze dropped to her lap. When she looked at him again, he saw fear in her dark eyes. Tanner laid a hand on her shoulder, as if giving her support.

"There's something I haven't told you, Bull," she said. "Something I should have told you when I first came here."

Little by little the story emerged—how the brother of Refugio Cabrera had raped her, how she'd waited until he came for her again, then killed him to avenge her foster parents and to save her own life. "I took the car and fled in the night, to the only place I could call home. I knew Refugio would never stop looking for me, but I hoped I would be safe here. I was wrong. And now I may have put all of you in danger."

"You don't know that for sure," Bull said.

"If Joaquin and Raul could find me, so could the cartel. For all I know, the two of them may have even been sent to track me down and report back." She shook her head. "I don't know what to do. I only know that this is my own fight, and I don't want to involve the people I care about."

"You could go to my family's ranch in Wyoming," Tanner said. "You'd be safe there, and I know my brother and his wife would be happy to have you."

She laid her hand on his. Seeing them together, Bull remembered what it was like to be so much in love with a woman that you'd do anything to protect her. He would have done the same for Susan.

"We don't know that we're in danger," he said. "If we were, it wouldn't be the first time. We know how to fight. We know how to defend our land and our loved ones."

"But it mustn't come to that," Rose said. "I would leave before I let it get that far."

"It's too soon to know," Bull argued. "Joaquin and Raul may be just what they say they are—two scared men running from the cartel. If that's true, the safest place for them, and us, is right here, where we can keep an eye on them. Send them away, and they're bound to get picked up by Immigration and deported back to Mexico. Now that they know you're here, we can't let that happen."

Rose's shoulders sagged. "I'm sorry for this mess, Bull."

"It's not your fault. If I'd brought you home like I promised, we wouldn't have anything to worry about, would we?" Bull rose, stretching his limbs. "Go on home to bed, now. I'll keep an eye on that pair, and we can sort all this out in the morning."

Bull watched the truck drive away. In the bunkhouse, all the lights had gone out. The bunkhouse phone was out of order, so nobody would be ringing their buddies in Mexico. But he needed a solution to the problem of Raul and Joaquin by tomorrow morning, which meant he would likely spend a sleepless night thinking about it.

Satisfied that everything was under control, he went back into the house and locked the front door behind him. On the way down the hall to his bedroom, he looked in on his sleeping boys. The sight of them tugged at his heart, or what was left of it after the loss of his wife. He swallowed the lump that had risen in his throat. Nothing mattered more than his boys. To keep them safe, he would give his life a hundred times over.

Would he have to make that choice in the days ahead?

Night-flying insects swarmed in Tanner's headlights as he drove back to Rose's trailer. Beside him, Rose was quiet, as if lost in thought.

"Are you all right?" he asked her.

"Just worried."

"I know." He slid an arm around her shoulders and pulled her close. "If it'll give you a diversion, I have some other news. I found out that it was Ferg who had your lambs killed. One of his hired thugs did it."

"Ferg! I should've known." She sighed and shook her head. "But why? The property's out of his reach now."

"He knows that. But he wanted to stir up trouble between you and Bull. It almost worked."

"Yes, it almost did. I'm really glad it wasn't Bull. He's no saint, but I've never known him to act out of pure meanness."

"When I went to see him, Ferg also admitted to having you

spied on. He claims it's his legal right to keep an eye on the neighbors from his own property. I met the little creep who's been watching you. He's just a kid—doesn't look dangerous. You could probably knock him over with one hand. But you won't want to give him any entertainment."

Rose was silent for a moment. "No!" she exclaimed.

"No?"

"Why did you go to Ferg, Tanner? You should have left that to me. Those were my lambs he killed, and I'm the one he's spying on."

"I was trying to protect you, Rose," Tanner said.

"I've had it with being protected!" Rose's fist came down on the dashboard. "And I've had it with Ferg Prescott. If he thinks he can bully me and make my life miserable, he's wrong! I've had enough! I'm going to drive out to the Prescott Ranch tomorrow and give him a piece of my mind!"

"Are you sure that's a good idea?"

"I don't care if it's a good idea or not. I'm sick and tired of being treated like a child—by Ferg, by Bull, and even by you."

"Do you want me to go with you?"

"No. I'm a big girl. I can handle this myself."

"Your choice, lady." He was secretly proud of her. His woman was all spunk. But Ferg was a sore loser and a dangerous foe. Tanner couldn't help being worried about her.

But at least, for now, he'd managed to take her mind off the two Mexicans.

They pulled up outside the fence, next to Rose's pickup. Switching off the engine, he turned to her. "Are we still friends? I want to make sure you're not mad enough to run me off."

She laughed. "Not a chance of that, mister."

Tanner locked his truck and took a moment to check around the trailer, in the trees, and across the creek. If Ferg's creepy little spy was around, at least he was nowhere in evidence.

Once he was satisfied, he followed Rose into the trailer and locked the door behind them. It had been an unsettling day for both of them. The last thing they needed now was to be disturbed again.

"Maybe you should get a guard dog," Tanner said.

"And have somebody kill it, like the lambs? I couldn't stand that. It would break my heart."

"For a tough woman, you're such a tenderhearted thing. Come here." He caught her close and swept her back to the bed. After unbuttoning her cotton shirt, he buried his face between her breasts—small, perfect breasts, the nipples as dark as raisins. Hearing her say that she loved him had thawed a frozen place in his heart. Until Rose, he'd stopped believing that he was worthy of love, or that he could ever love again. But he'd been wrong. They were two broken people—but somehow the shattered pieces seemed to fit together, making them whole.

He left her before dawn, bending down to kiss her sleeping face. She opened her eyes with a whimper and caught his neck to deepen the kiss. Once his first rotating partner arrived at the new office, he would miss these nights with Rose. But he wouldn't subject her to the gossip that would arise if he openly spent his nights with her. They could only make the most of the time they had.

After checking the yard for signs of intruders, and finding none, he climbed in his truck and drove away. Right now, the future was too uncertain to make plans. But he could no longer imagine a life without Rose. Somehow, he would find a way to make things work out for them. Meanwhile, he had a job to do.

Rose woke again at first light. For the space of a few breaths, she lay still, her body warm with the memory of Tanner's lovemaking. Then the concerns of the day flooded in on her—first and foremost, Raul and Joaquin. Were they all right? Was Bull's family all right? What if she'd made a terrible mistake, trusting them enough to leave them at the Rimrock?

She flung herself out of bed, pulled on her clothes, splashed her face, and tied back her hair. After feeding the chickens, she grabbed her keys off the hook by the door, locked the trailer, and headed for the Rimrock in her pickup.

In the east, a flaming sunrise greeted the day. The rains had ended, leaving the land summer dry. Soon the Rimrock cattle in the lower pastures would be coming to the water tank to drink, testing the strength of her fence. If she didn't want her yard trampled, she would have to think about reinforcing the posts and wire.

A plume of dust trailed behind her wheels as she drove into the ranch yard. The place looked surprisingly peaceful, with cows and calves grazing in the paddocks and a couple of ranch hands filling the water troughs.

Bull was sitting on the porch, drinking coffee. He stood as she drove up and parked below the steps. "I've been wondering when you'd show up," he said as she climbed out of the truck. "Come on in and have some breakfast."

She took the steps two at a time. "Where are Joaquin and Raul?" she demanded. "Is everything all right?"

"Everything's fine. At least I hope it is. Raul and Joaquin are on their way up to the line shack in the mountain pasture. Jasper and Sam took them in the pickup this morning, with a load of supplies. Our Mexican boys will be up there tending cattle for the summer months. They'll have horses, but no vehicle. If they stay put, they should be safe enough, and hopefully so should you."

"What if they don't stay put?" Rose was still worried.

"Let's hope we won't have to answer that question." The dark look Bull gave her expressed more than words. There was another side to this man, a side she'd only glimpsed at times like this. When it came to protecting his land and his family, there were no limits to what Bull Tyler would do.

Something told her that the decision to send the two men to the line shack had not been made lightly.

"Come on in," he said with a jovial smile that didn't fool her. "Bernice is making flapjacks. I'll have her throw on a couple extra. Will and Beau will be in once they're ready for school. They'll be glad to see you."

"Did you tell them about the lambs?"

"I told them. They cried, but it's time they learn that life on a ranch isn't always pretty. Bad things happen."

The table was set in the dining room. Rose took a seat and

helped herself to some coffee. "Tanner found out who killed the lambs. It was somebody working for Ferg."

"I could've told you that." Bull forked a couple of flapjacks from the platter on the table and dropped them onto Rose's plate.

"What I can't understand is why."

"I could've told you that, too. Ferg hates sheep even more than I do. But I'm guessing that what he really wanted was for you to blame me so he could move in and show some sympathy, maybe worm his way into your good graces and eventually get some concessions on the water rights. Think about it. It almost worked."

"It's not just that." Rose poured syrup on her flapjacks. "He's having me watched. He even admitted to it. He said it was perfectly legal."

"It sounds like I need to go have a talk with him," Bull said. "I can set the bastard straight on a few things."

"No." Rose put down her fork. "Not you, Bull. It has to be me. Ferg needs to know that I can stand up for myself. I don't need a man to stand up for me. Not Tanner, and not you."

They might have fallen to arguing, but just then Will and Beau came into the dining room, scrubbed, combed, and dressed in fresh school clothes. Laying their backpacks on the end of the table, they sat down, speared two flapjacks each, and drowned them in syrup.

"We feel bad about your lambs, Rose," Will said. "That was a mean thing to do."

"It was Ferg who had them killed," Bull said. "Ferg is a mean man. Remember that if you ever have any dealings with that family. Trust a skunk before a rattlesnake . . ."

"And trust a rattlesnake before a Prescott. We know." Beau's jaded tone suggested he'd heard it all before. "Can we ride our ponies after school?"

Bull frowned. "We'll see. Ask Jasper when he gets back from the mountain."

Rose had finished her breakfast. "If you'll excuse me, I'll be going now," she said, rising. "Thanks for the flapjacks. You boys have a good day at school."

She was out the door before Bull could repeat his warning about Ferg Prescott. She didn't want to be reminded one more time that she was only a woman and not fit to deal with the powerful and unscrupulous boss of the Prescott Ranch. Now, while she was still riled up, would be the perfect time to face the man who'd become a thorn in her side.

Climbing into her truck, she started the engine and roared away from the house, toward the back road that connected the two ranches. Glancing in the rearview mirror, she saw Bull standing on the porch. He was shaking his head.

# CHAPTER SIXTEEN

WHEN NO ONE ANSWERED THE BELL ON THE SECOND RING, ROSE opened the door and stalked into the house. By then she'd worked herself into a seething rage. If Ferg Prescott thought he could harass her and get away with it, she was about to prove him wrong.

She found Ferg breakfasting alone at the dining room table, surrounded by the mounted trophies that had given her the creeps when she'd been there as a dinner guest. The massive bison head, with its staring glass eyes, loomed directly above him. Over the window, the mounted body of a snarling cougar crouched on a long shelf.

As Rose walked into the room, Ferg looked up and smiled, showing bits of egg yolk on his large front teeth. "Hello, Rose. I don't recall inviting you at this hour, but please sit down and have some breakfast. I'll have Curly bring you a plate."

"I've already eaten breakfast. And I'll stand, thank you. It won't take long to say what I've come to say."

Ferg sipped his coffee, then set the cup down and added some liquid from a silver flask. "So, please go ahead," he said. "Take your time. I've always viewed you as an entertaining little woman."

"I'm not an entertaining little woman!" Rose snapped. "I'm a legal property owner and a citizen of the United States. And you have no right to send your man onto my land to kill my livestock!"

He gave her a blank look. "My dear, I have no idea what you're talking about."

"Don't give me that." Rose could feel her anger boiling over. Only the awareness that he was goading her gave her a measure of self-control. "Tanner McCade had you dead to rights. He saw blood on the shoe of your hired thug, and he saw the man coming out of this house."

"That doesn't prove a damn thing," Ferg said. "And even if you could prove it, sheep aren't livestock. They're vermin. No court in the state would convict a man for killing them—no more than they would for killing coyotes or prairie dogs."

"I'm not here to prove anything," Rose countered. "I'm only here to warn you. Keep your people off my land. I have the right to protect what's mine—even if I have to shoot somebody to do it. Believe me, I have a gun and I know how to use it."

His expression went cold. "I know you do, Rose. I haven't forgotten the night you murdered my father."

A thread of fear uncoiled in the pit of her stomach. "It was self-defense, not murder," she said. "Your father had a pistol in his hand. He was going to shoot me because I'd seen him kill my grandpa."

"But you were never arrested or tried."

"That's because you blamed Bull when you knew better. Do you want me to tell the sheriff that you lied?"

For the first time, he looked uneasy. "That's old news," he said. "Nobody cares anymore."

"Then let's leave it at that." Rose chalked up a small victory. "But while I'm here, I want to ask you why you're having me spied on. Tanner said you even admitted to it."

"As I told your boyfriend, I have the right to know what's going on next to my property—like those two Mexicans who showed up at your trailer last night. What's to stop them from crossing the creek and robbing me blind?"

"You've no need to worry. They're gone. But I'm a woman alone. All I'm asking for is my privacy. Can't you at least give me that?"

"Not if it means I can't protect my own property. I have that right, too." His hand came down on a bell next to his plate—the kind of bell a business might keep on the counter to summon service. The ring brought the cook from the kitchen.

"Curly, it's time for Miss Landro to leave. Would you please escort her to her vehicle?"

"Don't bother. I can find my own way." Rose turned and strode out the front door. She had said all she'd planned to say, but being thrown out of the house was the final humiliation. For all her righteous indignation, she had barely made a dent in Ferg Prescott's arrogance.

By the time she started her truck, she was trembling. She drove back by way of town. Tanner would be working, but just to talk to him, and maybe feel his quick, reassuring hug, would ease the sting.

The TSCRA ranger post was on the right side of the road. Tanner's truck was outside, but—her heart sank—another official truck was parked next to it. Tanner had mentioned that he was expecting a partner. The partner must have arrived. Rose sighed and kept driving. Tanner didn't need to be embarrassed by her stopping to cry on his shoulder.

She drove on into town. As long as she was here, she might as well pick up some groceries. Cooking and storage space were limited in her tiny kitchen, but at least she could look for foods that could be easily warmed up the next time Tanner came to visit.

The new grocery store was well stocked. Rose had to rein herself in to keep from buying more than she could use. Next to the frozen pie case, she paused. The pies looked delicious, but if she bought one, she would have to cook it today. There was no room for a pie in her freezer.

She was about to give the pies a pass when an idea struck her—an idea so ridiculous and daring that it just might work. In any case, she had little to lose. Resolving to take a chance, she chose a frozen apple pie and added it to her cart.

Back in the trailer, she put the groceries away and set the frozen pie on the counter. She couldn't be sure that Ferg's spy had shown up, but since she'd complained about being watched, she had a feeling that Ferg would send him just to prove he could.

Keeping an eye across the creek, she gathered the eggs and weeded her garden. By the time she'd finished, she could see the willows moving in a way the wind wouldn't have blown them. Ferg's spy must be in place. Tanner had mentioned that he was very young and looked harmless. She could only hope that was the case.

Going back inside, she heated the small oven, put the pie inside, and opened the trailer windows. The pie took nearly an hour to bake, but by the time it was done, its mouthwatering aroma was drifting out of the windows, around the trailer, and across the creek. Rose set it in the open doorway. When it was cool enough, she cut a slice, put it on a saucer with a fork, and walked to the edge of the creek.

"Hey, you," she called. "I know you're there, keeping an eye on me. How would you like a nice, warm piece of apple pie? Can you smell it? Come on out and it's yours."

Scarcely daring to breathe, she waited. Was she taking a dangerous risk or playing a brilliant hunch?

The willows stirred and slowly parted. A skinny young man in a camouflage print shirt stepped into the open. Homely, with an oversized nose and bad skin, he couldn't have been more than eighteen or nineteen. Not much more than a boy, and so shy that he could barely meet her eyes.

"Would you like this pie?" she asked again, more gently this time.

"Yes, please, ma'am," he muttered.

"Come here and sit down." She motioned to a cut log that served as a seat. He hesitated, then crossed the creek in the shallow place. Like a timid animal, he approached the log and lowered himself onto it. Rose handed him the saucer and the fork.

"My name is Rose," she said. "What's yours?"

"Reuben. Reuben Potter. This sure is good pie."

"I'm glad you like it. Do you work for Mr. Prescott, Reuben?"

"Uh-huh." Reuben spoke between bites. "He wouldn't like it if he knew I was talking to you."

Rose smiled. "Then we won't tell him, will we? I know he pays you to watch me. But I want to be your friend. Would you like that?"

He hesitated. "I guess."

"I won't always have pie, but if you get hungry while you're watching, I can make you a sandwich or something, and we can visit a little. Will you let me know when you come, so I won't be afraid?"

"Sure. I don't want to scare a nice lady like you."

"Then there's something else you can do. It can be dangerous, living alone like this. As long as you're here anyway, will you watch my place to make sure I'm safe and that nobody comes around to make trouble? That shouldn't be too hard, should it?"

"No, ma'am." He finished the pie and handed her the fork and saucer. Rose was tempted to offer him another piece. He looked hungry enough to eat the whole pie. But no, one slice was enough. It would be best not to get his expectations up.

He rose from the log. "Thanks for the pie, ma'am. I'd better get back to work."

"You're welcome," Rose said. "Let me know the next time you come around. And thank you. I'll feel safer, knowing you're there."

"Yes, ma'am."

She watched him cross the creek and vanish behind the screen of willows. Had she taken shameless advantage of the boy? Or had she just shown him some needed kindness?

Never mind, she honestly liked Reuben. She even sensed a kinship between them. He struck her as something of an outcast, someone who didn't quite fit in, not unlike herself. And she did feel safer, knowing that the person watching her was not a stranger.

All the same, she couldn't deny a feeling of smug satisfaction. In her own subtle way, she'd finally gotten the better of Ferg Prescott.

Tanner's new partner, Special Ranger Joe French, was a divorced man in his early thirties, friendly and easygoing. By the end of the first week, he and Tanner had settled into a comfortable routine, with one of them manning communications in the office and the other going out on calls. When a troubling situation arose, they went out together, each serving as backup for the other. By the end of the second week they'd closed two cases, brought five rustlers to justice, and recovered fourteen head of stolen cattle.

After Joe learned that his partner had a sweetheart, he was happy to cover the office and give Tanner an occasional night off with Rose. It wasn't enough time to suit Tanner, but the work was satisfying, and he was as contented as he'd been in a long time. Someday he would have the means to marry Rose and settle in a cozy home somewhere, surrounded by the family they would have. For now, having a good job and an amazing woman who loved him would have to be enough.

Rose was doing all right, too. Her garden and chickens were thriving, and Bull was paying her a little to do his bookkeeping and help his sons with their schoolwork. Rose's late grandfather, a retired professor, had educated her well while she lived with him. She could have been a teacher, Tanner thought. Maybe one day she would have the chance.

Over time, he and Joe had been interviewing the ranchers who held properties in the canyons below the caprock. The interviews were nearly finished, except for a visit to one isolated ranch, located in a remote canyon at the end of a long dirt road. Getting there and back would take the better part of a day.

"Why don't you drive out and do that interview tomorrow?" Joe suggested to Tanner. "Take your honey along. Make an outing of it. I can manage things here for a day."

Joe's offer was a gift. "Thanks," Tanner said. "I'll tell Rose when I see her tonight. She'll like that."

"I'd tell you to marry that girl and make an honest woman of her," Joe said. "But I know what this job can do to a marriage. My wife couldn't handle it—the hours, the time away, and the worry that I'd get shot and wouldn't make it home. She left me for a tax lawyer."

"I'll keep that in mind." Tanner had had the same concerns

himself. Rose was tough and accustomed to hardship. But he wanted to give her a good life and be around to enjoy it with her. For now, that would have to wait.

The closest thing to a fancy date in Blanco Springs was pizza and sodas at the Burger Shack. Tanner and Rose didn't go out often, but he enjoyed showing her off. She was a striking woman, and he loved the way she displayed her birthmark with pride. When he was with her in public, he could sense the envy of the men who glanced their way.

Tonight they'd taken the corner booth, where they sat close together, enjoying their combo pizza and talking. Earlier they'd seen Reuben Potter walk up to the counter and order a cheeseburger. Reuben and Rose had exchanged glances but hadn't spoken. Their friendship was known to Tanner but was otherwise a secret.

It tickled Tanner that Rose had won over the young man Ferg had hired to spy on her. And it was reassuring to know that an extra pair of eyes was watching her place, helping keep her safe.

So far there'd been no sign of the cartel and, after two weeks, no word from Raul and Joaquin on the mountain. But the worry was always there, in the back of Tanner's mind. He wouldn't rest easy until he knew that the threat was gone for good.

"I'm excited about our outing tomorrow," she said. "Do you want me to pack a lunch?"

"Nothing fancy, and not unless you have time. I'll bring some snacks and plenty of water. We can stop for a meal after we get back from the interview."

She stirred the ice in her Diet Coke. "I've been thinking," she said. "As long as we're out in the truck, how much time would it take on the way home to circle around and stop by that line shack in the Rimrock's mountain pasture?"

A subtle alarm went off in Tanner's head. "I've never been there, but I've seen it on an aerial map. It's not that far out of the way. Maybe an extra hour. But are you sure that's a good idea?"

"I've thought about it," she said. "I know it's the usual thing for cowboys to work out of the line shack for weeks at a time. But I'm worried. Raul and Joaquin were like brothers to me once. What if something's happened to them?"

Uneasiness crept up Tanner's spine and tightened a knot in the pit of his stomach. He didn't like this. But he knew Rose. She'd made what seemed like a reasonable request, and she wouldn't take no for an answer.

"We'll go on one condition," he said. "I want you to let Bull or Jasper know what we're planning. If they say we shouldn't go to the line shack, promise you'll at least listen."

She sighed. "All right, we can stop by the Rimrock tonight. Why don't we box up the rest of this pizza for Joe? I've had all I can eat."

"Fine." Tanner signaled the server and asked for a take-out box. Minutes later they were back in the truck, on their way to the Rimrock.

They found both Bull and Jasper sitting on the front porch. Bull's boots rested on the porch railing. Jasper's cigarette glowed red in the darkness. He tossed it over the side as Rose and Tanner came up the steps to join them.

"What are you youngsters up to?" Jasper asked. "You look way too serious for such a nice evening."

Rose told them about her plan to go to the canyon ranch with Tanner. "I hope you can spare me for a day, Bull," she said.

He lowered his feet to the porch. "That shouldn't be a problem," he said. "The books are up-to-date. And with school ending next week, the boys don't have much mind for their classwork. Go and have a good time. I know you could use a break."

"Thanks," Tanner said. "But there's more. Tell them, Rose."

"If you two are running off to get married, that's fine with us," Jasper teased.

"Not that," Rose said. "But I've been concerned about Joaquin and Raul, alone up there in the line shack. I'm trying to talk Tanner into paying them a visit, just to make sure everything's all right. We could even deliver them more supplies if you want."

"But I'm not so sure that's a good idea," Tanner said. "We've agreed to let you two make the call."

"We have?" Rose raised an eyebrow. "I said I'd *listen.*"

"I'm with Tanner," Bull said. "Before they showed up here, those boys were running drugs for the Cabrera cartel. Whatever they told you, I don't trust them. Neither should you."

"What about you, Jasper?" Rose asked. "You drove them up to the line shack. What do you think?"

"I think you'd best leave well enough alone," Jasper said. "We sent those two boys up the mountain to keep you safe. I know they're like family and all, but the less you have to do with them, the better. As for your bein' worried about them, they're big boys. They can look out for themselves."

"And if they're up to no good, that's for me to deal with, not you," Bull added. Tanner caught the cold glimmer in Bull's blue eyes. At that moment he realized, with chilling certainty, that the legends he'd heard about the man were true.

"So I'm outnumbered three to one," Rose said.

"Don't go up there," Jasper said. "If you want anybody to check on those boys, we'll do it."

"When?" Rose demanded.

"Tomorrow," Bull said. "It shouldn't take that long. Satisfied?"

Rose sighed. "All right. Take me home, Tanner. I'll see you in the morning."

At her trailer, he walked her to the door and took her in his arms. She came to him without resistance, nestling against his chest. "Are we good?" he asked. "Are you sure you're not mad at me?"

"I'm fine. Bull and Jasper are probably right," she said, stretching on tiptoe to kiss him. "Let's relax and have a good day tomorrow."

As always, he checked around the yard and gave a wave toward the other side of the creek, in case Reuben was watching—which he likely wasn't, since they'd seen him in town tonight.

Driving back to the ranger post, Tanner realized that his earlier unease hadn't gone away. His worry about visiting the line shack had come to nothing. He was looking forward to a day with Rose tomorrow. So what could go wrong?

In his law enforcement work, he'd learned to trust his gut instincts. But maybe this time he was just overthinking. Take it easy, he told himself. Everything is going to be fine.

Rose was waiting when Tanner came for her at seven-thirty in the pickup with the TSCRA logo on the sides. The sky was clear, the weather mild with a light breeze, perfect for a long drive through beautiful canyon country. As she climbed into Tanner's truck and fastened her seat belt, Rose was glad she'd been overruled last night. This was a rare day to relax and enjoy being with Tanner, not to worry about what might be happening at the line shack.

Leaving the Rimrock far behind, they drove north along a narrow paved road while Tanner watched for the unmarked turnoff to the Jacobsen Ranch.

"It's more of a homestead than a ranch," Tanner explained. "Families settled these canyons generations ago. They built houses, raised some stock, and pretty much lived off the land. We like to keep in touch with them. If they trust us, they can help by being our eyes and ears in this back country."

Tanner was dressed in his ranger uniform—white shirt and jeans, with his badge clipped to his belt. A holstered pistol rode his right hip. His Stetson hung behind the seat. "You look very handsome today, Mr. Special Ranger," Rose teased him.

"Today the outfit's mostly for public relations," Tanner said. "We want people to know who we are and that we're here to help them when they need us. If there's trouble, having met them ahead of time makes things easier on both sides—hey, here's the road. We might have to eat some dust."

He swung the pickup onto a narrow dirt road that wound among ledges and knolls, and hoodoos of sandstone, laid down by water when the dinosaurs were on the earth. Prickly pear and cholla grew on the slopes. Tumbleweed and rabbit brush flourished along the roadside. Where springs bubbled out of the ground, cottonwood trees lent touches of fresh green.

"This country is beautiful," Rose said. "Thank you for bringing me along today."

"Would it make any difference if I told you that my inviting you was Joe's idea?"

"Really?" Rose laughed. "He's a gem. I'll have to bake him a batch of cookies when I get home. I might even save one or two for you."

"You'd better." He touched her knee, his eyes on the winding road.

"Is Wyoming this beautiful?" she asked. "I've never been there."

"It is," he said, "but in a different way. There are high mountain peaks, covered with snow most of the year. Lots of pine trees and open, grassy plains with deer and elk and pronghorn antelope. Horses to ride and cattle to tend. The winters are pretty rough, and hard on the cattle. But even the snow is beautiful in its own way."

"Would you ever go back?"

He hesitated. "Maybe someday. I like my job here, but sometimes I miss the family. It would depend on a lot of things, like whether my brother can manage our ranch without me."

"And the memories?" Rose had to ask the question.

"I survived the memories when I was there for two weeks. Again, I guess it would depend."

He fell silent, leaving Rose to wonder whether he would want to take her if he went back north, and whether she would go. She could no longer imagine life without Tanner, but she had her own roots here in Texas.

The country had opened up into a broad canyon surrounded by hills and buttes and dotted with stands of cedar. Above the Rimrock Ranch, the escarpment was high, steep and narrow. Except for the red soil and rocks, this place was very different— broad and open with massive formations. Until today, she hadn't even known it was here.

The road had straightened out but was still dusty and uneven. Far ahead, she could see tall, green cottonwood trees surrounding a sprawl of adobe buildings. "Is that the ranch?" she asked.

"It looks that way. We'll soon know."

A few more minutes brought them to the ranch, a pretty place with a windmill in the yard and laundry blowing from a clothesline. A few spotted, mixed-breed cattle ranged around the yard, grazing on the abundant spring grass. Chickens pecked grain in a wire coop.

A tall man with an unkempt gray beard came around the house. Rose stayed in the pickup while Tanner climbed out to greet him. With the truck windows rolled down, she could hear most of their conversation.

"Howdy," the man said, extending a hand. "I can see who you are, but it's been years since you fellers made it out here to visit me. I haven't paid my TSCRA dues in a coon's age. Hope you're not here to collect. I haven't got the cash, and anyway, who'd want to steal cows like these?"

"You're fine, Mr. Jacobsen." Tanner shook the man's hand and introduced himself. "We've set up a new post in Blanco Springs. For starters, we're trying to get acquainted with the ranchers and homesteaders in the region. It can be helpful, knowing who our neighbors are."

"Well, you're welcome to come on in. Bring your lady friend, too." He glanced toward the truck. "I can't offer you much in the way of hospitality, but I just took a batch of bread out of the oven. Tastes pretty good when it's hot."

"We'll take you up on that," Tanner said, opening the door and giving Rose a hand to the ground. "Does anybody live here with you?"

"Nope." Jacobsen led the way inside to a primitive but clean kitchen. "My woman lit out and took the kids twenty-three years ago, and I've done for myself ever since."

He seated them at the kitchen table and gave them each a thick slice of warm, buttered bread. It was delicious. "Milked the cow and churned the butter myself," he said. "Better than that store junk that's full of Lord knows what."

"Don't you get lonesome out here alone?" Rose asked. "You must not get many visitors."

"I do fine with my own company," Jacobsen said. "But come to think of it, you've made this the second day I've had visitors. Yesterday I had some that left me shaking my head. Strange bunch. They were lost—and you have to be pretty damned lost to make it clear out here. They said they were looking for some kind of cattle camp with a shack. I said I couldn't help them, and they left."

"What was strange about them?" Tanner asked.

"They were Mexicans. Not the wetback kind that swim the Rio Grande. I get a few of those now and then. I feed 'em and send 'em on their way. But these were *rich* Mexicans—three men, driving some kind of big custom four-wheeler. They had nice clothes, fancy watches . . ."

He trailed off, thinking. "The big one—the boss, I think—he had this gold ring. Real gold, I could tell. It was made to look like an eagle's foot, with the talons holding a ruby as big as my thumbnail. Can't even imagine how much a ring like that might be worth."

The bread dropped from Rose's fingers. She froze, feeling as if the blood were being drained from her body.

Tanner gave her a worried look. "Are you all right, Rose? What is it?"

She found her voice, barely. "Those men. They're the Cabreras. The one with the ring is Refugio."

# CHAPTER SEVENTEEN

*B*ULL SHIFTED INTO LOW GEAR AS THE PICKUP ROUNDED A HAIRPIN curve in the narrow dirt road. The rear tire on the right side slid off the crumbling shoulder, but a stomp on the gas pedal gave the truck a forward burst, pulling the big vehicle back onto solid ground.

Beside Bull in the front seat, Jasper gave a low whistle of relief. "Want me to drive?" he asked, half teasing. "Like I've said before, we need to get a crew up here to fix this road."

"You're not the one who'll have to pay for it," Bull muttered, shifting again. "Remind me later."

They passed a few minutes in silence before Jasper spoke again. "Want to make a bet?"

Bull paused at a fork in the road, which had many branches along the high escarpment. He shifted down again, then turned left. "What kind of bet?" he asked.

"I'll bet you a beer at the Blue Coyote that when we get to that line shack, we'll find the horses gone and our two boys lit out."

"I'll take that bet," Bull said. "Why wouldn't they be there? They're scared of getting caught by the cartel, and they've got no place else to go."

"What if they're not really scared? What if the cartel sent them to track down Rose and report back? They could ride the horses back to civilization, steal a car, and be out of here."

"In that case, you'd win your beer. But we'd have to go after them first, wouldn't we?" Bull thought of the heavy Smith and Wesson .44 he kept under the seat of the truck, along with the 12-gauge shotgun that had belonged to Rose's grandfather. He swore silently. Maybe he shouldn't have taken a chance on the pair. If he'd assumed the worst from the beginning, he and Jasper wouldn't be here now. He'd let himself go soft because he knew Rose cared about them. But hell, they were drug runners for the cartel. What had he been thinking?

"Do you think Rose will be all right?" he asked, changing the subject.

Jasper chuckled. "Sure. She's with Tanner. He's a tough man, and I've seen the way he looks at her, like he'd take on an army to keep her safe."

"But what if the cartel shows up?"

"Then Tanner might need a little help from us." Jasper's reply said it all. A danger to Rose was a danger to the Rimrock family.

The sun was descending the arc of the sky. Its rays made a filigree pattern through the leaves as the truck wound its way up the road. Now they could see the line shack, a simple clapboard cabin with a chimney for the iron stove inside and an outhouse around the back.

"No sign of life," Jasper observed. "Not even the horses."

"It's early yet," Bull said. "Maybe they're out riding herd."

They pulled the truck off a wide spot in the road, climbed out of the truck, and hiked up the short, grassy slope to the line shack. "Anybody home?" Jasper called.

There was no answer.

When they rounded the corner of the shack, they saw that the door was open.

"Something's wrong." Bull had taken his .44 out of the truck. He paused to check the chamber and cock the weapon before they moved forward, cautiously now.

They had nearly reached the threshold of the shack when the smell hit them—a sickening odor they both recognized. "Oh, good Lord," Jasper murmured as he stepped into the doorway.

Raul and Joaquin lay sprawled faceup, their blood spreading

around them in clotted pools. One had been shot in the chest, the other in the forehead. Black flies filled the awful silence with their buzzing.

The sight of the dead men was shocking enough. But there was more. Scattered over, around, and even partway under the bodies were dozens of bloodstained fifty- and hundred-dollar bills, sticking to their hands and clothes and lying in the blood. The total, Bull estimated at a glance, amounted to several thousand dollars. And suddenly, chillingly, he understood.

"What the devil . . ." Jasper swore, staring at the money.

"It's a message," Bull said. "Those two weren't running from the cartel. They were leading their boss to Rose, for a reward. Somehow—and I'm guessing they used a horse to get down the mountain to a phone—they got the word out about where they'd be. The cartel thugs showed up, learned what they needed to, handed over the reward, and then shot these two dead—as if to say that anybody who'd betray their own family would be just as likely to betray their bosses."

"Damn it, we've got to find Rose," Jasper said

Bull studied the death scene. "I'm guessing they were shot sometime late yesterday. That means the killers could be anywhere. Let's go. We can call the sheriff when we get back to the ranch."

Jasper took a quick look around the outside of the cabin. "Saddles are in the shed," he said. "But there's no sign of the horses. They must've spooked and run off. Never mind, let's get going."

Bull drove the hairpin road as fast as he dared, aware that a slip-off could delay his warning Rose—a delay that could be tragic. Rose was a fighter, but she'd have no chance against the people who were after her now.

Why had he let things go this far? He'd suspected that Raul and Joaquin were up to no good. Hell, Rose had even suspected them. They'd been like brothers to her; she'd said so herself. If he'd known they were here to betray her to the cartel, he would have shot them himself and buried their bodies, without a heartbeat of regret.

Beside him, Jasper was mumbling something he could barely hear. "What is it, Jasper?" He swung the truck around a sharp curve. "Speak up so I can hear you."

"Ignore me," Jasper said. "I haven't prayed in a long time, but I'm praying now!"

"You can't go home now, Rose." Tanner swung the truck onto the asphalt road. "I'm taking you to the ranger post. You'll be safe from the Cabreras there. Now that I can get a signal, I'll radio Joe and have him call the Rimrock. They need to know what's going on."

"But what about the trailer—and my truck, and even the chickens? How can I just leave everything I own? Can't we go back just long enough to get—"

"No, Rose!" It was the first time she'd heard anger in Tanner's voice. "If those two Mexicans could find out where you live, so can the cartel. And you know even better than I do what they're capable of. Now be still while I call in."

Rose slumped in the seat while Tanner radioed his partner. In spite of the warm afternoon sun, she was shivering. Only one thing could have brought Refugio Cabrera to Texas. Joaquin and Raul had somehow contacted the cartel and let them know where to find her. She had been betrayed by men she had once loved as brothers.

What now? Tanner had gotten a detailed description of the vehicle and the men from Jacobsen. It would make sense to give it to the police and let them hunt the criminals down. But she knew that might not be enough. The men of the Cabrera cartel were expert at eluding the law. They would take care of the business they'd come for and disappear like morning fog, leaving scarcely a trace.

She wondered briefly who Refugio had brought with him. Lucho had been his only brother. But he had several cousins in the cartel, all sworn by blood and fanatically loyal. Any of them would kill at a word from their boss. Women, children, it didn't matter. She had seen it with her own horrified eyes.

The radio crackled as Joe's voice came back on. He had reached the housekeeper at the Rimrock. Bull and Jasper had driven up to the mountain pasture to check the line shack. They should be back anytime. Meanwhile, she was just leaving to meet the boys at the school bus stop. She would leave a note on the front door.

Tanner laid a hand on her shoulder. "Try not to worry too much," he said. "I'm here, I'll protect you, and this nightmare will soon be over."

"Yes," Rose said. "And when it's over, I'll either be free or be dead."

Bull drove into the ranch yard, tires spitting gravel as he pulled up to the house. Bernice's station wagon was gone, but then, as he checked the time, he realized she would have left to pick up the boys when they got off the bus.

"There's a note on the front door," Jasper said. "Hang on, I'll get it." He took the steps two at a time and was back in seconds. "Rose and Tanner know about the cartel," he said. "Tanner's taking her to the ranger post. He'll call you when they get there."

"Thank goodness." Bull breathed a sigh of relief. But he knew the danger was far from over.

They could hear the ringing phone in the ranch office. Bull raced inside to answer it. Tanner was on the line.

"I got your note," Bull said.

"We're here," Tanner said. "Rose is all right, and I've phoned a description of the men and their vehicle to the sheriff. They'll have patrols out looking for them."

"Wait—you saw them?"

"We talked to a rancher who did. They asked him for directions. He had a good memory. One of the men matches the description of Refugio Cabrera, the cartel boss."

"The one who's after Rose." It wasn't a question.

"It looks that way," Tanner said. "Call us if you get any news, and we'll do the same."

Bull was about to hang up when he remembered. "Oh—I don't know how you'll want to handle this with Rose, but we found Raul and Joaquin dead in the line shack. The cartel got to them before we did."

"The little bastards got what they deserved. I'll tell her, but she won't be surprised. She already knows they gave her up to Cabrera."

Bull hung up the phone. At least Rose was in a safe place. But the rest of what he'd heard was bad news. If Cabrera had taken the risk of crossing the border and coming this far, he wouldn't go back without taking his revenge. Rose was in even more danger than he'd realized.

He glanced at the clock. Bernice and the boys were usually back by this time. What could be keeping them?

Jasper had been waiting on the porch. Now he walked into the house, a stricken look on his face. "You need to see this, Bull," he said. "Come on outside."

Bull followed Jasper back onto the porch. Jasper pointed in the direction of Rose's property, where a thick, black column of smoke was rising into the sky.

Bull swore. "That would be the trailer and probably the truck, and maybe the blasted chickens, too."

"Rose will be heartsick," Jasper said. "But at least she isn't there."

"Damn," Bull muttered. "I'd like to get those bastards in my sights and blast them off the face of the earth." He glanced at his watch. "It's past time for Bernice to be back with the boys. I'm going to drive out to the bus stop and see what's holding them up. You stay here and listen for the phone."

"I'll be right here." Jasper was still gazing at the distant smoke.

Bull climbed into the truck, turned around, and headed down the gravel lane that intersected with the highway to town. The bus stop wasn't more than ten minutes away. Maybe the bus had had some kind of engine trouble. If Cabrera and his buddies were still at large tomorrow, he would have Bernice keep the boys at home. Better safe than sorry.

The bus stop was just ahead. Bull slowed the truck, eyes scanning the empty corner. No bus. No Bernice. And no sign of his sons.

He drove closer, his hands gripping the wheel in a frenzy of disbelief. An instant later, he spotted Bernice's brown station wagon. It lay in the deep bar ditch, where it had rolled partway onto its side.

Heart in his throat, Bull slammed on the brakes, leaped out of the truck, and half slid down the grassy slope.

The station wagon was empty.

From the safety of the ranger post, Rose had heard the sirens that summoned the volunteer fire department. The first thing she thought of was her property. If Refugio had looked for her there and found her gone, it would be like him to torch everything.

Tanner, standing behind her chair, seemed to read her thoughts. He rested a hand on her shoulder. "You don't know it's your place," he said. "It could be anything."

"I know." She touched his hand. Her home was burning—she could feel it. And whoever had set the fire would be long gone by the time anyone else got there.

Tanner had told her that Raul and Joaquin were dead. She shouldn't be sorry. They had been like family, and they had betrayed her in the coldest way imaginable. But she would always remember them laughing, joking with her, teaching her how to ride and herd sheep. They had been good men once, but the cartel, and the lure of money, had changed them.

Rose gazed at the silent phone on the desk, willing it to ring with good news. She thought of her friends on the Rimrock—Bull, Jasper, Bernice, and the boys. They could be in danger, too. She could only hope to hear that they were safe. But the phone remained silent, leaving her in the hellish limbo of not knowing.

Bull burst in through the front door, wild-eyed and out of breath. Jasper watched him struggle to bring himself under control. "Any word?" he asked.

Jasper shook his head. Even before Bull could say more, Jasper guessed what had happened.

"They're gone—Bernice and the boys. I found Bernice's car pushed off the road. Nobody in it. Give me the phone. I've got to call the sheriff."

Sick with fear for his sister and the children, Jasper forced himself to stay calm. He dialed the sheriff's number before handing the receiver to Bull. It was the female dispatcher who answered.

"Get word to the sheriff." Bull's tightly reined voice hid his anguish. "The Cartel's taken Bernice and my two sons. If anybody sees the vehicle, be aware that they have hostages, so nobody can go in shooting. Get the word out! And, for God's sake, get some help! Call the FBI! Call anybody!"

Bull slammed down the phone. "Damn it," he stormed, "why can't they find those monsters? They've got a vehicle description—unless they've stolen a different one. Maybe I ought to go after them myself."

"You know better than that," Jasper said. "You need to be here in case somebody calls." And Jasper knew that somebody would. He knew exactly why Bernice and the boys had been taken. But there was no point in mentioning it to Bull. He would figure it out soon enough.

Bull stared out the window as the sun sank toward the escarpment. "It'll be dark before long," he said. "Then the bastards will be even harder to track. How can I just stand here and do nothing?"

Just then the phone rang. Bull jumped to answer it. He listened, said a few words, and hung up before he relayed the message to Jasper.

"The highway patrol picked up Bernice. She's all right except for some scrapes and a sprained wrist from being shoved out on the road. Cabrera gave her a message to deliver. He said that if the cops didn't back off, he'd kill one of the boys. I'm to wait for his call—it'll come later, when he's ready."

"Where's Bernice now?" Jasper asked.

"A medic's checking her over. Then one of the cops will bring her here and stay to monitor any phone calls. But you know that drug lord is too smart to let his calls be traced." Bull cursed again.

"Damn it, I just want my boys back. I'll give Cabrera every cent I've got. All of it!"

Jasper met his eyes with a calm gaze. "Bull, Cabrera doesn't need your money," he said. "There's only one thing he wants, and you know what it is."

Half an hour later a young deputy came in with Bernice. Her cheek and hands were skinned, her wrist in a brace. Her eyes were red and swollen from weeping. "Bull, if I could have done anything to stop them—Lord help me, I would have died for those boys."

"I know, Bernice. This isn't your fault," Bull said, and it wasn't. He was the one who should have realized what Raul and Joaquin were and taken care of them while he had the chance.

Jasper led his sister to a chair and brought her some coffee. She looked as if she belonged in bed, but it was a given that she'd want to be here, helping any way she could.

"How were the boys?" Bull asked her.

"Scared and quiet. As far as I know, they weren't hurt. They weren't crying." Tears welled again. She wadded the tissue in her hands and dabbed at her eyes. "I'm so sorry."

The young deputy appeared unsure of what to do. Jasper found him a chair and brought him some coffee. Then they waited.

It was getting dark when the call came. Nerves screaming, Bull picked up the receiver.

"This is Bull Tyler."

"Mr. Tyler. It is a pleasure. This is Refugio Cabrera." He spoke good English but with a heavy accent. Bull put the phone on speaker. "You have fine sons. They have been very brave."

"Can I talk to them?"

"Not just now. But I assure you, they are fine. We haven't harmed a hair on their little heads. Give me what I want and they can be back in their beds tonight. Otherwise . . . But we will not talk about that now."

"So tell me what you want, Cabrera."

"I think you know." The voice deepened, roughened. "I want Rose Landro, the bitch who murdered my brother in cold blood. Turn her over to me, and your sons will go free."

"And if I don't?"

Cabrera's chuckle was the most evil sound Bull had ever heard. "If the wait is too long, we start with fingers, one by one, then maybe ears, and then . . . But I am sure you get the picture."

Bull battled nauseating fear. No doubt Cabrera would do what he said and more. "She isn't here. If I can bring her, tell me where and when."

"No *if.* Not if you want your sons back alive. There is an old barn on a back road south of the town, with a dead tree outside. Do you know it?"

"I know it. It's the old Gunther place."

"Seven forty-five. One vehicle, just you and the woman. No tricks and no police, or your boys will die. All I want is the bitch who killed Lucho." The call ended with a click.

The four people in the room stared at one another, all of them knowing what had to happen next. "I'll do it," Bull said. "I'll call Rose."

When the phone rang, it was Tanner who took the call. "Bull, is there any news?" he asked, then paused and handed the receiver to Rose. "Bull wants to talk to you," he said.

"I'm here, Bull," she said.

Rose could hear the strain in his voice. "Cabrera has my boys. We're meeting them at the old Gunther place at seven forty-five."

The icy grip of terror closed around Rose's heart. She fought against it, knowing what had to be done and that only she could do it. Nothing could be allowed to happen to Bull's precious sons. If she had to go to Refugio, that's what she would do.

"I'll meet you at the ranch in a few minutes." Rose hung up the phone. Bull hadn't asked it of her, but he didn't have to. It had to be done. She could only say a silent prayer for courage.

Turning to Tanner, she forced herself to speak calmly. "I have to go to the Rimrock right now," she said. "Can I take your truck?"

"I'll drive you," Tanner said. "What's happening?"

"I'll tell you on the way." She raced for the door, fearing that if he knew, he might try to stop her.

"Can I do anything to help?" Joe asked as Tanner followed her.

"This isn't your fight, Joe," Tanner said. "Take care of the place."

They climbed into his truck. "What is it?" Tanner asked.

"Just drive," Rose said.

"Not until you tell me what's going on."

"Just go. We can talk on the way."

He pulled into the street and headed back through town. Rose could tell he was getting impatient. But what would she do if he stopped the truck and refused to take her to the Rimrock?

"Rose?"

She took a deep breath. "Refugio Cabrera has Bull's sons. He's demanding to trade them for me or he'll kill them."

His mouth tightened. A muscle twitched in his jaw. Several seconds passed before he spoke. "We can't just let them take you," he said. "We'll need a way to fight them."

*I should never have doubted him,* Rose thought. He was with her all the way. "Not until the boys are safe," she said. "Agreed?"

"Agreed. I've got my .38 under the seat. I could go in after them once the boys are out."

Suddenly she was afraid for him. "Cabrera and his men will be armed to the teeth. It's too dangerous."

"Blast it, Rose, I'd rather die with you than have to live without you."

She pressed her head against his shoulder. "I think that's the most beautiful thing anyone's ever said to me. We'll talk to Bull. He might have some ideas. But we won't have much time."

She was doing her best to sound brave. But Refugio Cabrera was the central figure in her nightmares, a tall, handsome monster capable of unspeakable acts. Even the thought of him triggered waves of sickening fear.

"I told you a story about how I gunned down a serial killer in a standoff by circling around the back of a cabin," Tanner said. "I could try it again."

"It won't be that easy," Rose said. "This time there'll be three of them. But I could hide a weapon on me—a knife or a gun. I've been a scrapper all my life, Tanner. I don't go down easy."

They had turned off the highway onto the gravel lane. At the end of it, they could see the lights of the Rimrock. Bull strode outside to meet them as they pulled up to the house. Wordless, he gripped Rose's hands hard enough to hurt.

"Let's do this," she said, showing him her brave face. "Let's get your boys back."

"I'm going with you," Tanner said.

"You're sure?" Bull looked at Tanner as if taking his measure. Earlier Tanner had changed his white shirt for a dark blue, long-sleeved tee. Before getting out of the pickup, he'd taken his pistol and thrust it into his belt.

"There's no way you're leaving me behind," Tanner said.

"Then you'll have to get out of the truck early," Bull said. "Cabrera's expecting two of us."

"I'll need a weapon I can hide," Rose said. "A switchblade would do if you've got one."

"There's one in my truck," Bull said. "Can we agree on a plan?"

"You get the boys out. I'll get Rose out," Tanner said. "That's about as much plan as we can manage."

Bull checked his watch. "We've got fifteen minutes. That's about what it'll take us to get there."

"Where are the cops?" Tanner asked.

"None close by. The police will have roadblocks on the routes out of town, but the Cabreras will anticipate that. I guarantee they'll have a trick or two up their sleeves."

They climbed into the truck with Rose between the two men. Bull found the switchblade knife in the glove box. Rose's fingers shook as she slipped it under her jeans. Would she live through the next hour? Would Tanner? She couldn't think about that now. Nothing could be allowed to matter except the lives of two innocent children.

Bull carried guns in his truck, the 12-gauge double-barreled shotgun Rose had given him and the heavy .44 pistol he favored. But he would have to appear unarmed before the Cabreras. His only chance to use them would be to keep them within easy reach until after his sons were safe. Where he sat, touching her, Rose could feel the tension in his body, and she knew he was afraid, not for himself but for his boys.

The Gunther farm, deserted years ago when the well went dry and the owners went broke, lay at the end of a rutted road beyond the outskirts of Blanco Springs. The house had been burned by vandals, but the barn, with its rotting timbers and dilapidated wood siding, still stood, along with what was left of the corral. The yard was overgrown with weeds.

Bull drove without headlights, the road just visible in the twilight. Ahead, through the murk, they could see the looming outline of the barn. With the dome light switched off, he slowed the truck just enough for Tanner to bail out onto the side of the road. Rose watched him vanish into the darkness, keeping low and moving from shadow to shadow.

The barn was dark, with no sign of movement. "What if they're not here?" Rose whispered, her pulse racing.

Bull glanced at the clock on the dash. "It's seven forty-five. They're here." He pulled up a dozen yards from the barn. "You stay in the truck for now."

Leaving the keys in the ignition, he laid his guns across the seat and climbed out of the truck. The beam of a flashlight flickered on in the doorway of the barn. Rose froze as the light found her through the windshield, lingering on her face.

"Cabrera, show me my sons." Bull's voice was firm, but Rose could imagine the gut-wrenching fear he must be feeling.

"First, show me you're not packing a weapon. Turn around and raise your arms."

Bull did as he was told. "My sons!" he thundered. "Now!"

"They are right here." Refugio's voice sent chills through Rose's body. But when the light shone on the two boys, each in the grip of an armed man, she took a breath of relief. At least Will and Beau were alive and appeared unharmed.

"Now, the woman," Refugio said. "Bring her out, we make the trade, and you can take your boys home."

Rose glanced down at the weapons Bull had left on the seat. She could take one of the guns, and . . . But what was she thinking? If she tried to save herself, Bull's sons would be the first to die.

Before Bull could come for her, she opened the door and slipped to the ground. "I'm coming, Refugio, you pig," she called. "Let the boys go."

A coldness crept over her as she walked forward.

# CHAPTER EIGHTEEN

*T*ANNER WAS PARTWAY AROUND THE SIDE OF THE BARN WHEN HE heard Rose's defiant shout to Refugio Cabrera. Fueled by her courage, he pushed through the thick growth of weeds toward the back corner of the barn. He had to be there for her. And he had to be ready to strike as soon as he knew the boys were safe.

This was his first time on the Gunther property, which put him at a disadvantage. His plan to ambush Cabrera and his thugs from behind would work only if he had some kind of opening. So far he had no idea what he would find when he reached the back of the barn.

Training had taught him that it was safest to assume there might be a lookout. He kept low, screened by the tall weeds. Thistles clawed at his clothes. A sharp briar gouged his cheek, drawing a trickle of blood. He kept going.

The big four-wheeler had to figure into the equation. Since he couldn't see it outside, he had to assume the vehicle was in the barn. In a gunfight, it could provide cover for the cartel thugs or for him. He wouldn't know which until he got inside. And even then it would be too dark to see much.

Did Cabrera plan to kill Rose right here or take her back to Mexico and prolong the torment? There was no way to know. All he could do was try to get her out of that barn and to safety as fast as possible.

He reached the back of the old barn and swore under his

breath. No opening, not even a window. But the boards that formed the siding had weathered over long years. They were so thin that he could see the flicker of a flashlight and hear voices through the cracks. When the time came, he would have to break through, most likely with a solid kick. And when he started shooting, he would have to make sure he didn't hit Rose.

Sweating, he tested a board with his finger. It yielded to the pressure. If he could smash his way through, it would give him the advantage of surprise. If not . . . But that was just one more unknown he was dealing with. The only certainty was that whatever the cost, he had to get Rose out of there alive.

After a dozen paces, Rose halted and stood still. She could see the boys, each one gripped by a man holding a pistol to his small head. Their moon-pale faces were frozen in fear. Rose's heart broke for them and for their father.

"Let the boys go now, Refugio, or I won't take another step." She shouted the words, hoping Tanner could hear her.

She willed herself not to think about dying. Refugio was holding all the cards. He could shoot her now and kill the boys out of spite. But giving her a quick death would spoil his fun. His sadistic streak was all she had to count on.

"Let them go, Cabrera," Bull shouted. "Tell your goons to take their hands off them. If anything goes wrong, I won't care who I have to kill or how long it takes."

"They can go. But you keep walking, Rose, or my men will shoot them." The cartel boss nodded to his henchmen. They released their grip on the boys. Will reached for Beau's hand and locked his around it. They stumbled a few steps, then broke into a run that took them all the way across the open yard to their father's arms.

Rose kept walking, aware of the switchblade knife under the back of her jeans. In her side vision she glimpsed Bull carrying his sons to the truck. *Go, Bull,* she thought. *Get them out of here. Nothing else matters.*

Bull's truck might have started and moved. But if it did, Rose couldn't be sure, because she had reached the entrance to the barn, and the two Cabrera cousins—she recognized them now—were stepping forward to take her arms, holding her between them.

Maybe this was her time to die—like Ramón and María and the good people of Río Seco, who'd been lined up against an adobe wall and shot, or killed in more imaginative ways for the amusement of the cartel. After all, everybody died. Why should she be anything special?

Then she thought of Tanner, somewhere out there, risking his life to save her. Tanner, who'd told her he would rather die with her than live without her. And she knew she had to keep fighting. She wanted to live. She wanted to raise a family with him, to grow old with him. And she wasn't about to settle for anything less.

It was dark inside the barn, but Rose could make out figures and faces. The vehicle—some kind of enclosed ATV with oversized tires—was a looming black shape, parked to one side of the barn, taking up almost a third of the space.

The two cousins, gripping Rose's arms, propelled her over to Refugio, who held a flashlight in one hand. As he holstered his gun and shone the light in her eyes, his cruel, handsome face broke into a smirk. "So we meet again, Rose. I can hardly wait for us to get to know each other better."

Rose spat in his face.

Refugio's chiseled features froze. Taking a handkerchief from his jacket, he wiped his face. "Cuff the bitch and throw her in the back," he snarled in Spanish. "Let's get the hell out of—"

A crash of splintering wood and the echoing sound of a gunshot shattered the night. The two men holding Rose's arms let go and went for their weapons. In a lightning move, Rose whipped out the switchblade and drove it into Refugio's body. The tip of the blade barely penetrated his black silk shirt. Too late, she realized that he was wearing a Kevlar vest underneath.

"Rose! *Get down!*" Hearing Tanner's voice, she understood that he was afraid of hitting her. Still gripping the knife, she dropped and rolled under the vehicle. "They're wearing body armor!" she shouted to warn him.

Frustrated by her helpless position, she lay in the darkness, listening to the deafening *whang* of the 9mm Glocks the cartel men carried and the blast of Tanner's .38. She could hear air escaping from a tire. That must have been where Tanner's first shot had struck.

A leg—clad in black pants, not Tanner's jeans—came into view below the vehicle's metal frame. Rose hacked at it from behind with her razor-sharp knife. Gasping with effort, she cut deeper and felt the hamstring separate with a snap. She was rewarded with a scream. The man had fallen a few feet away, crying and holding his maimed, useless leg. She could tell it wasn't Refugio. Too bad, she thought. But if she could get the man's gun, she could help Tanner.

Hugging the barn's earthen floor, she came in low behind the wounded man, wrenched the loosely held 9mm Glock from his hand, and aimed. A single, deafening shot to the back of the head ended his worthless life.

As the sound cleared her ears, she realized that the gunfire had stopped.

Scarcely daring to breathe, she lay still. A flashlight came on, its beam moving over the carnage in the barn. The man Rose had killed lay nearby. The other Cabrera cousin, also dead, sprawled a dozen feet away. And Tanner . . .

Rose's heart contracted. Tanner lay facedown at Refugio's feet, a crimson flood spreading over the back of his shirt.

Refugio let the light linger on him. "He is still alive, Rose. Toss that gun over here. The knife, too, or I will finish him right now."

Rose did as she was told. "Let me help him," she said. "Please."

"All right. Do it. Any tricks and I'll kill you both."

Rose moved to cover Tanner's prone body with hers. She could feel his heart beating, but he was badly hit, losing a lot of blood. She tried to stop the bleeding with pressure from her hands. It was useless. "He needs a doctor," she said.

"Come with me, and I will leave him alive. Maybe Bull Tyler will come back and find him."

*Maybe,* Rose thought. But there was no guarantee that Bull would come back at all, and Tanner didn't have much time. If she left him, he would die alone.

"No." She clung to Tanner's unconscious body, covering as much of him as she could. Tanner's words came back to her, and she knew they were true for her as well. She would rather die with him than live without him. "I'm not leaving him," she said. "If it matters that much, you'll have to kill us both."

Refugio cursed in Spanish. Rose tried to imagine what he was thinking. His men were dead, and the police would have the roads blocked, watching for his vehicle. He might be able to slip away alone and on foot, disguised as a common migrant worker, but with Rose as his prisoner, that kind of escape would be impossible. And for him, mercy was out of the question. *Kill her now. Kill them both.*

With the flashlight still in one hand, he raised his pistol and cocked it.

Rose glimpsed a tall silhouette in the open doorway of the barn. In the same instant, the deafening roar of a 12-gauge shotgun, firing on both barrels, shattered the air. The close-range blast could have dropped a thousand-pound steer. Even in a Kevlar vest, Refugio didn't stand a chance.

Bull steadied his balance, lowered the weapon, and rubbed his shoulder. "Damn, but that old gun's got a kick," he said. "How's Tanner?"

Rose found her voice. "Alive, but barely. He's losing a lot of blood. We've got to get him to a hospital."

Bull stripped off his shirt to use as a temporary dressing. "Better not to move him without help. Let's put a patch on him, and you stay here with him. The patrol cars are out. First one we pass, I'll have them call an ambulance . . ."

*Eighteen hours later*

Tanner opened his eyes. As his murky vision cleared, he saw that Rose was bending over his hospital bed, red-eyed, disheveled, and so stunningly beautiful that all he wanted to do was look at her.

"Hello," she whispered.

"Hello," he said. "You look like an angel. Am I in heaven?"

"You were knocking on the gate," Rose said. "But the doctors brought you back. You needed three pints of blood. Even so, you were lucky. The bullet didn't hit anything vital."

"What about Cabrera and his pals?"

"They're shaking hands with the devil."

"All I remember is a lot of shooting. Then I got hit and everything went dark."

"You got one of them," Rose said. "I got one, and Bull finished off Refugio. Good teamwork, I'd say."

"Sorry, I really wanted to save you by myself—you know, ride in like a knight in shining armor and slay all your dragons."

"You did save me." She took his hand and pressed it to her cheek. "Without you, I wouldn't be here."

"You should get some rest." He touched her tangled hair.

"There'll be time for that. Right now I need to go call the Rimrock and tell Bull and Jasper you're awake. I'll call Joe, too. He'll want to know."

After she left the room, Tanner lay in a fog of uncertainty. He could feel the pain under the dressings that bound his ribs, covering the entrance and exit wounds where the shot had gone through his chest and back. Crazy. He didn't even know which way the bullet been traveling when it hit him.

He groaned as the worries flooded over him. How long before he'd be ready to work again? What about his job? He didn't even have a place to live, except the ranger post. Worse, his injuries weren't related to his work, so there'd be no compensation.

And what about Rose? He knew that he wanted to marry her, and it couldn't happen soon enough. But what did he have to offer her? Nothing but a modest savings account and half ownership of a struggling Wyoming ranch. How could he provide the best future for Rose and peace of mind for himself? Could he make it here in Texas, with Rose wanting to stay on her beloved land, or would he be better off joining Clint's family in Wyoming? Only one thing was certain—he couldn't have it both ways, and neither could Rose.

He had some hard decisions to make, and they needed to be made soon. He could only hope those decisions wouldn't cost him the woman he loved.

By the time Rose returned to Tanner's hospital room, he was nodding off again. She bent over the bed and kissed him awake, working her way around monitor cords and an IV. He opened his eyes. "Joe sends his best," she said. "He talked to Clive. Your job will be waiting when you're mended. Bull's with his boys, but Jasper's coming here. He wants to talk to us. Since he'll have to drive from the ranch to Lubbock, he won't be here for an hour. You might as well get more rest."

"You too," he murmured and closed his eyes.

Rose curled up in the armchair next to the bed. It wasn't comfortable, but she hadn't slept in nearly two days, and she was exhausted. It seemed as if she'd barely drifted off when Jasper walked into the hospital room, startling her awake.

"Thank God you're both all right. Don't get up, Rose. I can see you're tuckered out." Jasper pulled a straight-backed chair up to the bed. "And you—" He laid his hand on Tanner's. "We've got a lot to thank you for."

"All I did was get shot," Tanner said.

"We've got some talking to do." Jasper took a deep breath. "Some of this is going to hit hard, Rose. That's why Bull and I decided to save it until we knew Tanner was out of the woods."

Something told Rose that bad news was coming. She was strong and she could take it, she encouraged herself.

"I guess you already know that when we drove up to the line shack, we found those two Mexican boys shot dead. After they gave you up for a reward, the cartel had no more use for 'em."

Rose struggled to ignore the hurt that was still there. "I know, and I wasn't surprised," she said. "I'd already figured out that they'd betrayed me to the cartel."

"There's more," Jasper said. "Your property. I went over and had a look after the fire. Everything's gone, Rose. They torched it—the trailer, your truck, even the damned chicken coop with the chickens in it. I'm sorry."

"Oh—" Rose knew she shouldn't be shocked after hearing the sirens and guessing the truth. But the news still hurt. Her hands balled into fists as she fought to hold her emotions in check. The trailer and truck were a loss. But the chickens were living creatures, and she had loved them.

Jasper paused, waiting for her to take in the news before he continued. "This is the worst part. When the sheriff's crew came to investigate, they found a body on the other side of the creek. A young man in a camouflage shirt. He'd been shot."

"No!" This time the news broke her. She pressed her face into Tanner's blanket to muffle the sobs that shook her body. Reuben had been a lonely, misfit boy, just needing a little kindness. And she had made him her friend for her own selfish reasons. "This is on me," she said. "I was nice to him. I asked him to watch the place."

"Don't, Rose." She felt the gentle weight of Tanner's hand on her hair. "Reuben's death isn't on you. It's on Ferg, and on the monsters who killed the boy just because he was there."

"But he didn't have a chance to grow up. He could have found his way. He could have become somebody."

"He had a friend who was good to him," Tanner said. "At least you gave him that."

"It wasn't enough." Rose took time to get her tears under control. "I just realized I have next to nothing," she said. "No home, no money, nothing but a piece of ground and the clothes on my back." She forced a smile, remembering how she'd come to the Rimrock as a fourteen-year-old girl after her grandfather was killed. "But I guess this isn't the first time, is it?"

"You've got your friends," Jasper said. "And the Rimrock will be your home for as long as you want to stay."

"And you have me." Something in Tanner's voice told Rose he had more to say.

"You can stay, too, Tanner," Jasper said. "You'll need a place to rest up and heal. You'll have it at the ranch."

"Thanks, I may take you up on that," Tanner said. "Meanwhile, I've got a lot of thinking to do and some big decisions to make."

She gave him a questioning glance, wondering if his decisions involved her. "Well, take your time," Jasper said. "As long as you do right by our girl, Bull and I will be happy."

After Jasper had gone, Tanner took Rose's hand. The whole time Jasper had been talking to Rose, the arguments had been warring in his mind. Now that the answer—the only answer—had fallen into place, he knew that, for her sake, he couldn't leave things unsettled.

"I have something to say to you," he began. "Hear me out. If you need time to think about your answer, I owe you that much, at least."

"I'm listening." Her eyes were soft and dark. She was a woman who'd lost almost everything, a woman who'd been terribly hurt. Was he about to hurt her again? Tanner cleared his throat.

"I love you, Rose. I want you at my side forever. I want to raise our babies and grow old with you. But here in Texas, I'll never be more than just a man with a job."

He saw the subtle shift in her expression, as if she'd already guessed what he was going to say next. He knew how much she loved her land and how hard she'd fought for it. But one of them had to make a choice. Maybe it would be him.

"Right now, that parcel of land is all you have. I know how much it means to you. But I have land, too. Land and family in Wyoming, a place to put down roots and bring up our children. We wouldn't have to live with my brother. We could rent a place in town while I build us a home on the ranch . . ."

Her face reflected shock. "You're saying you want us to go back there?"

"I'm not saying. I'm asking. More than anything else, I want a life with you, Rose. If that little parcel means so much to you, I'll try to stay and make things work. But think about the constant struggle you've had there, and the danger. Think about what we could have in Wyoming—our own land and cattle, satisfying work, safety, and plenty of family around."

Seeing her unreadable expression, he trailed off. Had he said too much? Did that parcel of creek land mean more to her than his love?

"What is it?" he asked.

After an agonizing pause she spoke. "My grandfather died for that creek land. He left it to me as a legacy. I came home to Texas, thinking that nothing was more important than making a home on it. But I've come to realize that the land will always be there, whether I choose to live on it or not. But if I make the wrong choice, I could lose what means even more to me—I could lose you."

"Rose—"

"No, wait. I need to know this. What about your memories? What about your wife and son?"

"We'd be building a new life. The memories will always be there, but they won't stop me from being happy. Not with you."

"Then I have just one question," she said. "And I need an answer now."

"Ask it." Tanner held his breath, sensing that the rest of their lives could depend on his answer.

A radiant smile lit her face. "Can I have chickens and goats in Wyoming?"

Three weeks later they were married on Rose's land. They stood next to the fallen tree where her grandfather lay, his grave marked by a granite stone that Bull had placed there as a token of thanks for saving his sons.

Bull had also cleared away the burned remains of the trailer, pickup, camper, and chicken coop. The earth lay bare and clean, ready for the new grass that was already beginning to sprout.

A justice of the peace performed the ceremony. In attendance were Bull and his sons, Jasper, Bernice, and Joe. They watched, smiling, as Rose said her vows to Tanner in a simple white dress with a garland of summer wildflowers in her hair.

After a farewell luncheon, it was time to take leave of their friends and start north for Wyoming. Rose was looking forward to a new home, a new family, and new adventures with the love of her life. But she would always keep her Rimrock family in her heart. Saying good-bye wouldn't be easy.

Joe had already gone back to work. Standing beside Tanner's loaded pickup, Rose hugged Bernice and the boys. "Can we come and visit you, Rose?" Beau asked.

"I hope you can. That will be up to your father," Rose said. But something told her that Bull's attachment to the Rimrock was so deep he would never tear himself away, even for a visit.

She flung her arms around Jasper's neck, almost weeping. He had been her dear friend and staunch ally. She would miss him most of all. "Things are gonna be a lot less interesting with you gone, darlin'," he said. "Take care."

With Bull, she was more restrained. They had been enemies for a time, but friends in the end, and once again he had saved her life. "Take care of my land," she said. "You can never tell when I might come back and want it."

"My offer to buy it from you is still open," Bull said. "Just let me know."

She shook her head. "Tanner and I talked about it. We could use the money, but when the land's gone, it's gone. Not yet. Not without a very good reason."

"We'll leave it at that, then." Bull shook her hand and Tanner's. Then Tanner helped Rose into the truck. She waved good-bye and then lost sight of the little group. She was still wiping away tears as he drove down the lane toward the highway.

"Are you all right?" he asked her.

"Never better."

"So, Mrs. McCade, are you ready for an adventurous new life?"

Laughing, she leaned across the seat and kissed him. "Bring it on!" she said.

# EPILOGUE

*Wyoming, three years later*

ROSE LEANED FORWARD IN THE SADDLE, WIND SWEEPING THROUGH her hair as she galloped her buckskin horse across the meadow. The runaway yearling calf dodged and twisted, but the well-trained gelding cut off its escape and herded it back to the branding pen.

Tanner, astride his tall bay, gave her a thumbs-up as she galloped off after another animal. There was no need for Rose to help with the roundup, especially now that Clint and Ruth's two older boys were old enough to do a man's work on the family ranch. But she loved being out in the fresh mountain air, riding through grass that was almost tall enough to tickle her horse's belly.

Behind her, pine-skirted mountains, still snowcapped in early summer, rose to the sky. A red-tailed hawk circled overhead and settled in the gnarled top of a dead lodgepole pine. A marmot whistled from its den in a clump of rocks.

Rose had fallen in love with this country the first time she'd seen it as a bride. She'd learned a great deal since then—how to rope a steer, how to make venison jerky with meat and brine, how to keep animals alive in a winter storm, and so much more.

She, a lifelong loner, had learned how to fit in with the big, noisy, close-knit McCade clan—when to step in, when to give advice, when to listen, when to lend a hand, and when to stand aside.

And she had learned how to be a mother. Rose and Tanner's two-year-old daughter, Maria, was a handful, but she had cousins to keep an eye on her while her mother helped with the roundup. In the McCade Ranch family, everybody pitched in. And thanks to the extra help Rose and Tanner had brought, the ranch was finally beginning to prosper.

Sometimes Rose thought of her own lonely, miserable childhood. What a blessing that her children—and there would be at least one more—would grow up surrounded by love and family.

Now the sun was low in the sky. It was time to end the roundup for the day, to douse the branding fire, box up the tools and medicines, and ride the horses back to the barn.

Tanner rode up alongside her and slowed his bay. "Good job today," he said, "but are you sure you should be riding with the baby and all?"

"The doctor said it shouldn't be a problem this early," Rose said. "Don't worry. I'll know when it's time to hang up the saddle."

They rode down the slope toward the big, sturdy barn. Tanner had built a beautiful three-bedroom log house on the far side of the ranch compound, close enough for easy access to the rest of the family but distant enough to afford some privacy. "I'll put your horse away if you want to ride ahead. You can get Maria and take her home," he said.

"Thanks," Rose said. "I put a pot roast in the oven this morning. With luck, it should be nicely done and on the table by the time you get to the house."

Nudging the buckskin to a trot, she headed downhill and left the horse at the hitching rail outside the barn. At Clint and Ruth's house, she picked up Maria, a curly-headed cherub, and carried her back across the yard.

"Da-da?" Maria pointed toward the barn. She was a daddy's girl from the get-go.

"Yes, he's taking care of the horses." Rose gave her a kiss. "You can help me fix supper. Okay?"

"Okay." It was her new favorite word.

Carrying her child into the house, Rose looked forward to sharing supper with Tanner across the table and Maria in her high chair, then, after putting the little girl to bed, snuggling in front of the TV with her man while they wound down from the day. At last they would go to bed, make tender love if they weren't too tired, and drift off in each other's arms.

Sometimes Rose thought of her old dream—living a solitary and independent life on her little strip of land. That dream had long since faded into the past. This was her life now—a life of honest work, family, and love.

It was the best life of all.

*Don't miss the start of Janet Dailey's heartwarming new Christmas Tree Ranch series, coming just in time for the holidays!*

## MY KIND OF CHRISTMAS

*Sometimes the best surprises are right at home . . .*

Returning to Branding Iron, Texas, is Travis Morgan's last resort, and the abandoned ranch he inherited isn't much more welcoming than the prison cell where he spent the last three years doing time for a tragic accident. Completely without funds or family, Travis finds celebrating Christmas is the last thing on his mind, but there's no escaping the holiday spirit in this close-knit little town—not with Branding Iron's longtime Santa retiring, and sweetly stubborn Mayor Maggie Delaney determined to find a replacement. When her no-nonsense façade slips to reveal the sensual, vulnerable woman beneath it, Travis realizes Maggie just might be as lonely as he is—and that this holiday season, love could be the gift that heals them both.

"The spirit of Christmas permeates this charming holiday romance."
—*RT Book Reviews* on *Merry Christmas, Cowboy*

$M$AGGIE DELANEY, NEWLY RE-ELECTED MAYOR OF BRANDING IRON, had driven out to check on Abner Jenkins, whose farm was a few miles out of town. Earlier that morning, when she'd called the old man to make sure he was prepared to play Santa in this year's Christmas Parade, his landline phone had rung without an answer. Worried about the old man, she'd climbed into the big Lincoln that had been her father's, and gone to check on him. She'd found Abner's truck gone from the yard. His house, when she checked inside, had been empty.

After leaving a note on his door, she'd been about to turn around and drive back to town when an impulse had changed her mind. The recently paved road, which cut off the highway and ran past Abner's place, had been an icy mess. Two passing farm trucks had almost slid into her. Maybe it would be better to go forward, following the less traveled part of the road where it looped through the back country and rejoined the highway a couple of miles to the south.

It had been a bad idea. The rest of the road was even icier. She was already late for her 10:00 meeting with the Library Board, and now her dad's beloved old Lincoln had slid, spun and crashed into a metal gatepost, causing a startled man to fall off his windmill.

From the car, she could see him lying on the frozen ground. He didn't appear to be moving. Good Lord, what if she'd killed him?

She flung herself out of the car, her kitten-heeled boots barely finding purchase on the ice-encrusted ground. The car had pushed the gatepost to one side, freeing the gate to swing open in the wind. She hurried across the bare yard to where the man lay at the foot of the windmill, sprawled on his back.

Approaching, she could see the faint rise and fall of his chest beneath the old woolen peacoat he wore. His long legs, clad in faded jeans and worn-out work boots, were moving slightly. At least he appeared to be alive. But he could be badly hurt.

Her gaze took him in. He was a stranger—tall and whip-lean, dressed in worn-out work clothes. Below the knit cap that covered his head and ears, the planes of his face were sharply chiseled, the closed eyes deeply set.

It was a striking face, almost handsome in a stubble-jawed, Clint Eastwood sort of way. But how could she be ogling the man at a time like this? She needed to be checking him for injuries and calling 911.

As she bent over him, his eyes opened—slate-colored eyes, their look so piercing that she drew back with a little gasp. His lips tightened. He cleared his throat. "What the blazes did you think you were doing?" he muttered.

With effort, she found her voice. "I was trying to decide whether you need an ambulance."

He stirred, wincing as he sat up. "I'm fine. That's not what I meant. You were driving like a bat out of hell down that icy road. You're lucky you didn't break your fool neck—and mine."

"You sound like a cop."

His mouth tightened. "I hope that's a joke," he said.

She stood as he hauled himself to his feet. Maggie was a statuesque woman, almost five-foot ten. He loomed over her by half a head.

"I was late for a meeting in town," she said. "I'm sorry for distracting you. And I'm sorry about your gatepost. My purse is in the car. I'd be happy to write you a check for the damage."

"Don't bother. I can fix it myself." He turned away from her and walked over to the metal gatepost, which stood askew against the front bumper of the car. Maggie could tell he was in some pain.

What was he doing out here? As she recalled, this run-down ranch had been abandoned for several years, since the people who'd been leasing it moved away. What was this ragged-looking stranger doing on the property? Was he some homeless derelict needing shelter from the cold? Or worse, a fugitive criminal, hiding out from the law?

Either way, it was clear that he didn't want her around. Maybe she should ask the sheriff to check him out. There was something raw and a little wild about the man. Something that whispered danger.

Her key was still in the ignition. If she was smart, she'd get back in the car, lock the doors, and pray that the engine would start.

—